P9-ARY-852

A FIDDLER AND
FIORA MYSTERY

THE ART
OF
SURVIVAL

A.E. MAXWELL

A Novel Idea
W. Main Street
Leesburg, Florida 34748
(904) 326-8558

HarperPaperbacks
A Division of HarperCollinsPublishers

If you purchased this book without a cover, you should be aware that this book is stolen property. It was reported as "unsold and destroyed" to the publisher and neither the author nor the publisher has received any payment for this "stripped book."

This is a work of fiction. The characters, incidents, and dialogues are products of the author's imagination and are not to be construed as real. Any resemblance to actual events or persons, living or dead, is entirely coincidental.

HarperPaperbacks *A Division of* HarperCollins*Publishers*
10 East 53rd Street, New York, N.Y. 10022

Copyright © 1989 by Two of a Kind, Inc.
All rights reserved. No part of this book may be used or reproduced in any manner whatsoever without written permission of the publisher, except in the case of brief quotations embodied in critical articles and reviews. For information address HarperCollins*Publishers*, 10 East 53rd Street, New York, N.Y. 10022.

A hardcover edition of this book was published in 1989 by Doubleday, a division of Bantam Doubleday Dell Publishing Group, Inc.

Cover illustration by Danilo

First HarperPaperbacks printing: June 1993

Printed in the United States of America

HarperPaperbacks and colophon are trademarks of HarperCollins*Publishers*

10 9 8 7 6 5 4 3 2 1

Praise for A. E. Maxwell

"Unnerving, mesmerizing and, when relief from fierce tensions is required, blessedly funny."
—*Publishers Weekly*

"A slick, well-crafted mystery . . . also a sensitive exposé on human nature written with knowing insight as well as plenty of humor and dry wit." —*Los Angeles Times*

"Maxwell is good, really good, able to create believable, engaging, and original characters and set them plausibly into a story of nonstop suspense." —*Chicago Sun-Times*

"Maxwell's style is sexy and hard-hitting."
—*Publishers Weekly*

"[The Maxwells] combine wit, humor, suspense and a believable plot with just the right mix of action and dialogue for a good read." —*United Press International*

and
Fiddler and Fiora

"One of the most interesting and engaging private eyes since Robert Parker's Spenser." —*Advertising Age*

"Weary of dreary police procedurals, morally ambiguous cold warriors, hypersensitive and much-too-introspective private eyes? Then you may be just the man or woman enough to ride shotgun with A. E. Maxwell's Fiddler."
—*Los Angeles Herald Examiner*

"The most unusual, up-to-date private eye with the hard-boiled characteristics of the legendary Sam Spade."
—*San Antonio Express News*

"Fiddler, like the legendary Philip Marlowe, is one of a kind . . . he tackles each situation with all the restraint of a rampaging bull. . . . A. E. Maxwell, like Raymond Chandler, is a master at creating atmosphere."
—*Saint John Telegraph*

"One of the slickest, most likeable detectives."
—*Mystery News*

Also by A. E. Maxwell

MONEY BURNS
JUST ANOTHER DAY IN PARADISE
THE FROG AND THE SCORPION
GATSBY'S VINEYARD
JUST ENOUGH LIGHT TO KILL

Available from HarperPaperbacks

ATTENTION: ORGANIZATIONS AND CORPORATIONS

Most HarperPaperbacks are available at special quantity discounts for bulk purchases for sales promotions, premiums, or fund-raising. For information, please call or write:
Special Markets Department, HarperCollins Publishers, 10 East 53rd Street, New York, N.Y. 10022.
Telephone: (212) 207-7528. Fax: (212) 207-7222.

For our editor
Shaye Areheart
who loves Fiddler enough to worry about him

ONE

It all started to go downhill on the High Road from Taos. The Cobra's right-front tire went off like a gunshot. The car wallowed to a lopsided halt in a turnout that overlooked the seventeenth-century village of Truchas. A few minutes later I was rolling around in the wet snow and half-frozen mud, struggling with the spare. I was also cursing whoever had tossed the blush-wine bottle out onto the pavement, creating the kind of urban land mine you don't expect to find in the New Mexican highlands.

I suppose I couldn't complain too much. It was my first blowout in the eight weeks and fifteen thousand miles since I'd left California. I hadn't stayed more than two or three nights in the same place, dodging the worst of the winter weather when I could and suffering the drawbacks of touring in an open-cockpit automobile when I couldn't.

The morning of the blowout I'd started in eastern

Colorado. When KOA, the Voice of the Mountain West, predicted snow at the higher elevations, I turned south, running before the late winter storm. I would have stayed clean and dry, too, except that I love the little villages along the High Road to Taos. I decided to chance a fast pass through the wild, fierce countryside, hoping to make Albuquerque before the freeway got too slick with ice and snow. As it was, I barely made Santa Fe.

The sky had been clear when I left Taos and drifted along the shoulder of the blunt, rugged range known as the Sangre de Cristo Mountains. The Blood of Christ. The name tells you a little bit about the New Mexican highlands. The culture—equal parts of *indio,* Hispano, and Anglo—is not what you could call "progressive." It's the kind of place where *penitentes* flog themselves raw, offering their blood to a savage God. Like the social philosophy, the level of technology in these villages is closer to Stone Age than to New Age.

If you aren't the one starving, the harsh land and subsistence farming techniques and crumbling adobe houses are starkly beautiful. It was the beauty I'd come looking for, the sense of touching something primitive, something real, something that would purge the bad taste that had been tarnishing my mouth for two months.

But not even a Shelby Cobra can outrun the modern world. It's scattered across the countryside like the jagged chunks of glass that ripped through the sidewall of my tire.

As I thrashed around under the Cobra's fender, trying to keep the wet sand and gravel out of the knock-off hub, I realized I was running on four tires that were nearly bald. I shouldn't have been surprised. I had all but lived behind the wheel of the Cobra since the morning I pulled out of Crystal Cove and headed south to bury Aaron Sharp. Somewhere between here and there I'd lost track of a great many things, including the tread on the tires.

By the time I got the spare on and headed down the hill to Santa Fe, I was damned cold. When I finally found the Goodrich tire store, the visibility was down to a hundred yards. Naturally the service bays at the tire store lacked any kind of heat. The mechanics didn't seem to mind the cold, but I'd had about as much of life in the open cockpit as I could take.

The Navajo wheel man spent thirty minutes in focused reverence as he slowly, slowly, slowly eased a one-ounce weight around the cast magnesium rim of the Cobra's right-front wheel, trying to divine the single perfect place to mount the weight so that it would both balance the wheel properly and not mess up the Cobra's esthetics. At any other time I would have appreciated a man who inhabited the difficult terrain between good and perfect, but I was too cold, too wet, and too irritated at that moment to appreciate anything except the chance of getting warm and dry.

When the mechanic started around the rim for the third time, I suspected I had stumbled into the equivalent of automotive High Mass.

"Does everybody in Santa Fe have to be an artist?" I muttered.

"It's the rim's fault, man," he muttered back.

"Sucker's out of true. You sure you don't want me to slap a whole new wheel on? Hate to mess up the way your car looks with weights, but I can't get a good balance unless I put 'em on the outside where they show."

"Haven't you heard? There's no such thing as perfect. I'll settle for a good ugly balance."

"Hey, man, I'll go down to the speed shop and pick out a new wheel myself. If it ain't true, I'll make 'em take it back."

I believed him. He was built like a forty-ton wrecker. Nobody with half a brain would argue with him.

Nobody except me.

"Stay put. Good and ugly will get it done."

Muttering what sounded like Navajo imprecations, the wheel man went back to work. I went out to walk myself warm.

The country along the High Road might be closer to Chihuahua than to Chicago, but Santa Fe itself is far from primitive. One look at the prices tells you that Santa Fe is top drawer, cutting edge, New Age.

The city is high, higher than Denver by 1,500 feet, and the atmosphere is as dry as the Kalahari. The galleries are part of the rich Southwest Art trap line —Santa Fe, Scottsdale, Palm Springs, and Beverly Hills—and the boutiques all brag about their branch stores in New York, London, Paris, and Milan. You can find everything from twelfth-century Anasazi artifacts to Andy Warhol soup cans, from assembly-line tourist art to Southwestern expressionist paintings. Santa Fe is a heady mélange of gauche, gouache, and grand, a mix that leads to all kinds of interesting trouble; because where there's art, there's money, and where there's money, there's trouble.

I was ready for some trouble. I'd chased too many personal shadows too many miles and had nothing to show for it except windburn, a beard that was as uncurried as the land, and an infuriating tendency to think of Fiora, the woman whose lack of faith had sent me on the road in the first place.

I walked down the narrow sidewalks toward the canyon, drifting through Gallery Row, looking at what other people were willing to pay thousands of dollars to own. Most of the time I wasn't impressed. There's an awful lot of bad painting and sculpture that passes itself off as "western" or "southwestern art"—chiseled cowboys, sloe-eyed Indian maidens, and come-hither cow ponies—but the best of the southwest art is like the land itself, clean and infused with unself-conscious strength. The best of the best can nail you right in your tracks.

When the black soapstone bear in the Nickelaw Gallery window caught my eye, I stopped walking and forgot I was cold. The bear was a riveting combination of two cultural traditions. Southwestern Indians were, and still are, animistic in their religion. Spirits are believed to roam the wild land in animal form, mingling with men in an intimacy that Europeans lost when they opted for one immaterial, indivisible god. Traditional Indian art is rooted in ancient animism and consists mainly of tiny carved religious fetishes—bears, wolves, eagles, and the other climax predators of the Southwest.

The bear that interested me had begun in the

traditional bear-fetish form, a humpbacked stone carving that was rather like an inverted U. But somewhere along the way a new vision of old verities had overtaken the carver. Instead of fitting easily in a man's palm, this fetish stood about three feet high at the shoulder. Carved from a single block of black soapstone, the bear had to weigh in at around 250 pounds. There was no traditional bundle of feathers and arrows tied to the bear's back, nothing to break the flowing, powerful lines of the animal itself. It was as though the beast had been born from an artesian upwelling of midnight stone.

The bear regarded the snowstorm and me with two oval turquoise eyes, weighing all aspects of the situation, trying to decide whether to hibernate or to hunt. His poised, muscular stance reminded me of Kwame Nkrumah, the Rhodesian Ridgeback that lives next door to me in California. Like Kwame, the bear was tuned to a different reality yet aware of this one. He reached out to me as directly and intelligently as though he were alive and capable of discussing mealy grubs, megabytes, and the meaning of eternity.

I'm not an art collector, but once in a while a work grabs me the way the bear did. Almost always, the art is a synthesis of traditions, a vision born of the seething, energetic, sometimes lethal slip face where two cultures collide.

The bear was something new under the sun. I wanted him.

I pushed through the door of the gallery, reaching for my wallet at the same time. On first impression, the place exuded the kind of discreet fine-arts schtick that would have amused Fiora even as she took a firmer grip on her purse.

Thinking of Fiora made me angry all over again. I had used up a lot of time and miles trying to wipe her from my thoughts, and now her name had popped up in my mind twice in as many minutes.

That's the trouble with good art. It puts you in touch with the raw spots on your soul.

A woman with dark hair stood behind the gallery's high counter. She glanced up, blinked, and looked me over the way a cat examines something it dragged into the house but can't remember why.

"The bear," I said, dripping meltwater onto the pale green wool carpet. "How much?"

Maybe it was my expression that put the woman's back up, or maybe she didn't like big men with ragged beards, or maybe it was just that my jeans and down parka looked like I'd been changing tires in them.

Her head came up high and proud as she walked out from behind the counter. She was tall, dark, more angular than most Indian women, and damned handsome. Her eyes and straight hair were the color of obsidian, and her skin was the smooth, living brown that tanning salons promise but never deliver. She wore a long skirt of rose wool, a loose burgundy sweater, and calf-high leather boots. A stylized squash-blossom necklace rested between the upward curves of her breasts. Like the bear, the woman was an arresting meld of two cultures, an Apache princess with a Bryn Mawr gloss.

"We have many bears," she said coolly.

A glance around told me she was right. There were other bears in the place. They didn't interest me.

"The black one with the turquoise eyes," I said.

There was an instant of approval in the woman's expression, but when she spoke, her voice matched the reserved stillness of her resting hands. "Unfortunately, that particular bear has been sold."

I glanced again at the bear. Next to him on the pedestal was a small card with a red dot on it. I swore beneath my breath. That bear was the first thing that had reached out to me since I'd left California.

"Would the new owner like to make a fast ten percent on his investment?"

She looked me up and down again. "The bear sold for ten thousand dollars."

A lot of upscale galleries try to intimidate their customers. It enhances the image of exclusivity. As a sales tactic, it irritates the hell out of me, but I wanted that bear. So I pulled out my wallet and gave the woman a smile the temperature of the snow that was melting in my hair and running down the back of my neck. Fiora really hates that smile.

"In that case, would the owner like to make a fast thousand?"

"Cash, check, or Christmas layaway?" she said, giving me back a feline version of my smile.

"Cash."

"You carry that kind of money around in your hip pocket?"

"It saves having to run to the automated teller every few minutes."

For an instant her black eyes glowed with anger. She didn't like being high-hatted any more than I did.

"Just tell me who the new owner is," I said. "I'll make the offer myself."

The woman shoved her hands into the deep pockets of her wool skirt. "We don't divulge the names of our clients."

I jerked my AMEX card out. There are times when its distinctive platinum finish works better than cash. This was one of them.

"Run a voucher on this for ten percent earnest money. Then call the owner and make the offer. His privacy is protected and so is his chance to make a fast buck on his investment."

The woman looked at me for a long moment, saying nothing.

"Lady, I'm not looking to start a war. I just want that bear."

The fingers that took the card from my hand were as cool and controlled as the woman herself. She walked off without a backward look and disappeared into a small suite of offices just behind the counter. She was so close I could hear her punching out a number on the phone.

In the sudden silence that followed, I heard the almost secretive whisper of the hot, clean-burning fire in the narrow little corner fireplace. It was a hell of a lot more inviting than a credit check, so I walked across the room, removed the wrought-iron fire screen, and knelt on the hearth. While I warmed my palms, I watched the double handful of flames and thought about the living hell that is reserved for intelligent, beautiful women born into small-town western poverty. The dark-haired gallery saleswoman was one who had escaped. Fiora was another.

Women with histories like theirs are proud, arrogant, obstinate—and endlessly fascinating to me. I suppose it's because they refuse to accept the narrow role into which they are born. I can understand that; I can understand a bright woman wanting something more or less or simply different from the life that left her mother hollow-eyed and defeated. Wanting something better is the kind of desire that can make for positive changes in the world, so long as the ambition finds a constructive focus. If ambition finds a destructive focus, the changes come along just the same, but they're the kind you don't want to write home about.

The black-haired woman in the other room had the type of intensity and intelligence that needs bigger challenges than a small town can offer. Obviously she had escaped. You don't acquire her kind of polish in Glendive or Tonopah or Medicine Hat. As I stared at the fire I wondered what she had gained and what she had lost . . . and who she was calling, what computer links were closing across the country, why it was taking so damned long to run a simple credit-card verification.

Or was she fishing around for more information, like how big a bite I could stand and whether my next of kin would laugh or cry at my funeral?

You're getting paranoid, Fiddler.

The comeback to that one is so old it voted in the last election. But it's also true.

Even paranoids have real enemies.

tWO

My AMEX card appeared suddenly above my hands, which were still toasting over the fire. A voice that was no longer quite so cool spoke close to my ear.

"A doctor from Chicago bought the bear a week ago. He'll be vacationing for three more weeks. At the moment we have no way of getting in touch with him."

I took the card and put it into my wallet.

"We have other pieces by the same sculptor," she added.

Her smile was more friendly this time, but it still fell short of inviting. I sensed the presence beneath her polished surface of some kind of private devil that had to be denied or appeased. I felt like giving her a comforting hug, but the gesture would have been misunderstood.

"Please feel free to browse," she continued. "You

might find something you like as well as the black bear."

Bending gracefully, she put a small piece of piñon wood onto the fire and replaced the screen. The wood caught immediately, wrapping itself in flames. The woman turned back to me. Her eyes suddenly lost their hardness.

"And don't worry about dripping on the carpet while you browse," she said, sotto voce. "The bears aren't housebroken either."

There was a three-beat pause while I dug snow out of my ears and wondered whether I'd really heard what I thought I'd heard. By the time I laughed, she was almost back to the counter. I know she heard me, though; I saw her teeth gleaming when she turned to go into the office once again. I waited for a few minutes. She didn't come back.

It was too soon for the wheel man to have resolved the esthetic problem of ugly weights and out-of-true rims, so I took a turn around the gallery. Except for the bear, the art didn't compel me, although everything in the gallery seemed to be "significant" and perhaps even "important" work, judging by the price tags.

The sculptures were elongated, supplicant *indio* figures almost hidden within flowing alabaster curves. There were Madonna and Child figures, similarly elongated and nearly overwhelmed by the very stone curves that were meant to support them. Scattered among the humans were heavily stylized sculptures of eagles and bears and wolves in rose-colored stone. But there was nothing as successful as the soapstone bear, an extraordinary offspring of the shotgun marriage of two cultures.

I found a collection of antique fetishes in a locked case. Judging from the workmanship, they were genuine and far more primitive in their execution than the contemporary fetishes. The artifacts were frankly sinister—demons who demanded prayers and other, more painful, offerings. Most of the fetishes carried a burden of arrowheads or a leather amulet pouch. All seemed invested with the power to do evil. I moved on quickly, not wanting to worship at that particular altar. As far as I'm concerned, evil is neither so novel nor so fragile that it needs to be enshrined.

There were paintings all over the gallery walls. Some of the art was doubtless quite good, but most of it was merely expensive. The paintings that most often caught my eye were from the Taos Masters, turn-of-the-century New Mexican landscape painters who took lessons from the French Impressionists. Like their California Impressionist brethren, the Taos Masters have gotten short shrift from the East Coast art establishment. But now that abstract expressionism is losing its intellectual allure, traditional forms are coming back into favor. That was the hidden message in the six-figure price tags on these landscapes.

A small side gallery was hung with lesser works. Their prices hovered between $200 and $5,200. One of the landscapes stopped me. I looked for a long time, wondering what there was in the work that had pricked my subconscious. The landscape had the spires and buttes of the Monument Valley at the left of the canvas and the horizon sliding away into a lemon-yellow sunset on the right.

I stepped back a few paces and studied the canvas again. Despite its appeal, the painting didn't quite work. The stone formations were too overwhelming. They kept me in the foreground. Yet the composition was meant to draw the eye into the middle and far distances. When I managed to look into the canvas, I saw that the farthest monuments and sky came together in a way that was indefinably sensual, each thrust of stone met and matched by clinging folds of cloud. That, and the brooding power of the stone buttes, had drawn me. For all its technical flaws, the painting had more life than some of the six-figure "masterworks" in the other room.

I walked forward until I could read the card on the gallery wall: Tenorio, *Place of Power*, $2,500.

As I backed up to study the painting again, I heard a light step and sensed the swirl of soft, fine wool behind me. When I turned, she smiled. It was a different smile from the professionally polite variety I had received before. There was warmth in her now as she stood watching me, her arms folded beneath her breasts. The silver of her heavy necklace shifted and gleamed with each breath she took. Despite her apparent relaxation, I could still sense the hum of fierce tension beneath. Perhaps it was simply a part of her, like her height or her black eyes.

"Find something else you like?" she asked.

Her voice was less cool than it had been, less tightly controlled. Just beneath her Sunbelt Scots-Irish tones lingered a faint thickening of the vowels, legacy of a type of Spanish distinctive to New Mexico.

I nodded at the picture. "This one speaks to me."

"But not as clearly as the bear?"

There was no need to answer; my wallet was still in my hip pocket.

"It's a bit too dramatic, don't you think?" she asked, walking up to me.

"I saw a sky just like that in Four Corners."

"You have a good eye. That's where this was painted. But it looks more like it was painted from a Frederic Remington canvas or a John Ford movie, not from real life."

"Remington and Ford were both real people."

The woman turned her head a bit, studying the canvas dispassionately with her peripheral vision. "The scale is off, as though the scene had been shot through an anamorphic lens. See the pinnacle on the far left? That should have been moved. It should serve as a counterweight to the foreground. It doesn't."

When she gestured toward the painting I became aware for the first time of her hands. Hands are an underappreciated aspect of the human anatomy, male or female. My interest probably springs from my own hands, which failed me as a violinist but have proved quite useful in less peaceful pursuits. As a result, I've picked up a few spectacular scars over the years, some of them visible.

The female hands sketching the limitations of the painting had no scars. The fingers were as long and beautifully tapered as altar candles. Her unpolished nails glistened with health. There was no sign that she had ever worn a ring on her left hand.

"If you moved these elements," the woman continued, pointing to some clumps of chaparral, "and then shifted that monument to, say, about here, you'd have a more balanced result."

She continued to study the landscape. I studied her. Her face was long, lean, with the high cheekbones and well-sculpted features that sometimes result from an amalgamation of races. Her faintly tilted eyes were both clear and very dark. When she sensed that she was being watched, she gave me a quick glance, then tried to divert my attention back to the painting.

"Don't you agree?" she asked.

I looked at the painting again and shrugged. "The artist must have had his reasons."

"Her reasons." She tilted her head to the side slightly, looking at me as though I were a piece of art gone awry. "I'm Maggie Tenorio. I painted that, and I say it's wrong."

Native Americans aren't usually encouraged to paint in the European landscape style, but I didn't doubt Maggie's claim to be the artist. She wasn't the type of woman to be cut down to fit anybody's preconceptions, especially a white man's—even when part of her job was to dazzle the mark with her exotic looks and intimate knowledge of painting.

Almost idly I wondered how carefully she had gone into my credit rating while I stood watching piñon burn. But why wonder when there's a fast way of finding out?

"How about dinner?" I asked.

You can usually tell when a woman wants to say yes but is kept from doing so by something beyond her control—a lover or a previous date, for instance. Maggie's hesitation was different, as was her tense, enigmatic smile.

"My only time to paint is after work. You know how it is."

"Do I?"

Maggie looked at me in surprise. "You're an artist, aren't you?"

I looked at my scarred hands. Not a chance. Not any more. "No."

"You seem more an artist than a collector. You look at the art before you look at the price tag."

I smiled and decided to push some more. At worst I'd be sent on my way. At best I'd have a tense, rather beautiful woman's company for a few hours.

"You sure about dinner?" I asked. "You're going to eat sooner or later tonight. Why not with me?"

She was good. She let me dangle just long enough to tell me that she didn't go out with every man who asked.

"Okay," Maggie finally said, the syllables slow yet tight, as though she were going against her better judgment. "I close here at five and I'll paint until eight. Where are you staying?"

"Nowhere, yet."

She hesitated again. Something in her expression suggested more than the usual singles-bar nervousness about revealing phone numbers and addresses.

"Meet me at the Tecolote Café on Cerrillos Road

across from the Indian school," she said after a moment. "Eight thirty."

"Tecolote Café. Eight thirty."

"Don't be late, *californio*. If you are, I'll eat without you."

Suddenly there was a faint tingle of adrenaline in my blood, the kind of kick a fisherman gets when he sees a trout as long as his arm rising to a well-tied fly. Maggie wouldn't have been able to tell I was from California from a routine check of the credit availability on my AMEX card.

But I said nothing. Whether Maggie's curiosity about me was personal or professional, dinner with her had to be more interesting than watching someone change the Cobra's tires. It also had to be less painful than thinking about Fiora.

Like too many times before, I was half right. Unfortunately, it wasn't the half that counted.

tHREE

Maggie's jeans displayed a handsome Pollock pattern of oils over the hips, as though she cleaned her brushes or wiped paint-stained hands on them. She wore a Pendleton plaid shirt and an old shearling vest with beadwork that looked more northern Athabascan than Southwest. She smelled faintly of solvent and wood smoke and night air. Her hand was cool and tense when I stood up from the table to greet her.

"You like *posole?*" she said.

"As long as I don't have to eat more than four bowls of it."

I seated Maggie and took the chair next to her. The fat white kernels of corn in the *posole* were tender, the chiles were fiery without being brutal, and the *carnitas* was succulent. Just right for a cold night with fresh snow on the ground. So were the *tamales, the rellenos*, and the red sauce. The green sauce made my eyes water, but it was nothing that a second beer and a fat white-flour tortilla couldn't handle. I ate silently and steadily, enjoying the food, letting Maggie set the pace for whatever she had in mind.

When I reached for my beer after a final round of green sauce, Maggie smiled. She looked tired but more relaxed than she had at the gallery. Maybe her painting had gone well.

"And here comes something you can't get in California," she announced as the waitress left a covered basket on the table. "*Sopaipillas.*"

Maggie removed the napkins reverently. I waited until she had filled the hollow fry-bread triangle with honey and had taken a big bite.

"How do you know I'm from California?"

There was a long silence while Maggie chewed, swallowed, and sighed. "You don't miss much, do you?"

I waited.

"It was your fancy card. I called American Express and said I needed your billing address. It came back to Pacific Rim Investments in Beverly Hills."

I waited some more.

"I've never met a man who lived in an investment house," Maggie said, licking honey from her palm.

"PRI is my bookkeeper's firm."

"Your bookkeeper must be very fond of you." She said it calmly, but there was a definite query in her voice.

"Meaning?"

"Meaning that somebody at PRI confirmed your

address. Then, ten minutes after you left this afternoon, I got a call from a woman named Fiora Flynn."

For several seconds I tried to think of something that would have surprised me more. I came up empty. It was a small goddamn world, getting smaller every day. I had the distinct feeling that I'd run to the end of my string when I wasn't looking.

"Benny," I finally said.

She gave me a sideways look. "You lost me."

"But I didn't lose myself," I said, disgusted.

"You were trying?"

"Yeah, sort of. But I guess I was carrying a transponder around in my wallet without even knowing it. What did Fiora want?"

"She wanted to know how you were. You sure she isn't your shrink rather than your bookkeeper?"

"She's a world-class money shuffler. An investment banker."

Maggie gave me a cool look. "Whatever you say."

"She's also my ex-wife."

"Oh."

"She's been 'ex' for a long time, so long we'd almost become friends again. That ended a couple of months ago. It all came apart. Done. Finished. Kaput."

"She didn't seem to think so."

I shrugged. Since our divorce, Fiora and I had both learned that we were too connected to one another to tear apart easily. God knows I'd tried, and never harder than in the past months. So had she, but not lately. We never could seem to let go of each other at the same time. A deeply buried part of me was glad. The rest of me was mad enough to kill.

"Actually, I met your wife—"

"Ex-wife."

"—at an opening last year," Maggie continued, ignoring my interruption. "Olin Nickelaw, my boss, has galleries in Palm Springs and Beverly Hills. Several of Ms. Flynn's clients do business with us."

I reached for a *sopaipilla*, tore off the corner as Maggie had done, and poured honey into the warm hollow.

Maggie studied her coffee cup, then gave me a look from underneath her eyelashes that was meant to appeal to my hormones. The impact was diminished because I could sense a tightness in her that had nothing to do with sex. When I didn't respond, she dropped the coyness and addressed me directly.

"Your name is Fiddler, and your mail is sent to one of the hottest investment firms in the U.S., and your ex-wife's voice isn't quite steady when she asks how you're doing." Maggie set her coffee cup aside. "So what do you do when you're not trying to buy black bears that are already sold?"

"Didn't that American Express computer tell you?"

"It told me enough to get you company for dinner. You may think you're special, but there are a lot of broad-shouldered, battle-scarred cowboys wandering around Santa Fe. A few of them have ten thousand dollars in their jeans, too."

"Would you be relieved or disappointed to find out that I'm not a coke dealer?"

"Relieved. Are you a coke dealer?"

"No."

She let out a long breath. "Okay. But I've got to tell you, you don't come across like an investment banker either."

"Now it's my turn to be relieved."

Maggie laughed. It was a nice sound, even though it was like her smile—too tight, too brief.

"What do you do?" she asked finally.

I wondered what she had in mind for me that went beyond my credit rating, but all I said was, "I'm retired."

"From what?"

That made me smile. From Maggie's reaction, the smile wasn't one of my more reassuring efforts.

"Benny describes me as one of Southern California's most forceful social critics," I said.

"What?"

"When I see something I don't like, I criticize it. Sometimes forcefully."

Maggie's expression changed. For a few moments she looked like the woman who had talked about sculptures that weren't housebroken.

"Sounds like a job I could get into," she said.

"It has its moments."

She looked at my scarred hands. "Yeah. I'll bet. Dangerous work, criticizing."

I let it go by.

Maggie frowned into her empty coffee cup. She looked around the steamy, fragrant restaurant as though surprised to find herself there. I ate some *sopaipilla*, licked stray honey from the back of my thumb, and thought about how bloody small the

world is. The first woman in months who had gotten past my anger just happened to know Fiora.

I hate coincidences.

"Maggie?"

"Hmm?"

"Why did you run a make on me?"

"I was curious."

"Why?"

"The way you look, you could be anything from a
dope dealer to a hit man to a Hollywood actor."

"Why couldn't I simply be a customer wanting to
buy a black bear?"

Maggie's expression shut down and her buried
tension all but hummed audibly. She caught a
strand of dark hair and pulled it back behind her ear
with a jerky motion. It was the same for her voice.
Jerky.

"Habit," she said tightly. "Olin likes to know who
he's dealing with."

That might have been partly true. I was interested
in the part that wasn't true.

"My credit rating should have reassured him, if
art is all he's selling," I pointed out. "Maybe he
deals something heavier than soapstone bears. A
gallery could launder a hell of a lot of dirty money."

She shrugged. "This one doesn't."

One of the waitresses across the room set a beer
mug down sharply on a table. Maggie flinched as
though she had been shot. The lady was very
jumpy.

"Social critic, huh?" she said, tapping her short
nails on the coffee cup. "Ever hire yourself out?"
She smiled to tell me she was half joking.

But only half.

I shook my head. "That's the problem with us re-tired types. We're penalized for working. Every dollar I made would be deducted from my Social Security check, and pretty soon I'd owe the government money."

"You'd like Olin. He's a cocky bastard too."

"So I only take on jobs that interest me," I said, ignoring her dig. "No charge for the service. What kind of social criticism did you have in mind?"

Maggie came close to accepting the invitation. I could see her rising, nosing the lure . . . and then sliding away once more, leaving my offer untouched.

"The only thing I have in mind right now is sleep," she said, pushing back her chair decisively. "Thanks for dinner, cowboy. If the bear becomes available, I'll tell Pacific Rim Investments to pass along the message."

We were the only diners left in the place, so I didn't argue about leaving the restaurant. I dropped a twenty on the table and followed Maggie to the front door, falling into step beside her on the way out. She hesitated, started to object, then didn't.

The sky had cleared. The ground and the rooftops were covered by four inches of snow that glowed silver-white beneath the moonlight. The air was still and cold, reminding me of Montana in February. I half expected to hear cattle bawling or a horse stamping and snorting in protest against a cold saddle, but the only sound was the thin cry of the snow being compressed beneath our boots.

The restaurant's parking area was empty except

for the newly shod Cobra and an American four-door sedan that sat in the shadows at the far corner of the lot, as though the car belonged to one of the kitchen help. Both vehicles were mantled by snow. Maggie glanced across the lot, then back at me. She pulled her thick collar higher.

"Thanks," she said, giving me a look from eyes much darker than the night sky. "This wasn't a good night to eat alone."

She turned away, ignoring the parking lot, moving with the long-legged strides of a woman accustomed to walking.

"Wait. Do you need a ride?"

Maggie looked back. I gestured toward the Cobra. Her teeth were a flash of white against her shadowed face.

"Thanks, but no thanks. It's only a few blocks. That thing looks like it would be lethal in fresh snow."

"Then I'll walk you home."

Again the hesitation as she examined my offer for hooks. "Okay. But that's all, Fiddler. Just a walk."

"If you're worried about my manners, I'll stay here."

Without answering, Maggie walked toward me until she could really see my eyes and I could see hers.

"I'm not worried. A guy like you can get all the women he wants without twisting any arms."

It could have been a come-on, but it wasn't. Maggie wasn't giving off any of the subtle, unmistakable signals. The lady had something on her mind, and it wasn't sex. So we walked down the street side by side and a hundred miles apart. Santa Fe is a quiet town after dark. The rasp of our boots on the freshly cleared sidewalk was almost as loud as the traffic noise from two streets over.

Maggie walked with her hands shoved into the pockets of her shearling vest and her eyes on the sidewalk. When we were about fifty feet from a side street, I heard the sound of an engine starting up in the parking lot of the restaurant we had just left.

"I didn't have the advantage of a computer credit check," I said. "Tell me about yourself, Maggie Tenorio."

Her shoulders lifted in a graceful shrug. "Not much to tell. I paint, but not well enough, and I work in a gallery."

I had said the same thing about myself years ago: *I play violin, but not well enough.* Then I had thrown the violin beneath the wheels of a southbound Corvette and watched while a piece of my soul was ground into the pavement. I'd been too young then to live with the difference between good and perfect. I wondered if Maggie was that young, or if she had made some peace with the limitations of her talent.

"You didn't learn to paint in Santa Fe," I said. "You're much closer to Impressionism than to R. C. Gorman."

"I got my start across the street, though." Maggie nodded back toward the shadowy buildings on the other side of Cerrillos Road. "That's the Institute of American Indian Arts." She pulled her hands out of her vest and spread her fingers wide. "Geronimo

was said to have perfectly formed hands. I'm de-
scended directly from him."

In the cold moonlight Maggie's hands were elegant, almost eerie in their flawless proportions.
Slowly she curled her fingers into fists and shoved
them inside her vest pockets once more.

"I have to get home," she said, moving away.

I glanced over my shoulder, listening for the
sound of a car turning onto the street and coming
slowly toward us. I heard only my own breathing. A
few steps brought me abreast of Maggie again.

"Did the Institute teach you Impressionist techniques?" I asked.

Maggie made a sound that could have been stifled
laughter or disgust. "I learned that on the East
Coast. Someone tried to turn me into a refined
white-lady painter. MFA all the way."

"It didn't take."

She gave me a look out of eyes like clear black ice.
"You're a Westerner. You know where I came from.
You know what reservations are like." Her voice
was soft, but it shook with repressed energy. "The
rich Ivy League guys thought I was real exotic, until
one of them tried to introduce me to rough sex. I
broke his little snub nose."

Her head turned just enough to catch my grin.
She grinned in return.

"Geronimo would have loved you," I said.

"Geronimo would have let his women string that
Ivy League white eyes up by the heels and cook his
brains over a slow fire." Maggie let out a harsh
breath. "I'd like to say my own kind have been better to me. They haven't. I learned how to handle

rutting boys in the river willows behind the reservation council house when I was thirteen."

"Boys?" I asked dryly.

"Yeah. Boys. The men are no problem. Budweiser Droop takes care of them. The sex drive is the first thing to go. Ask any Native woman."

From the willows by the reservation river to the gallery beside the high-ticket tourist plaza. That's a long way to go, running on a combination of ambition and rage. Maggie's nights in the willows weren't anything to cherish; I wondered if her days in the gallery by the plaza were any better.

I listened carefully for cars. Nothing but the brittle scrape of boots over frigid cement.

Maggie turned off Cerrillos onto a side street that hadn't been plowed. I followed. The rasping of our boots became a soft grinding sound as we walked on unmarked snow. The street went for two blocks before it dead-ended against a head-high adobe wall that surrounded a cluster of houses. Once this had been a barrio. Now the street jogged to the left and found a gap in the barrio wall. Maggie stopped at the entrance to the little neighborhood. I looked over my shoulder. Nothing was moving on the street.

"I can make it alone from here," she said.

"You sure?" I asked, listening, listening for the sound of a car.

"I live right over there."

She pointed toward a small adobe house a hundred feet away, then stepped close to me and turned her face up as though to be kissed. Before I could take her up on the invitation, she stood on tiptoe and whispered a question.

"Is he close?"

"Who?"

"The man following you."

I kissed Maggie's cool cheek like a dutiful cousin and said, "He's parked half a block over, and he's following you, not me. Feel in need of a little constructive criticism yet?"

fOUR

"What makes you so sure he's following me?"

There was more curiosity than doubt in Maggie's question, so I gave it to her by the numbers.

"There was a car in the far corner of the parking lot at the Tecolote. Now there's a car of the same make and color parked half a block over from here. I can see its front end just sticking out past the wall at the end of the block. Only difference between this car and the one in the Tecolote's lot is that the snow on the hood of this car has started to melt, like the engine's been running in the past few minutes."

Maggie didn't turn to look. Either she had no curiosity or she wasn't surprised somebody was watching her.

"He could still be following you," she said.

"Not likely. I didn't know where I was going. He did. He was parked and waiting while we were still talking about Geronimo's hands. Then he pulled out of the restaurant lot and took the long way here. Either he's a mind reader or he knew where we were going."

"Shit," she said softly.

"You know who it is?"

Maggie stepped away, kicked at a mound of snow with the toe of her boot, and gave the car a quick glance from the corner of her eye. "I can't tell who's inside."

"Guess."

There was a silence; then she shrugged. "I was going out with this man. He was married and his wife turned real ugly. I broke it off a few weeks ago, but she may have hired somebody to follow me and see if he's still hanging around."

Maybe it just wasn't Maggie's night for telling lies, or maybe it just wasn't mine for believing them.

"Well, there's a fast way to find out," I said, turning toward the car.

Maggie grabbed my arm before I could take a step.

"What the hell do you think you're doing?" she demanded in a fierce whisper. "You can't just walk up and ask who he is!"

"Why not?"

She stared at me, blinked, then tilted her head and laughed with a fierce kind of pleasure—Geronimo's offspring down to the tips of her perfectly shaped fingers.

"All right, cowboy. You're on."

"Get your house key ready."

She fished in her hip pocket. A few moments later her hand emerged. A key gleamed in the moonlight.

"We're going to walk toward your front door," I

said. "Once we move out of his line of sight, you keep going. I'll hop the wall and get around behind him."

"Do you have a gun?"

"No. I'm not dressed to be a social critic tonight. I thought I was just going out to dinner with a genteel art dealer from the Nickelaw Gallery. So if you hear shots, do me a favor—call the paramedics before you call the cops. Ready? Good. Let's go."

We went through the gate and up the front walk. There wasn't much yard. The fresh snow hadn't been marked up by a prowler's footprints. As Maggie moved into the shadows beneath the overhang at her front door, I turned and crossed the side yard in a rush, brushing aside the low branches of an evergreen as I went. There was a flicker of movement on the wall ahead. A handful of snow dropped off. It was too far away for me to have knocked the snow loose.

The peeper had been more aggressive than I expected. He had gotten out of the car and watched us over the wall.

There were rapid footsteps, a skidding sound, and a hissed curse from the other side of the wall. I grabbed the top of the wall and levered myself up in time to see a man wearing a dark parka and trousers scramble to his feet.

"Police! Freeze!" I shouted as I vaulted the wall.

It was a lie, but it usually works better than "Citizen! Freeze!" This guy didn't seem impressed, though. He just ran, skidded again, then scrambled up and leaped for his car. The driver's door was standing open. He grabbed it, rebounded, cursed, and went headlong into the driver's seat. The key must have been in the ignition, because the starter began grinding right away.

The car was badly tuned. He was still cranking on the starter when I hit the driver's door, yanked it open with one hand, and grabbed a handful of parka collar with the other.

There was a bad smell inside but I was too busy to be offended. I got a glimpse of a white face staring at me and of a hand covered by a black leather glove. The hand came looping off the steering wheel in a back-handed swipe. I swung the door in, hoping he would crack his knuckles on something less tender than my face.

Safety glass exploded inches away from my head.

Even as I ducked, I realized what had happened. The son of a bitch was wearing sap gloves. The lead inserts along the back of the fingers were guaranteed to put a little zing in even the most mediocre punch. Whoever this clown was, he played hardball. That made me feel a whole lot better. I'd have hated to unload eight weeks' worth of anger on a middle-aged loser who was trying to pay off his MasterCard before his liver turned to Swiss cheese.

I still had hold of the parka hood with one hand, and he was still cranking on the starter. I took an extra turn of cloth around my fist just as the engine finally caught. He stabbed the accelerator at the same moment that he jerked the shift lever into DRIVE. The back wheels spun viciously in the fresh snow, sending clots of white flying. A few seconds later, rubber spun down to pavement and bit hard.

The car lurched forward and simultaneously slewed sideways.

The surge broke my grip on his coat and ruined my balance. I was falling backward when the rear fender gave me a flying kiss as it went by. The blow knocked the wind out of me and flipped me into a snow-covered shrub. I dumped out on my knees, wiped snow from my eyes, and tried to catch a license number on the car. The streetlight on the corner was bright enough that I noticed something I hadn't seen before. The car had California plates.

That explained why he was such a lousy winter driver. He fishtailed all over the place until he slid out onto a plowed street. Then he straightened out, whipped around the corner, and vanished.

The snow stung my bare hands and ate into my knees. When it comes to insulating against cold, denim isn't worth a damn. I pulled myself to my feet, brushed off, and learned how to breathe again. About the third breath I realized that it was an incredibly beautiful night, with a glittering wash of brilliant-cut D-flawless stars in the west, a bright moon poised 15 degrees above the mountain in the east, air so pure it was more heady than wine. . . .

And I was alive to enjoy all of it.

Maggie's voice came from the other side of the wall, a single anxious word. "Fiddler?"

"It's safe. He's gone."

"Are you all right?"

I looked at my bleeding palm, felt the ache in my knees, shook glass from my jacket, and began laughing.

"I'm fine, Maggie. Hell, I'm better than fine. I haven't felt this good since I left California."

Maggie came down the sidewalk, stopped, and stared at me. "You're crazy."

"Probably." I laughed again and stretched. Everything was still connected. "You know anybody in California who wants to give you grief?"

"What?"

"The guy watching you had California plates on his car."

She gave me a blank, expressionless look. "You're the one from California. You tell me."

I shook my head. "What kind of trouble are you in?"

There was a pause, then a curse. "Nothing I can't handle." Her voice was like her face. Blank.

"Can you handle sap gloves?"

Still blank, as though she didn't understand.

"He was wearing the kind of equipment that professionals use—cops and leg-breakers and other people who hit folks for a living."

Maggie blinked, then let out a long breath.

"I've lived alone for the past ten years in towns that are a lot rougher than Santa Fe," she said finally. "I have deadbolts front and back, alarms on the windows, Mace on the bedside table, and a loaded twelve-gauge shotgun under the bed, if it comes to that."

A single look at Maggie's face told me I wasn't going to get to hear her story tonight and probably not tomorrow night, either. If the damsel was in distress, it didn't show.

"Good night, Maggie."

I was halfway down the block before her voice came back to me over the creak of the closing gate.

"Good night, Fiddler. And . . . thanks."

"My pleasure."

And it had been.

I collected the Cobra and went looking for a place to get in out of the snow. The first VACANCY sign I saw was on La Fonda. At their prices, I wasn't surprised. The desk clerk took my magic platinum card and gave me back a warm place to sleep. As soon as I got to my room, I called the Santa Fe Police Department. The desk officer claimed he couldn't take a prowler report, or order extra patrols in Maggie's neighborhood, unless I gave him my name. I stayed anonymous and hung up, figuring that Santa Fe was a small enough town that the night-shift cops might get the word anyway.

My second call was to Benny. I let it ring forever, not because Benny's in a wheelchair but because he's an independent sort who only answers the phone when he feels like it. Sometimes it takes sixteen rings to get him in the mood. Most times it takes longer.

I had counted twenty-seven rings when an answering machine cut in. I almost dropped the receiver in surprise. Benny had never had an electronic secretary before; if he wasn't home when you called, tough. The recorded message was another surprise.

"Listen, you stiff-necked sod, if you don't get your bleeding arse home soon you won't have anything worth coming home to."

Benny must have figured I was the only person in

the world who would wait twenty-seven rings to see if he felt like picking up the phone.

The machine gave the customary piercing beep and waited obediently for my message.

"Find out who belongs to California plate number one Charlie delta Mary fiver two four," I said. "Then find me. And bugger you too, old pal."

fIVE

We all leave a paper trail on the way through life —bank records, credit-card chits, telephone tolls. The problem has gotten worse with computers. The only way to avoid it is to carry cash and use public telephones. I hadn't been that interested in hiding during the last two months. Still, it irritated me to know that Fiora had been less than an hour behind me when Maggie ran my credit card through her validation machine at the Nickelaw Gallery.

There's no magic to tracing someone, at least not with the help of a guy like Benny Speidel. Benny has friends in all kinds of strange places—including, obviously, the computer room at American Express. That was how he got the trap put on my card.

The trap probably consisted of nothing more than a computer signal. Every time a merchant in the United States ran my card through his electronic validator, the AMEX computer executed a little two-step. First it told the merchant I was good for the tab. Then it relayed the time, place, and purchase to Benny's friend, who immediately called Benny, who immediately called Fiora.

God save us from clever friends.

If it had been anybody else I would have gone hunting, but Benny is different. Before Fiora betrayed me to the FBI, there were two people in the world I thought of as friends. Now Benny is the only one. All the rest of the people I've known are acquaintances or lovers or enemies, sometimes all three at once. Benny doesn't fit in any category. He's never betrayed me, nor I him, which is more than I can say for either my acquaintances or my lovers. Or my wife. My *ex*-wife.

Maybe Benny and I get along because we see the world pretty much in the same way. He's a hell of a lot brighter about it, of course. He has a genius for understanding how the world really works, as opposed to how idealists such as Fiora would like it to work or how pragmatists like me try to make it work.

Benny's a free-lance computer and high-tech consultant to every spooky agency in the Free World, but for him the hardware is only a means to an end; the end itself is information. He uses his battery of personal computers, mini-mainframes, and 1200-baud modems to reach around the world, tapping data bases and computer banks that contain most of the information extant in the world, free or otherwise.

Thanks to a Geneva science consortium Benny belongs to, he can even query unclassified data bases in the U.S.S.R. as easily as most people use an automated teller machine. Actually, Benny says the Soviets are probably as open with access to their data bases as any country in the world. It's the computers they put under lock and key.

Benny's electronic talents seem magical to lots of people, but I've gotten used to him. Which is why I was not at all surprised to find a La Fonda phone slip under my door the next morning. The message was succinct: *NIF.* Followed by *Piss off, mate, we got tired of waiting for a postcard.*

Benny is the only man I know who has a command of slang in three foreign languages and all dialects of English.

While I thought about the ramifications of the fact that the license plate was Not In File, I showered, dressed, and ate breakfast at a French bakery in the shadow of the Archbishop's Cathedral. I took a second cup of coffee back to my room and sat looking over Santa Fe's low-roofed adobe sprawl, trying to choose among the possible explanations of why a California license plate would not be in the California Department of Motor Vehicles file. The most common reason was that the car had recently changed hands and the new paperwork hadn't been fed into the computer. Another good possibility was that the plates had been "salvaged" from a wrecked car that previously had been written off by an insurance company and the DMV.

The most interesting possibility was that the license plate was NIF because the number had been issued to an undercover police vehicle. Crooks are almost as adept at running license numbers as cops are, and the quickest way in the world to blow an undercover narcotics investigation is to have the customer's plate go back to the U.S. Drug Enforcement Administration, Washington, D.C.

I reached for the phone and started punching in Benny's number. He would know the answer. If not, he was in a better position to make an expert guess than I was, and he knew it as well as I did. Usually he would have included his guess along with the NIF.

That was why I could sense Benny waiting for me to pick up a phone and call him. My hand stopped short of the final numbers as I realized that I wasn't ready to deal with all the broken pieces I'd left behind in Southern California. At the very least, I sure as hell wasn't ready to contend with both Benny and Fiora.

We got tired of waiting for a postcard. Not *I*, but *we*.

I hung up the phone and went for a walk. The snow on the plaza was so clean it squeaked beneath my feet. The sky was a pure, frigid blue. The temperature was in the teens, and a sharp little coyote wind gnawed at my ears. The air shone like polished crystal. I spent an hour in Los Llanos, the best bookstore I'd seen in a year. The Cobra couldn't have held half of what I wanted, so I had the store ship everything to California and went outside again.

Wind swept through the arcade in front of the Governors' Palace. As cold as it was, two dozen silversmiths and jewelry makers were huddled along the adobe wall, seeking shelter from the wind. They wore bolo ties and ear cuffs and had neat rows of

cultured turquoise rings spread on blankets in front
of them.

Most of the time I suppose the jewelers did a
healthy business, particularly when the lack of overhead is figured into the profit. Santa Fe is a nexus
for more than New Age planetary forces; conventioneers cluster here as well. Today the city was
hosting a national meeting of real estate appraisers.
Folks from Keokuk and Paducah and Wind Gap
shuffled back and forth, hunched against the cold,
bending over now and again to examine the silver
jewelry and the sand paintings. Bolo ties seemed to
be moving well enough, but nobody was getting
rich. The Indian merchants sat on their heels, swad-
dled in colorful wool blankets, polite and pro-
foundly bored.

A silversmith with a gold incisor stood wrapped in
a green three-point Hudson's Bay blanket, stamping
his New Balance 675s to warm his feet. His vendor's
badge identified him as Johnny Begay from Nambe
Pueblo, up toward the federal nuclear weapons lab
at Los Alamos. His rings were well above the standards of the arcade bazaar. They had heavy silver
shanks and genuine turquoise beautifully marbled
with brown matrix.

"Local stone?" I asked, hefting a ring that
weighed four or five ounces.

He shook his head. "Afghanistan. The *mujahedeen*
have been bringing out all kinds of stuff—turquoise,
lapis lazuli, faceted crystal. They're trading it for
guns." His brick-colored face shifted around a wide
grin. "Wars ain't all bad. I've never seen rough
stone this good."

Without haggling I paid him what he was asking for the ring. Benny's politics are retrograde enough that he would love the ring for its political significance alone. The fact that the ring was masculine without being clunky, and wouldn't catch on all the drawers in his workshop, was a bonus.

I left the plaza and wandered the narrow winding streets, letting the wind push me as I had been doing for the past eight weeks. Before I realized it, I found myself on the block behind the Nickelaw Gallery.

The art business must have been better than a license to steal. There was a dirty black Lamborghini Countache in the gallery parking spot marked "NICKELAW." The mud streaks made me pause. A guy shouldn't let a $150,000 piece of art get dirty. Of course, I had no room to talk, the way I'd let the Cobra go to hell recently.

The alarm on the gallery door chimed pleasantly as I came in a step behind a lanky kid in a shearling coat carrying a small framed canvas wrapped in brown paper. Two voices from the back room had stopped talking at the sound of the chimes. The gallery itself was empty but for the whispering of flames in the corner fireplace.

"Here's your Fechin, Maggie," the kid called toward the office. "You were right. It couldn't take the heavier frame."

"Just leave it. Olin and I are busy." Maggie's response sounded both preoccupied and curt. The kid from the frame shop caught the off note too. He glanced at the office door, made a sour face in response, then laid the painting on the counter and left. The chimes sounded again on his way out.

Maggie and Nickelaw must have thought they were alone again. The last resonance of the door alarm hadn't faded before the argument resumed.

"You'll do as you're told." Nickelaw's voice was male, calm and certain, the kind of voice used to giving unquestioned orders. "Hear me, Maggie?"

I had only had dinner with the lady, but I knew Nickelaw was taking the wrong approach. I heard the flat, unmistakable sound of an open hand striking flesh. At first I thought he had tripped Maggie's hair trigger and gotten himself smacked for his efforts. Then I heard a guttural snarl and a voice so enraged that it took me a moment to recognize it as hers.

"Touch me again and I'll cut off those *cojones* you're so proud of and feed them to the ants."

"Listen, bitch—"

I was already moving toward the office when the front door chime went off again and the voices stopped. A short, light-skinned Latina in a fur cap and a Postal Service uniform breezed in, a leather pouch over her shoulder. She glanced at me, then around the gallery.

"Anybody home?" she called. "Certified letter here. Somebody's gotta sign."

Nobody answered. By now I was close enough to the office to see in at an angle. There was an incredible apparition just inside the office. Slender yet deeply curved, artfully blond, the young woman made me understand the meaning of drop-dead beautiful. She was lounging with a dancer's grace against a desk, her arms crossed over her chest and held so that they pushed up her full breasts. From the lack of expression on her expensively tanned face, she could have been watching a TV soap opera instead of a real-life slapping match.

There was something faintly familiar about the girl's face, but before I could place it, the twilight hazel of her wide, feral eyes and the flick of pink tongue over her lush mouth distracted me.

She moved out of the office doorway, only to be replaced by another apparition, a male too beautiful to be turned loose among mortals. Nickelaw moved with the kind of spring-loaded grace that a dancer or a gymnast sometimes achieves. Like the girl, he was slender, well-built, and blond. But his hair was cropped rather than long and he had the kind of blue eyes that are invariably called sapphire because no other description gets the job done. Clean-shaven, supple, muscular: he had it all, and the black leather outfit he wore showed it all, including the balls Maggie had just threatened to remove.

Abruptly Maggie appeared behind Nickelaw. Her black eyes burned with cold energy. There was an open pocketknife in her hand. She held the weapon waist high, blade turned up, telling anybody who cared that she understood the basic techniques of fighting with a knife. I thought of the willows behind the reservation hall.

A single sapphire glance from Nickelaw took in the mail carrier and me. He hissed something under his breath and moved to block my view of Maggie, but not before I saw her glance down at her hand as though surprised to find the knife there. She folded it quickly and closed her fist over it.

"I'll sign," he said impatiently, coming out of the office. His movements were quick, clean, hard, reminding me of the blade Maggie had put away.

The letter carrier read the address off the envelope. "Are you Olin Nickelaw?"

"Yes." His voice was neither deep nor high, simply curt.

Nickelaw took the letter, signed with his left hand, and shoved the certified receipt back at the letter carrier. He turned and looked at me again, his eyes narrowing as they took in my jeans, scarred boots, and generally scruffy appearance. My facial proportions weren't close to his perfection, but his expression suggested that he wouldn't have been impressed by God himself.

"Was there something?" Nickelaw asked me with clear disdain.

In case I was as thick as I looked, he raised his left eyebrow to underline his aristocratic contempt of the peasantry.

"Yeah, there's something, but it will wait." I gave him a smile that said I wasn't knocked out with him either.

The letter carrier sensed the tension. She dropped a sheaf of generic mail on the counter, glanced at the two of us, and quickly withdrew.

"What is it?" Nickelaw demanded as soon as the door chimes faded.

He stood with his legs spread a bit, weight forward on the balls of his feet, like Baryshnikov or Carl Lewis. His blond hair was cut as close as a working quarterhorse's mane. A handmade white shirt set off the black leather pants and jacket very nicely. A five-pound concho belt gleamed around his flat middle. When he moved I could see that the leather was as supple as chamois and nearly as thin. One of the gallery lights caught the soft glint of silver in his left earlobe.

"Well?" Nickelaw demanded.

Because he had moved, I could see Maggie again. Clearly. The mark on her cheek was dark and angry.

"Don't fold up that knife on my account," I said to her. "I've seen blood before."

Nickelaw took a step foward. "Listen, cowboy, I don't know who you are, but you're in the wrong picture show."

"I'm just a customer who wants to buy that black bear," I said, gesturing toward the sculpture. "The one that's already sold."

Nickelaw looked over his shoulder at Maggie, showing me a Greek profile that hadn't come from a surgeon's knife. "Is this the guy?"

Maggie brushed past Nickelaw and came to stand between us. The red warmup suit she had on wasn't the kind women wear to soak up sweat. The fabric had been hand-painted with a silver squash-blossom necklace around the collar and elegantly stylized medicine feathers along the outside of the leg. When she moved, the suit molded to her, revealing a frankly voluptuous body.

"This is Fiddler," Maggie said calmly. "He left a deposit on the bear in case Dr. Demberg backed out."

Nickelaw looked at me again, more carefully. "So you collect stone. Who have you bought lately?"

The tone of his voice said he didn't believe I had the money or taste to collect anything more than flies. As a tactic for interrogation, arrogance can be fairly successful, especially when used by someone you want to impress. Nickelaw was accustomed to people wanting to impress him for no better reason than his handsome face.

"You're half right about me," I said to Nickelaw. "For you, I'll bet that's a pretty good average."

"Fiddler's not a collector," Maggie said quickly. "He's a walk-in who fell in love with that bear."

Nickelaw absorbed that. Between one blink and the next, he changed his stance. "A walk-in, huh? You still interested in the bear?"

"Did Dr. Demberg change his mind?" I asked.

"For the right price, I might be able to do something for you. A deal's not done until I say it's done." Nickelaw's smile turned on and off like a strobe light. "Besides, the doctor doesn't know soapstone from cement blocks. He collects what I tell him to collect and sells what I tell him to sell. For fifteen grand he'll sell the bear."

Nickelaw was pushing, trying to decide whether I was rich and stupid or simply eager to get close to him. Dope dealers use the same ploy to separate undercover cops from real customers. No righteous doper would pay more than the going market rate. Addicts are crazy but they aren't fools.

I gave Nickelaw a bland smile and said, "For fifteen grand, I'd sell the bear too."

Nickelaw's smile faded, as though he had suddenly lost interest in me. He turned away, grabbed a black leather portfolio case with silver buckles from beneath the counter, and straightened up again. He put his hand on Maggie's arm and bent over her. He spoke in a quiet conversational tone but he didn't bother to hide his words, as though he didn't care about being overheard.

"Listen, cunt. You're good, but in this business, good is just another word for second-rate. You walk out, and it'll take me maybe five minutes to find someone just like you. You stay, and I'll put your stuff right out there with the best. Hear me?"

Maggie's dark eyes narrowed, but before she could lash out with the knife in her hand, he was out the back door. The drop-dead blonde was a few steps behind him. A few seconds later I heard the Countache caterwauling out of the parking lot.

"If he treats that car as bad as his help and his clientele, he's going to lose all three," I said. "Along with his balls."

"His customers are the nouveau riche. They don't know art but they know what Olin likes. They love it when he talks dirty to them."

"What about you? Do you love it?"

Maggie gave me the kind of look that reminded me of the knife in her hand. She didn't love Nickelaw's act any better than he would have loved singing soprano.

"Want to talk about it?" I offered.

She didn't say anything.

I shrugged. Dealer's choice, and in this game Maggie was the dealer. I headed for the door and some fresh air. "If you change your mind before I leave

town, try La Fonda," I said, but I didn't hang
around for an answer.

The door opened before I got there: another customer, or another tourist tired of the cold.

"Fiddler—wait."

I stood in the open door, letting the fresh air pour
over me for a moment. Then I looked back at Maggie.

"Meet me at the Fine Arts Museum," she said.
"One o'clock."

Before I could answer, Maggie turned to the
shivering customer and went back to work selling
art.

S|X

The Fine Arts Museum was just off the plaza. The wind and I went in together. The warmth felt good. Even in the dry highland air, cold weather gnaws away your energy one calorie at a time. The lobby of the building was quiet and soothing in its almost medieval Spanish architecture.

The museum's ambiance of spacious peace didn't last beyond the door of the main gallery, which was filled with the works of some frenetic splatter painter who made me feel edgy all over again. The modernists seem to be everywhere, even in Santa Fe, like blush-wine bottles on back-country roads. After a few minutes the canvases got on my nerves. I retreated to the gift shop off the lobby.

The shop had a big selection of books on the Taos Masters. I skimmed the shelves, refreshing myself on the history of the school. The best of the Taos Masters had been pioneers as well as artists. Two of them were art students looking for a new visual fix. They stumbled across the little village of Taos in the 1890s and became the nucleus for the colony of landscape and portrait painters, photographers, and writers who eventually settled in the New Mexican highlands.

As with most art colonies west of the Hudson, the Taos school was idiosyncratic, eclectic, and carefully disdained by Manhattan. The southwestern painters didn't have time to notice the snub. Realism, impressionism, cubism, even art deco competed for influence over the energetic pioneers, but the New Mexicans always put their own twist on whatever style of art they tried.

I felt an affinity for the early artists. They were restless, unruly, and secretly hoping to leave the world a better place than they had found it. As I leafed through glossy art books, I couldn't help wondering if any of the Taos Masters had dangled in their own minds and times over the chasm between "good" and "great."

The only answer to my question was obvious; whether through confidence or desperation, they had kept on painting. If they hadn't, other names and faces and landscapes would be separating the covers of the gift shop's books. Cold comfort for the fiddler without a violin.

"He's not great, but he's not that bad," said Maggie's voice by my elbow.

My head snapped up from the color plate of a Nicolai Fechin painting. "Are you a mind reader?"

"You don't have to be a *bruja* to read your frown."

"I was just wondering whether arrogance or desperation kept some of these guys painting."

"Fechin kept painting because people kept buying," she said nonchalantly. "He wasn't in it for the art. He had to make a living."

"But he had to realize he was no Georgia O'Keeffe. Hell, he wasn't even fit to clean her brushes." I flipped a few pages and pointed to a painting of a single crimson poppy. There was lush invitation in the flower's petals, oblivion in its black center, and a shimmering enigma at its core. The flower was vital, sensual, challenging, and . . . dangerous. "Look at it. O'Keeffe's poppy reminds you that flowers are as fiercely alive as tigers."

"The feminine principle," Maggie said, as though she were quoting someone, "source of all life and, because of that, dangerous." She looked at me oddly. "Do you like O'Keeffe's flower paintings?"

Like was a pretty flat word for what the poppy accomplished. "They speak to me—like the bear."

"Most men prefer these," Maggie said, reaching past me and turning pages.

She pointed to O'Keeffe's famous variations on a cattle skull hanging in the desert sky like a bleached, sand-blasted sun. Then came variations on the *penitente* crosses dividing a dry land into bleak, uneven quadrants. As I looked at the O'Keeffe color plates, I was aware of Maggie watching my face.

"Well?" she asked after a time.

"Well what?"

"Do you like these?"

"Not as well as the poppy."

The sexy, amused smile Maggie gave me was unlike anything I'd ever seen on her face. "Know something, Fiddler? I'll bet no girl was ever forced to break your nose."

I laughed. "So far so good."

Maggie's smile broadened. "Have you been upstairs yet?"

"No."

"C'mon. I have a treat for you."

She took the book from me, shelved it, and pulled on my hand. Not knowing what to expect, I followed her. She darted up the stairs with the eagerness of a kid climbing up to Christmas.

"What—" I began.

"Nope," she said, cutting me off. "If I tell you it won't be the same."

When we reached the top of the stairs, Maggie pulled me around a corner. I came to a dead halt, feeling as though I had walked into the pages of an art book. The walls were hung with seven of Georgia O'Keeffe's ravishing, eccentric visions. Maggie let go of my hand and watched me, saying nothing as I wandered among the paintings.

Intelligent, independent human beings are rare. Intelligent, independent artists are even rarer. O'Keeffe was both.

"She lived in New Mexico for fifty years, off and on," Maggie said as I began a third circuit of the room. "Her most significant work was done at a small ranch community north and west of Santa Fe. She liked the solitude, and she enforced it. Her arrogance matched her talent. Until the last years of her life, she refused to exhibit in New Mexico, as though she thought the galleries and museums here were beneath her."

I thought of the safe, arid paintings on the first floor of the museum, the ones so firmly modern, the ones no critic or curator would reject as being out of the intellectual mainstream.

"Maybe they were," I said. "O'Keeffe took risks. A lot of them." I glanced around. "Not all of them worked. At least, not for me."

"This isn't her best work," Maggie said quickly. "The powerful museums and collectors in New York and Chicago and San Francisco have carried off all the monumental O'Keeffe canvases—the skulls and the flowers, the crosses and the clouds." Maggie looked at the walls in silence. "But for people who will never see anything of O'Keeffe's work outside of a book, these seven canvases let you know what it's like to stand in the presence of a unique artistic vision."

Maggie walked over and touched the wall next to a painting. As she spoke, she moved around the room, pointing to other paintings. No longer tense or angry, she was wholly absorbed in the art. Only a faint mark remained on her cheek to remind me of Nickelaw's bad manners.

"O'Keeffe began with billowing abstract forms when she was young," Maggie said. "Then she used concrete objects in her middle age. In her old age she returned to the abstract, but in a more disciplined, less emotional manner. Her last paintings are a distillation of a mature artist's understanding of color, form, space, density. They're exquisitely balanced."

Maggie's words were infused with a bittersweet passion. I recognized the inflections. I had used them myself, long ago, when I tried to explain the genius of great composers to people who had not the slightest idea what I meant. Beethoven always caused a particularly sharp reaction in me. He had hated the violin, but he had been commissioned to compose a violin concerto. His revenge was as cruel as any man has ever taken. He used the E string mercilessly throughout the concerto. In the hands of even a very, very good violinist, the result is as tedious as listening to cats mate. In the hands of a truly great violinist, no more ravishing piece of music has ever been played. It was Beethoven's violin concerto that taught me about the unbridgeable gap between good and great.

I wondered which O'Keeffe painting was Maggie's personal violin concerto.

"Whoever put this exhibit together did a very clever thing," Maggie said, gesturing toward two paintings that commanded a large section of the wall.

It took me a moment to realize what she meant. The first of the paintings was dated 1940. It was a deceptively simple landscape of a river winding through a dry land. On either side of the flat river valley rose rounded piñon-studded hills. The curves of the hills had the soft allure of a woman's breasts beneath the prickly reality of the desert's hair shirt. The river's sweeping bend reinforced the sense of life existing in the middle of an arid landscape. The contrast between the sensuous and the bleak gave the painting a peculiar tension.

The second canvas had been inspired by the same river and the same landscape, but it was painted twenty years later. All that remained of the original vision was the blue line of the river itself. The desert, hills, and sky had been erased. What had been an individual vision of a landscape was now a minimalist statement concerning color and form.

As Maggie talked and compared the two paintings, I could appreciate her educated enthusiasm for the abstract rendition of the river's curve; I just couldn't work up any enthusiasm of my own. In fact, the retrograde part of me kept whispering that someone could have painted a ringer and hung it next to an original O'Keeffe.

"This is the artist's vision distilled by time and experience to the absolute essence," Maggie said. "It's as though O'Keeffe had seen the Chama River twenty years before, painted it to the best of her ability, and then spent the next twenty years haunted by what she hadn't accomplished in the first painting.

"Finally one day she took up her brushes and painted what had always been the core of her private visual experience of that landscape—the elusive geometry of the river's bend."

I wondered if Maggie would be haunted by the limitations of *Place of Power* for the next two decades, or if she would be like me and find something else she could do better.

"You don't like the second painting, do you?" Maggie asked.

"You keep talking to me long enough and I'll be

able to work up an academic appreciation for it. But that's all it will be—academic."

"And you believe that art should be an emotional experience?"

"For me, yes. If I want abstract intellect, I'll get a book full of mathematical equations."

"But that poppy you liked wasn't a photographic rendition of a single, particular poppy. It was O'Keeffe's statement of what a poppy *is*."

"Yes, but I didn't need a guided tour to understand what was going on in that painting. I could enjoy the experience in solitude, just me and the poppy, no priestly intercession required."

"You don't know what art is but you know what you like, right?" Maggie asked dryly.

"Close. I know what I dislike on sight."

"And you dislike that," she said, touching the wall near the abstraction of a river curve. "You prefer the real and emotional over the abstract and intellectual."

"To me," I said, "water is one of the most graceful things on earth. Rivers, even the hard-bottomed, hard-assed rivers of Montana, are essentially graceful. If I were going to abstract the concept of river from a landscape, I'd try for some grace. That"—I hooked my thumb at the second painting—"has damn little grace."

"But the second painting says so much more about O'Keeffe's growth as an artist."

"Maybe, and maybe it just gives the blue-smoke-and-mirrors crowd so much more room to maneuver."

"What?"

"The critics, academics, and art pushers, the folks who make their livings by standing between art and the audience," I said bluntly. "Anybody with twenty-twenty vision can have an opinion as to whether a landscape painting succeeds. Good eyesight doesn't help when the painting is a red square on a white background and is titled Number Thirty-four."

Maggie smiled unwillingly. "Are you hinting that it's easier to sell a mediocre abstract than a mediocre landscape to an uneducated buyer?"

"Yeah. The average Joe on the street looks at a muddy landscape and knows that something's wrong with the painting. But show him a muddy abstract and he could be talked into thinking he's too dumb to appreciate important art." I shrugged. "I look at that second O'Keeffe and figure the blame is about equally divided between my mediocre taste and her mediocre canvas. In fact, I find myself wondering if she really painted the damn thing."

"She did," Maggie said without hesitation.

"You're very sure. Did she work in front of a notary?"

"Hardly. O'Keeffe was very reclusive."

"Then how do you know that's her painting?"

Maggie's dark eyes examined me. "You're serious, aren't you?"

"It's warm in here and cold outside. That's about as serious as anything needs to be."

She laughed softly and then with more confidence, as though relearning a lost skill. I smiled and wished she would relax enough to tell me what was really bothering her. She wasn't ready for that. Not yet. She wasn't used to trusting anybody but herself and the twelve-gauge under her bed.

"There are a dozen ways to authenticate a painting," Maggie said. "X-ray diffraction, pigment anomalies, fiber count of the canvas itself. . . . My favorite is pictology," she continued, her expression both casual and subtly amused, as though she were remembering a private joke. "Most painters use certain shapes or colors in the same way again and again. That is, they put them in the same area of the canvas—background, foreground, center left, center right, and so on."

"That abstract doesn't have a foreground or background," I pointed out, "so pictology isn't much help."

"Yes, but in both paintings the river occupies the central vertical third of the canvas. If that doesn't convince you, there's the fact that brush strokes are as individual as a person's handwriting. Some artists are known for clam-shaped strokes, or strokes that begin forcefully and trail off quickly, or for heavy vertical and light horizontal strokes.

"Each artist is different," Maggie continued. "Forgers who copy a picture use brush strokes that are mechanical and controlled. There's no character in them. There's nothing spontaneous. The force applied to the brush remains the same throughout the stroke instead of varying as brush strokes do when an artist is creating. The result is a more wooden painting, even though it might be a precise copy."

"Wooden," I said, baiting Maggie, enjoying her sudden animation. "That sounds like an art-critic word again. Blue smoke and mirrors."

"Then how about analyzing the artist's body of work and the way a particular painting fits within it?" she retorted. "If the abstract river had come to the museum with a 1940s date, the canvas would have been immediately suspect. Such a painting would have been completely out of sync with the artist's known works at that time." She looked at the pictures and looked back at me. "Trust me, Fiddler. That's a genuine O'Keeffe."

"Okay."

Maggie looked surprised. "Okay?"

I nodded. "See how easy it is? You say 'trust me' and I do. Now it's your turn. Trust me, Maggie. Tell me why you decided not to cut off Nickelaw's nuts."

The animation vanished from Maggie's face as thoroughly as the land and sky had vanished from the second O'Keeffe painting. What remained looked every bit as strained as the abstract river. Maggie reached into her purse and brought out a cream-colored envelope. She handed it to me without comment.

I opened the envelope. Whatever I had expected, it wasn't this. The Nickelaw Gallery letterhead was the height of dramatic masculine elegance. So was the engraved card inside. It was a formal invitation to a 7 P.M. gallery party being hosted that night by Olin Nickelaw. In the right-hand corner, the invitation noted that the preferred attire was "Santa Fe Casual."

"I didn't know I was on Nickelaw's 'A' list," I said.

"Neither does he."

I glanced at Maggie, then at the face of the envelope again. This time I recognized Maggie's flowing script.

"Am I coming as your date or your bodyguard?" I asked, glancing at the faint bruise on her cheek.

"Does it matter?"

I thought about it. "Does a handgun fit under Santa Fe Casual?"

SEVEN

Santa Fe Casual turned out to be a cashmere turtleneck sweater underneath a suede shirt. There would be plenty of room for the flat Detonics Combat Master in the small of my back, under the hand-tooled, silver-trimmed belt. Leather pants were optional. I passed on them and invested in new 501s. Indian jewelry was de rigueur: the more the better, with ten-pound necklaces being preferred. I borrowed Benny's new ring, threw in a tin of boot polish, and was good to go. Six hundred and eighteen bucks, not including the boot polish or the ring. Santa Fe might be casual but it ain't cheap.

By the time I emerged from the store carrying the new gear, the cold coyote wind loping across the plaza had finally swept away the silversmiths and scoured most of the daylight from the western sky. Commuter traffic wound its way around the traffic circle in a dazzle of lights. The bells in the cathedral a block off the plaza were announcing the time in tones so clear I felt as though I could touch them.

I should have stayed outside and tried. As I opened my hotel-room door, I discovered that the Ice Cream King of Saigon, aka Benny Speidel, wasn't the only man who had me in a computer trap, but the long weeks on the road had turned my brain to suet.

As soon as I opened the door, I was looking down the bore of a large-caliber revolver. The room smelled like eau de cat box with an overlay of rancid ashtray, but that wasn't my biggest problem. The light from the hallway behind me was strong enough that I could see the hollow-point loads in the exposed chambers of the cylinder. I couldn't see the chamber under the hammer, but I had no reason to think it was empty.

"April Fool, asshole. Step right in and keep those hands out where I can count the fingers."

Never argue with the man holding the gun. I stepped right in and kept all ten of my fingers in view, even though I wasn't sure he could count that high.

He was well below average height, even with the elevator heels he wore. Too short to be FBI or DEA, the army or the marines. Too short for even a local cop, probably. Too old, too; he looked close to early retirement, although with smokers it's hard to separate the results of addiction from the normal battle fatigue of life. He had worn a flattop for so many years that the haircut had come back in style. I doubt if he knew it, or cared. His eyes were round and mean and set deep, like those of an old boar hog. He smelled better than a skunk and worse than wet feathers.

I'd smelled him before, on a snowy side street where I'd tried to use the car door to gnaw off his arm.

"You don't need the gun," I said. "All you have to do is breathe on people."

"Think you're a real stud, don't you? That kind of attitude can get you in all kinds of trouble. Already has."

My insult hadn't shifted the gunman's focus one bit, which meant that things stayed the way they were: he had a gun and I didn't. It was a business-like gun, too. Short-barreled .44 Magnum, probably the same model Son of Sam used. So I waited and watched for an opening, knowing he wanted some-thing from me—and it wasn't my life. An assassin would have dumped me and walked out before I hit the floor.

The man's right hand reached into his hip pocket, producing a leather wallet. He held it at my eye level and let it fall open. The movement was smooth and practiced. He had spent a lifetime cutting people off at the knees to make up for his own lack of stat-ure.

"Special Agent Harvey Durham, Internal Revenue Service, CID. Know something, big man? You're in shit so deep your balls are dragging."

That explained the smell but I didn't say anything, because Harvey wasn't just a straight bureaucrat. Revenue agents have rules they must follow, just like every other government functionary does. Bu-reaucrats are powerful, but they can be had.

IRS CID is a different matter altogether. The difference between Internal Revenue Service and Internal Revenue Service Criminal Investigation Division is the difference between tax avoidance and tax evasion. It's the difference between back taxes plus penalty and back taxes plus penalty plus fines plus twenty years in federal prison.

CID doesn't screw around checking the math on your 1040EZ form; they start out by attaching a tax lien to your bank account. Then they get arbitrary. They're the only guys who ever made charges stick against Al Capone. In the ways that count, they're more powerful than the FBI or the DEA, whose agents have to pay attention to abstract Constitutional concepts such as "due process" and "innocent until proven guilty."

The tax collectors don't know individual rights from lukewarm piss and don't care. No matter how clean my finances might be, I was in as much trouble as good old Harvey wanted to put me in, and I knew it.

Harvey knew I knew it.

"I don't need a gun for meatballs like you," he said, putting his cannon away smoothly, shifting his shoulders like a boxer. "You big guys think you own the world, but you don't. Uncle Sam does, and I'm here to collect the back rent."

Harvey turned away, showing me his back, absolutely confident. The gun had just been a handy way to make sure I didn't tear off his arm the minute I walked in the door.

"You were about to offer me a drink," Harvey said.

He walked over and started rummaging around in the liquor caddy La Fonda provides for its high-ticket customers. He pulled out a shot-sized bottle of Chivas Regal, cracked the seal, and took a pull of the scotch.

"Don't stand on formality," I said, tossing my packages onto a nearby chair. "Help yourself."

He tipped up the bottle and drained it. Then he grinned, pulled out another bottle, and broke the seal on it. He lit a cigarette and dropped the match into the empty miniature.

"Meatballs like you really give me a pain. You can get just as drunk on cheap booze, but you're too good for that. You can get laid by the girl next door, but you're too good for that too. So you run around the place drinking fancy liquor and banging fancy women in a fancy room that costs two hundred bucks a night, and you look down on everyone who makes an honest living."

"What makes you think my living is dishonest?"

"Shit," Harvey said, dragging hard on the cigarette. "All the honest guys in town are flaked in front of a TV set with a beer in one hand and a hard-on in the other because that's the only piece of ass they can afford after making alimony payments."

Harvey exhaled, working hard at it. His lungs were going bad, and the thin air of Santa Fe didn't help. He ashed his cigarette on the floor and looked at me as though I were the source of the bad smell in the room.

"But sooner or later the meatballs take a fall. I'll

bet you've got enough on you right now to go away for twenty years.''

"Keep talking, Harvey. Sooner or later you'll say something that makes sense.''

"It all makes sense. At first I thought you might be an undercover cop of some kind, sniffing around that Indian bitch. I went to the computer and pulled your files. Even the DEA doesn't bother to make up a phony set of Ten-forties that go back as far as yours do. So I guess you are just who your motor vehicle registration says you are, a rich flake who stumbled into Santa Fe in a snowstorm.'' He shrugged. "For all I know, you carried some snow in with you."

"They call it 'blow' now.''

Harvey gave me a look out of his boar-mean eyes. "Your reported income went from the low four figures to the high sixes in just one year." He smacked the curve of the empty miniature against his palm. "No one who's honest can double his money and hang onto it past April fifteenth. You haven't done your fair share to feed the poor and disabled. You took money out of the mouths of hungry babies in Harlem."

"Your social conscience is breaking my heart."

"I'd rather bust your ass. Meatballs like you are the reason Uncle Sam can't afford decent pensions for working stiffs like me."

Harvey ashed the cigarette, sucked hard, and ashed again.

"But like all crooks, you got impatient. Why launder money by the handful when you've got a warehouse full of the stuff?"

"I do?"

"Whether you do or don't, I'll screw you over but good looking for it, and there's no way you can stop me. Don't count on your fancy bookkeeper, either. She's going to be busy with problems of her own. Got that, big man?"

"I got that the second I saw your badge. Cut to the chase, Harvey. What do you want from me?"

"From you? From you I want nothing. Not trouble, not hassle, not interference, not even a Christmas card. All I want is a view of you disappearing into the night."

"Why?"

The question surprised Harvey. He started talking low and hard and quick. "Listen, asshole, if you're here tomorrow, you'll be audited by the CID. On criminal fraud cases, we don't bother with a statute of limitations like the regular auditors do. We can go back to your first paycheck and your first short form ten-forty, looking for evidence of criminal evasion. We'll find it. Everybody is dirty if you dig hard enough. And while we're digging, we'll tie you up in knots and give you the kind of grief that makes you shit blood just to verify your medical deduction for piles."

Harvey dumped his cigarette butt into the empty scotch bottle and capped it with his thumb, suffocating the fire. "If we find out that you sleep in God's right hand, we apologize by computer form letter and go on to the next smart-ass big shot that catches our eye. My pension's the same whether I work on you for five years or on five other people for one year each."

Harvey waited for me to say something.

I waited for him to tell me something I didn't already know.

Harvey crossed the room, opened the door, and looked back at me out of cold hog eyes. "Climb in that fancy goddamn car of yours and head east, west, north, or south. There's nothing in Santa Fe worth the grief I'll give you if you stay."

The door closed hard.

It took twenty minutes with both windows wide open to make a dent in the smell Harvey left behind. I sat on the bed and stared at the wall above the television set, cursing my luck and wondering how the hell I could tell who the players were when no one would sell me a program.

The best possibility was the one most guaranteed to sic the CID on me for the next five years. Good old Harvey was probably a cog in one of Uncle Sam's law-enforcement gears. When no other way works, competing arms of the federal bureaucracies enter into a short-term shotgun marriage known as a task force. That's where five FBI agents, five DEA agents, a few IRS investigators, some Customs officers, a bomb technician from the Bureau of Alcohol, Tobacco, and Firearms, and a botanist from the U.S. Department of Agriculture are turned loose on a criminal conspiracy that looks big enough to guarantee headlines for all.

It usually works. The Justice Department has used task forces from Aspen to Miami. Maybe Santa Fe had developed a dope problem that warranted a full-court press from the Feds.

And maybe Maggie and Nickelaw and the drop-dead blonde were more crafty than artsy. Nickelaw could be using his string of high-ticket galleries as a front for a billion-dollar cocaine ring or a multimillion-dollar laundry or even as a fencing operation for stolen art. Any one of those activities could warrant a task force investigation, especially in a state with a small population. A few million dollars would go a long way toward corrupting the whole damned government of New Mexico.

Whatever the game, my presence wouldn't be welcome. That was no surprise to me. Harvey wasn't the first federal badge to give me the bum's rush.

None of my conclusions made me feel any better. If this was indeed a task-force operation, I'd end up on the IRS hit list real quick and stay there for as long as Harvey remembered my name. My 1040s are as clean as Fiora and a brace of highly trained tax types can make them, but when your personal fortune is based on a steamer trunk full of used tens, twenties, and fifties that you claim was left to you by a late and unlamented uncle, you've got more vulnerability than the average taxpayer.

Oh, I've paid inheritance tax on the cache, and Fiora is always careful not to be on the cutting edge of dicey stock transactions when she's investing the money; even so, the pragmatist in me knew that good old Harvey had a handful of the hair my barber doesn't cut.

But maybe Harvey had a sense of humor. I doubted it, yet you never know. Besides, as Uncle Jake used to say, *If you can't take a joke. . . .*

eIGHT

At seven I drove over to meet Maggie. She must have been waiting at the window because she was out the door and across the snowy lawn before I could park. She wore a white wool dress with a full, clinging skirt and a white parka with ermine trim on the hood. The pale fur made her dark eyes more mysterious and made her skin glow as though she spent most of her winter days on the Taos ski runs, like Nickelaw's blond girlfriend. In fact, Maggie reminded me of the blonde in an odd way. Maybe it was just the contrast of light head covering and dark skin. Or maybe it was the arching line of the eyebrows and the elegant facial structure. Then Maggie smiled briefly, and all similarity between her and the savagely beautiful blonde vanished.

Maggie touched my forearm as I reached over and opened the Cobra's low door. "Thanks for coming,"

she said. "I really don't want to face Olin alone tonight."

Her voice was tight. So was the rest of her. She
had to remind herself to breathe deeply every now
and again.

We drove to the gallery in a silence that wasn't
quite comfortable. The party was already in full glitter. Indian teenagers in white coats and long shiny
ponytails—probably students at the art institute—
trotted around the room carrying trays of Moët, William Hill Reserve Cabernet, and southwestern-style
finger food. The air was redolent of wood smoke,
cleverly cooked chiles and expensive perfume.

Most of the guests were just what you would expect to turn out for a Santa Fe gallery party. Or a
Scottsdale gallery party. Or one in Palm Springs or
Beverly Hills. There are faint regional variations, of
course. Palm Springs and Beverly Hills tend toward
diamond pavé bracelets, whereas Scottsdale and
Santa Fe favor oversized conchos and hunks of matrix turquoise. Some of the women looked as if they
had been training all week at the Nautilus studio
just to carry the weight.

It wasn't only the women who went in for heavy
armor. Native American males looked quite comfortable in their magnificent squash-blossom necklaces. The Anglo males wore necklaces too. They
also wore turquoise rings that went from the first
knuckle to the last and bracelets that could have
doubled as shields.

Underneath the jewelry, the crowd was com-
prised entirely of almost-familiar faces, the kind you
recognize or think you recognize, people whose

bearing says they are somebody whether you recognize them or not. It took me about ten seconds to pick out a stately white-haired former senator. He had put on a few pounds and lost a few hundred million in real estate in the last decade, but he still had the faintly flushed skin that deepened the color in his blank blue eyes, giving them the appearance of focus.

The rest of the group measured up to the politician's standard very handsomely. There was an aging pop singer who once had made a quarter of a billion dollars singing about mountains, a Hollywood actress noted for her devotion to the New Age, and a New York ballet dancer with a chronic case of sniffles that was rumored to be the result of cocaine rather than allergies.

The crowd was as far away from the cowboys-and-Indians end of the western art continuum as you could get. If you asked, these folks would tell you they were patrons of the fine arts. There wasn't a bolo tie in the lot, and the only Stetson I saw was being worn by an Indian. In honor of the occasion, Nickelaw had left his leather at home. The blonde hadn't. She was wearing a scarlet suede ensemble, a solid gold fetish necklace, and breasts that defied gravity. She watched the party with the same lack of interest she had shown when Nickelaw smacked Maggie.

A battery of Minicams and still photographers were staged in close order at the far end of the gallery. The media types were sucking up wine and food as fast as they could, trying to believe that Nickelaw had invited them because of who they were rather than what their publicity machinery could do for him.

"That's a surprise," I said as I helped Maggie out of her parka. "I figured Nickelaw would be the type to keep the paparazzi freezing out on the sidewalk."

"Olin never offends anyone who can be useful to him."

I touched the almost invisible bruise on her face and asked, "Where does that leave you?"

Maggie didn't answer.

With my hand lightly on the small of her back, I guided her through the crowd toward the press position. I like to cultivate reporters. Most of them know a hell of a lot more news than ever gets into print, even if they don't always realize it.

Besides, the press is entertaining to watch. It's a study in constant agitation. Reporters and cameramen are always anxious. They worry that the story won't pan out. They worry that the story will pan out but they'll miss it somehow. They worry that they'll get the story but the opposition will get a better angle. They worry that they'll get the story and the best angle but lose the lead news hole to a different story happening to a different reporter in a different place.

As a result of all the worrying, pack journalists are like predators newly arrived at the zoo. They pace and snarl and snap at one another and at the wire cage separating them from reality. But the cage is of their own making, which means they'll never get out.

Nickelaw's press corps was unusually anxious, as though this were an important press conference rather than a society cocktail party thrown in the name of fine arts and fantastic profits. Even more surprising, the logos on the Minicams stated that all three Albuquerque stations were represented. The still photographers were longtime pros carrying Nikons and Hasselblads. The pencil-press reporters had a quiet competence suggesting that they worked for the major dailies of the region rather than the *Mesquite Weekly*.

That was damned curious. No matter how charming and handsome Nickelaw was, no gallery owner can command that kind of media attention just by calling in a few favors.

A familiar face popped out of the middle of the pack. I had to think for a moment before I placed him. The camera put twenty pounds on his gaunt form and managed to conceal the anxious, fidgety manner he exhibited in person. His name was Joe Ballard and I'd seen him the night before, filing a report from the ABC bureau in Houston. Santa Fe has a certain national cachet, but a gallery party hardly seemed worth the time of a $400,000-a-year on-air correspondent.

The heady aroma of big money and big power in the room got thicker, competing with the scent of perfume, burning piñon, and nervous sweat.

"Nickelaw must have a lot of clout," I said softly to Maggie. "He drew a national network news crew all the way from Texas."

She nodded, sending a whisper of dark hair over her cheek. "One of the network news honchos collects fetishes and medicine bags. Olin's been cultivating him for months."

"Why?"

Maggie acted as though she hadn't heard me.

I excused myself and moved away. A few moments later I was easing along in back of the camera position, trying to look as though I belonged. It wasn't hard. Once, long ago, I'd been a reporter. Like riding a bike, you never forget the moves.

"Nice piece tonight, Ballard," I said, stopping near the network reporter.

"Thanks." He took a drink from the glass of champagne in his hand, then took another gulp to finish it. "But the idiots in New York cut almost thirty seconds out of it. They don't care about anything west of the Hudson."

"Then what are you doing here? Last time I checked, Santa Fe was west of the Hudson."

He grinned. "Yeah, but this is a great story, something even New York can understand. Missing art masterpiece, recovered art masterpiece, starving Indians, starving artists. Hell, it's got everything but sex, and I'm working on that. This will be the hottest thing in the art world since they found all those Wyeth pictures of what's-her-name, that plain-faced bimbo with the great tits."

"Helga?"

"Yeah, that's it. This one is in Helga's league. I got a great little sidebar this afternoon. Nickelaw took us out to the place where the picture was found. Dumpy little mud house clear to hell out in the boonies. We got some dynamite footage of this doe-eyed Pocahontas describing how her auntie hid the painting for all these years because she was so ashamed of . . ."

A waiter slid by with a tray of champagne, distracting Ballard. He hooked another glass of bubbly and was taking a healthy swig when Nickelaw stepped out of the crowd and into the lights from the bank of Minicams. Ballard swallowed hastily, wiped his eyes, and straightened his blazer.

"Show time," he muttered.

Ballard's cameraman swung the Minicam on its tripod to focus on Nickelaw. It was worth the effort. Dressed in a perfectly fitted tux, his hair and smile equally sleek, Nickelaw was handsome as sin.

"May I please have your attention?" Nickelaw asked calmly. "Thank you. I want you to know that you are among the few people in history who have been privileged to stand on a watershed in contemporary American art."

For a moment the entire room was so quiet I could hear the muted sizzle of piñon being consumed in the corner fireplace. The sound was like the excitement I sensed in the air. I took another breath and caught a familiar scent mingling with the wood smoke and perfume. It was the astringent smell of trouble brewing somewhere in the room, a pot of black coffee about to boil over.

Fiora is right. I love that smell more than I should.

There was a stirring just behind me. I looked and saw Maggie standing so close that I could feel her body heat. Her expression was calm. Her eyes were not. They watched Nickelaw and the room as though she were trying to read minds.

If Nickelaw was nervous, he didn't show it. He let the silence build for a perfect count of five before he made an elegant, dismissive gesture with his left hand and resumed speaking.

"There's a lot of hyperbole in the art world, but I've never been a part of it and I never will be. I mean what I say . . . and I say that tonight will be remembered long after all of us are dead."

Nickelaw looked to another quarter of the room, giving the camera a different view of his Greek profile.

"The Southwest has produced many painters and much art," he continued in a voice as firm and masculine as the line of his chin. "Some of it is fine art in the best sense of the word. Yet the Southwest has produced only one great world-class artist. Her works are among the most valuable in American art. I would like to talk about this woman tonight.

"Georgia O'Keeffe was an extraordinary, prodigious talent," Nickelaw said, turning to a different quarter of the room, making everyone present feel as though he were speaking directly to them. "We who are gathered here tonight know Miss O'Keeffe's greatness. We also know that she was an exceptionally complex and difficult human being. She guarded her personal life closely, even from those few whom she called friends."

On my left, Ballard was scribbling notes madly while his videotape machine recorded Nickelaw's presentation. The other reporters were doing the same, making sure that their audiences would be included among the elect who stood on this watershed of American fine arts. Deftly, Nickelaw made sure that the philistines in the audience weren't left to wonder what all the bells and whistles were about.

"History tells us that Miss O'Keeffe married Alfred Stieglitz, who was the father of modern art in America and a man of considerable intellectual vanity. Stieglitz was first O'Keeffe's mentor, then her lover, and finally her husband. When she married Stieglitz she was twenty-nine years old. He was fifty-seven. He was famous. She was not. He was at the end of his career. She was at the beginning. It was a difficult alliance.

"In the late nineteen twenties, Miss O'Keeffe suffered a nervous breakdown. She retreated from the East Coast. In an effort to recapture her health she came here, to New Mexico."

There was a murmuring among the crowd as they absorbed the fact of their own good taste in sharing a piece of geography with an artist of O'Keeffe's stature.

"When Georgia O'Keeffe arrived in Taos, she was a woman in torment. She was caught between the demands of her aging, imperious husband and the urgency of her own art. She had not painted well for several years. She found renewed strength in the Southwest's far horizons. The glittering night sky, the bones and the skulls she found in the desert, gave her new inspiration. She painted, but not in great volume. Sadly, much of what she painted she also destroyed."

Nickelaw changed his orientation again, looking directly into the bank of Minicams. Without warning the gallery lights dimmed except for spotlights illuminating the wall behind and to Nickelaw's left, where a drapery rippled softly.

"One painting escaped destruction."

As though to punctuate his sentence, the drapery rustled aside with a breathless sound, revealing a painting of a skull hanging in a blue-white desert sky.

*n*INE

The canvas was not large, except by O'Keeffe's standards. It was three by four feet, but careful lighting made it seem to overwhelm the room. Although the subject of the painting had been made familiar by time and constant exposure, the combination of bleached skull, ash-gray shadows, and sun-drenched sky was still arresting. The perspective on the skull was oddly changed. With its lower half eroded away by sand and sun, the skull was neither horse nor cow nor any instantly identifiable animal. It was a bleak, merciless, generic reminder of mortality.

"The flower," Maggie murmured. "My God, it looks so *red* in this light. Like fresh blood."

And like fresh blood, the half-opened flower appeared to be bursting out of the skull's forehead. But it was the skull that kept drawing my attention. The more I looked at it, the more I saw eerie echoes of humanity in its round, forward-facing eye sockets and pronounced cheeks. Yet the skull's proportions were wrong to be human. The missing chin would have been down to a man's shoulders.

The eye sockets were inhabited by malevolence rather than emptiness, giving me the uneasy feeling of being watched.

"In her other skull paintings she used cloth flowers," Maggie said. "Pale ones."

"This flower looks real enough to crawl out of the frame."

"It looks . . . hungry."

"Do you blame it? There's not much nourishment in death."

Maggie turned and stared at me for a moment before giving her attention back to the painting. No one heard our quiet comments for the simple reason that everyone was murmuring and whispering, caught in the moment and in the painting that dominated the room. Applause broke out on the left and spread like a wave in a quiet pool. The cameras swung around to capture the reaction. Reporters and correspondents scribbled more rapidly in their notebooks.

Maggie was right. The poppy looked hungry. The painting had a leashed, brooding power that was disturbing. It seemed to hover just above the canvas.

A muted spotlight came on, picking out the figure of Olin Nickelaw standing to one side of the painting.

"Naturally," he said, resuming his presentation as though nothing had happened, "in the case of such finds, provenance is a primary concern. The Nickelaw Gallery has been fortunate to be able to call upon the country's most prominent expert on the work of Georgia O'Keeffe, Dr. Lillian Bradley, chair-woman of the Fine Arts Department at Yale University. Dr. Bradley?"

Nickelaw yielded the spotlight to Dr. Bradley, who was more the "chairperson" type. She stood close to six feet in flat shoes. The shoulders of her chalk-striped business suit didn't need pads in order to look square. She had the short-haired, fiercely scrubbed look of a doctrinaire feminist, but her face had good-natured lines, as though she frequently found life amusing. Tonight there was a barely suppressed current of excitement about her.

"Thank you, Mr. Nickelaw. Ladies and gentlemen, we are indeed privileged to be here tonight."

Bradley turned and looked over at the canvas with both triumph and humility in her expression. "Marvelous," she whispered before returning her attention to the audience.

"Art never exists outside of its own history. To understand what we are seeing, we need to understand where the artist had been before she created this painting. During the summer of 1930, O'Keeffe stayed with Mabel Dodge Luhan, the doyenne of Taos. During the worst heat of the summer, O'Keeffe left Taos, seeking relief from the temperature. She went west across the Jemez Plateau toward Hernandez and Abiquiu, exploring the primitive landscape. It was her first trip into country where, as we all know, she finally settled."

Bradley glanced at her notes and then back up at the rapt audience.

"The diaries of other guests indicate that O'Keeffe set out in August to visit several friends of Mrs. Dodge in the little town of Abiquiu. That much is clearly documented. From other sources we know that O'Keeffe's car broke down and she was forced to lay over in the small town of Las Trampas while parts were shipped in from Santa Fe. She spent several days sketching and painting in the surrounding countryside before she returned to Taos. We know this because she stayed with the Quinones family.

"Mr. Nickelaw, will you be so kind as to play the tape of Victoria Quinones' sworn deposition?"

The spotlight on Bradley faded. As it did, a tape recording started. The moderately accented voice was that of a young woman, husky and yet clear.

I, Victoria Quinones, do swear that the painting titled Private Skull *has been in the possession of my family since the summer of 1930. It was the property of my aunt, Juanita Sanchez Quinones.*

The artist, Georgia O'Keeffe, painted the canvas while she was a guest in our house, using a skull she found there as a model. When she was finished, she stared at the painting for many hours. Then she took it from its stretcher. My aunt, at the time a teenager, asked Miss O'Keeffe what she intended to do with the painting. Miss O'Keeffe said she was going to destroy it because it was "unworthy." With that, she put it out on the rubbish heap beside the barn.

After Miss O'Keeffe left, my aunt retrieved the canvas and hid it. Later she mounted the picture herself and hung it on the wall of her bedroom behind a Navajo blanket. I didn't know the painting existed until one day when I brought the priest to my aunt's sickbed. It was cold. I took the blanket down to warm her and recognized the painting's value. My aunt swore me to secrecy, saying that people would call her a thief if the painting were ever made public. She made me promise never to talk about the painting while she lived. I obeyed.

After her death, the painting became mine. I didn't believe it should be hidden any longer.

The mesmerizing voice stopped. The muted spotlight came on Bradley again, but few people in the room looked away from the odd skull and its ravenous crimson poppy.

"In her quest for privacy," Bradley said, "Miss O'Keeffe resisted any kind of linkage between her own thoughts, her own femininity, her own person, and the art she created. It is my belief that O'Keeffe sometimes destroyed her own paintings not because they were inferior but because they revealed too much of the artist's personal life. *Private Skull* is such a painting."

The crowd parted to allow a pair of waiters to come forward, each carrying an easel on which was mounted a covered photo blowup. When the easels were positioned on either side of the canvas, the waiters withdrew.

With a quick, assertive motion, Bradley flipped the cover off the closer easel, revealing a photo of Georgia O'Keeffe. It was a Stieglitz shot that captured the brooding intensity of the artist and suggested a pervasive sensuality in the young woman herself. Somehow I was reminded by the photo of Maggie, who regarded the world with that same dark, well-shielded intensity.

"This photograph of O'Keeffe was taken at about

the time her husband's decline became apparent. Quite obviously, she is a woman whose life lies ahead rather than behind her."

When Bradley walked to the other easel, she moved carefully, as though much of her own life lay behind her. She threw off the cover on the second photo.

"This is Albert Stieglitz."

The father of American modern art was gaunt, with the burning eyes of a prophet or a madman. There was darkness in those eyes, an intensity of emotion that could have been rage or creation, bleak ecstasy or manic destruction.

Looking at those two photos, I almost felt sorry for Stieglitz. Whatever his faults as a human being, he had been a passionate Pygmalion who had had to watch his Galatea ripen into a strong, sensual woman during the time when he himself was slowly withering into an old man whose only strength lay in his fierce will.

"That poor son of a bitch," I muttered.

Maggie stared at me. "He was a son of a bitch, period. He ran O'Keeffe like she was on little tin rails."

"That's how it is with independent women—run them or lose them, and God help you if you try running them."

"I take back everything I said about your unbroken nose."

"It wasn't my nose that took the cheap shot."

Maggie's eyes widened for an instant; then she looked away. "I'm not sure about you, Fiddler, but

I'm certain that Stieglitz was one cast-iron son of a bitch.''

"O'Keeffe was an angel?"

Dark hair moved as Maggie shook her head. "No one is an angel."

"It always sounded to me like O'Keeffe and Stieglitz were well matched. Or as my ex-wife once said to me, 'It's God's wondrous plan—a bitch for every son of a bitch.' ''

Soft, humorless laughter came from Maggie. "I think I'd like your ex-wife."

"So did I. Once."

Bradley began speaking again.

"The contrast between the two photos is as great as the contrast between the poppy, which is almost violently alive, and the skull, which is death, the antithesis of the senses. O'Keeffe was hardly unaware of the difference between herself and Stieglitz. It must have bothered her intensely, so much so that she was driven to paint her troubling insight."

Bradley signaled. Nickelaw flipped the covering over O'Keeffe's photograph and repositioned Stieglitz's picture until it was in front of the painting, next to the skull.

"Look carefully. This is not an animal skull. Not quite. Nor is it quite human. Like Stieglitz, the skull lies between material reality and immaterial death; and the viewer who misses that point has only to look more closely. The likeness of Stieglitz lies within the skull itself. The eyes are almost identical to the eyes in the photograph. There is a ghostly ring around the skull's eye sockets, a suggestion of glasses. The shape of the cheekbones, the shadows that could be either sand-etched bone or beard stubble, the . . ."

A rising babble of conversation made it impossible for Bradley to be heard. She nodded to Nickelaw, who covered and removed the photo.

"There is little doubt that O'Keeffe, consciously or unconsciously, painted the likeness of her aging, declining, and arrogant husband into this symbol of death. And from death's forehead, like a mythical goddess, a poppy is born, a fierce and determined flower which could only be Georgia O'Keeffe; but she must struggle to free herself from death, to unfold the petals of her own genius before Stieglitz takes her down into the obscurity of the grave with him."

Bradley stepped back a few feet and viewed the painting without comment. Her expression was complex, like a mother looking at a difficult, much-loved child.

"Georgia O'Keeffe avoided portraiture," Bradley said finally, turning back to the audience. "Beyond classroom sketches, few human likenesses appear in her oeuvre. This painting is a remarkable portrait of a man and a relationship that O'Keeffe both loved and hated. *Private Skull* is a savage personal statement about time and man and woman. It doesn't surprise me that O'Keeffe was unable either to live with the painting or to destroy it entirely, so she temporized by leaving it on a rubbish heap for a simple woman to discover and salvage for the ages."

Bradley looked at the painting again, as though unable to see enough of it.

"There is no doubt in my mind that, despite its

technical flaws, this painting came from the hand of Georgia O'Keeffe.''

There was a barrage of flashes from the still cameras. The sudden, repeated *snick* of apertures was all but deafening. The crowd began applauding heavily as Bradley gave the spotlight and microphone back to Nickelaw.

Ballard, the ABC correspondent, gave me an elbow in the ribs and a triumphant grin. ''I knew there was a sex angle!''

Ballard's cameraman lifted his head from the viewfinder of his Minicam and looked around the room with eyes that had seen it all a thousand times. Cameramen are the last realists in the world. They know how the illusions are created and destroyed. Cameramen know where to look and where not to look. Aim that lens in the wrong direction, and it spoils the illusion for all those folks out there in Television Land. Keep the focus tight to make sure nobody can see the magician's smoke generators and light sources and rotating mirrors. Life is entertaining as long as you watch it through the camera, but lift your head and look around and you may begin to figure out how the illusion works. For most people, that's when the fun disappears.

For me, that's when the real fun begins.

Nickelaw acknowledged the crowd with a wave and a nod, and the lights came on full once more. There was a shoving match among the reporters. Both Bradley and Nickelaw were all but buried in microphones. The question of the day was, ''How much is the painting worth?''

Bradley launched into a discussion of the difference between esthetic and historical worth. Nickelaw remained discreetly silent. I turned to Maggie.

"How much is it worth?"

She was about to answer when I heard a familiar voice at my elbow.

"Two million bucks."

I spun around and stared at the woman who once had shared my bed and my life. Fiora's hair was still a honey shade of blond. Her eyes were still a changeable hazel-green. She still barely came up to my breastbone. She still was more beautiful to me than any other woman.

The past months on the road hadn't separated us at all—and knowing it made me furious.

tEN

"Hello, Fiddler," Fiora said. ""You're looking . . . good."

Beneath the assured smile and rather severe outfit, Fiora was even tighter than Maggie. There were brutal circles beneath Fiora's eyes, which at the moment were a troubled shade of green. I remembered what Benny had said: *We got tired of waiting for a postcard.*

"You're working too hard, pretty lady. It shows."

Her expression didn't change, but I know Fiora well enough to know that she flinched. She hates being called "pretty lady," probably because I only do it when I'm mad at her and I look at her and I discover all over again that she's still beautiful to me no matter how pissed I might be.

Fiora smiled, showing me a set of small, perfectly matched teeth. "Is this your latest distressed damsel?"

Before I could open my mouth, Fiora turned to Maggie.

"You *are* distressed, aren't you? No other kind of damsel seems to satisfy Fiddler. But don't worry. If you aren't distressed at the moment, you will be. He has that effect on women."

"Maggie, this is my ex-wife," I said, leaning a little heavily on the prefix. "I think you probably can understand why, too."

"Ms. Tenorio and I have already met," Fiora said. "It was more profitable for her boss than for me, but that's what the art business is all about."

"For people who care only about money, yes," Maggie said coolly.

I gave Maggie a look out of the corner of my eye and hoped she knew what she was doing. Standing up to Nickelaw with a pocketknife was one thing. Picking a fight with Fiora armed only with your wits was another thing entirely. I had the scars to prove it.

"Dear God, Fiddler," Fiora said, giving me the benefit of her shadowed, haunting eyes. "You've cornered another earth mother." She looked at Maggie with ersatz sympathy. "It must be hell to soil those elegant hands of yours on something as ignoble as money, especially when every artist's secret dream is to starve in a paint-spotted garret. Too bad that the Olin Nickelaws of this world always come along and corrupt artists by putting little price tags on their souls. Tell me, Maggie, which was the greater insult, the idea that your soul could be bought or the fact that the price was so cheap?"

Maggie took a sharp breath through clenched teeth, telling me that the shot had gone home.

"I've seen all I need to see here," I said quickly, putting my hand beneath Maggie's elbow. "Let's go."

"Don't worry about me," Maggie said, stepping away. "I'm a big girl."

Fiora was shaking her head. "That's not the way to his heart. You're supposed to swoon and fan your eyelashes and . . ." After a glance at me, she decided not to pursue the subject. "Well, you get the idea."

For a moment Maggie looked almost as amused as she did angry. "Yeah, I get the idea." She gave me a glance from between dark, unblinking eyelashes. "Thanks for the ride. I'll be okay now."

"I brought you and I'll take you home."

"Listen, cowboy, this Indian will go home however she wants to. Tonight I want to be alone."

"That's another one of the reasons I'm an 'ex,' " Fiora said idly. "Fiddler is very old-fashioned. He hasn't learned to let a woman go home alone, even when she wants to."

Maggie tilted her head up, gave me a long look, and smiled oddly, all irritation gone. She stood on tiptoe long enough to brush her lips across mine.

"It wouldn't have worked anyway," she said. "Your ex would be a real hard act to follow."

I watched Maggie turn and weave her way through the crowd without looking back. If I'd thought going after her would have done any good, I'd have gone, but I knew it wouldn't. Despite Fiora's crack, I *have* learned when a woman is determined to go home alone. Hell, Fiora should have known that. She's the one who taught me.

So I turned to her and looked her up and down as though she were a painting for sale. She was wearing a dark brown silk blouse and a narrow, long skirt that was as black as the skull's eyes. Her shoulder-length hair was pulled back and held with a severe black velvet bow. She wore earrings and a matching choker of irregular black pearls. Even with the heavy shadows beneath her eyes, Fiora still put every other woman in the shade.

"You in mourning for something?" I asked.

"Benny was right. You're determined to be a prick."

"Being betrayed does that to people."

The dark clothes only emphasized Fiora's sudden pallor. "Cheap shot, Fiddler."

"You should know, pretty lady. You've got a patent on the process."

"There you are, Fiora," said a male voice. "You're such a little thing it's easy to lose you."

"Don't bet on it," I muttered.

A mask closed over Fiora's face. It was like turning off a light switch. I'd forgotten her ability to do that, just to shut out the world.

"Roger, this is Fiddler," said Fiora. "Fiddler, Roger Valenti, one of the truly brilliant investors on the West Coast."

I didn't offer to shake hands with the truly brilliant investor, because his right hand was busy massaging Fiora's shoulder. I waited for her to tear off Valenti's fingers and feed them to him. She didn't, which meant there was more than money-shuffling between them. It shouldn't have mattered to me.

But it did.

"Fiddler, huh? That means the Cobra we saw in La Fonda's garage is yours."

"It looks like hell," Fiora said.

That settled any question of who "we" might be.

"I suppose it does need a little work," Valenti said to her. He turned to me. "Want to sell it?"

"No."

"Direct and to the point," he said. "I could pay a premium price, so long as the car is structurally sound. I rather enjoy putting a classic into shape for the Concourse."

I didn't give a damn what or who Valenti enjoyed, but I had just enough grip on my temper not to say it.

Finally he shrugged. "I only wish Olin were as direct in his dealings as you are."

Valenti smiled, but his eyes stayed shrewd. He was a smart, hard piece of business. That didn't surprise me; Fiora doesn't like her men soft or stupid. From Valenti's accent, he had learned his trade in some of New York's less desirable neighborhoods. Under other conditions I might have liked him. But the conditions were what they were, and I didn't like Valenti worth a damn.

"Fiora and I flew over in my Gulfstream for the unveiling of the O'Keeffe," Valenti continued. "I didn't expect to find quite this much of a media circus."

I tried to look interested. Fiora's expression told me how far I missed the mark.

"Not that it matters," Valenti continued confidently. "*Private Skull* is going to hang in my Museum of Southwest Art by the end of the week."

"That will come as news to Nickelaw," I said. "You don't throw this kind of media bash unless you have an auction in mind."

Valenti shook his head. "What I want, I get. I'm preempting tonight. That's why we're here."

"Hope you stuffed your Gulfstream with large bills. Nickelaw has orchestrated a national media event that will make the Helga pictures look like baseball cards. He intends to milk that canvas for all it's worth and a few hundred thousand bucks more."

Fiora glanced at me and put away the knife for the moment. "That's what I've been trying to tell Roger. I haven't seen a guest list, but I'll bet Olin Nickelaw has some of the most important collectors in the country here tonight, as well as curators from the top museums. He's trying to sandbag Roger."

Valenti just smiled. "Of course. Olin knows how to maximize his price. That's fine, sound business. Two million dollars is the place where the bidding ought to start. That would guarantee a clear record for an O'Keeffe painting. It would also be just the sort of price that would make a statement about the importance of this painting—and of the museum that ultimately acquires it."

"I think it could be bought for a lot less," Fiora said.

With a shrug Valenti dismissed what was obviously a well-chewed difference of opinion. "There's more than money at stake." He gave me an amused glance. "You look disapproving."

"Just wondering what Nickelaw's cut of all this artistic validation will be."

"He has already agreed to take a five percent commission," Fiora said. "That's considerably less than usual. Beyond publicity for his galleries, Nickelaw won't make much for his time and trouble verifying this painting."

"How much trouble is it to send a plane ticket to an expert?"

Fiora gave me a slanting, sideways look. "If you think I would advise my client to invest in a painting on no more than one art historian's good opinion, you shouldn't be let out in public without a keeper. *Private Skull* has been thoroughly authenticated in New York—everything from fiber count in the canvas to chemical analysis of paints and fixatives.

"Those things aren't a matter of opinion in the way Bradley's psychobiographical background of the painting is. The tests are precise, delicate, time-consuming, and expensive. Nickelaw paid for all of them and was looking around for more. He even paid an expert to vet the brush strokes. They were consistent with surviving O'Keeffe paintings done during the same time."

"I wasn't doubting the quality of your advice," I said, "just whether your—er, *client* was of a mind to listen."

Valenti looked amused again. I doubt if I did. Fiora looked formidable to anyone capable of seeing past the sleek feminine exterior. She also looked sexy as hell.

"My client pays the same price up front whether he listens to my advice or not. The downstream cost of not listening," Fiora added coolly, "can be quite high."

Valenti laughed and shook his head. "She's right, you know. Every time I haven't taken her advice I've regretted it. But this painting transcends finances and financial advisers."

Transcends finances? Not bloody likely. The room was alive with money. But I kept the thought to myself.

"Five percent of two million equals a hundred thousand," I said idly, thinking that would be a lot of money for ninety-nine percent of the world's population. Nickelaw was in the one percent to whom one hundred big ones was a good week's work. "That will barely keep Nickelaw in leather pants, not to mention drop-dead blondes."

Valenti laughed outright. Fiora's smile became genuine for the first time.

"She's something, isn't she?" Valenti asked, looking to the left as though he had some internal radar that kept the blonde on his personal scope.

The blonde was standing well off to the side of the crush around Nickelaw. She wasn't fazed by the scramble of cameras and microphones and blinding lights. I had a feeling she didn't ruffle easily. I also had a feeling that Valenti hadn't looked at the O'Keeffe with a tenth as much interest as he had shown for Nickelaw's silent bed partner.

"Yeah, she's something, all right," I said. "I can't

figure out whether she's too dumb to know what's going on or too coked out to care."

"With a face and body like hers, a brain would just be excess baggage."

I watched Fiora, wondering how she was taking Valenti's remarks and roving eye. Like the blonde, Fiora appeared unfazed.

"It's been very pleasant, Fiddler," Valenti said, clapping me lightly on the shoulder, "but Fiora and I really have to move along. We're meeting Olin a bit later at the Coyote Café to iron out a deal."

"I wouldn't want to stand in the way of artistic history," I said dryly.

Fiora gave me a look which dared me to try.

"Don't glare at me, pretty lady. I'm not the one drooling over Nickelaw's stand-up toy. Your client must have a thing for blondes, just like I do for damsels in distress. *Ciao*."

Before Fiora could show me her teeth, I showed her mine and slid away into the crowd.

I smiled even more when I got back to La Fonda, spent a couple of twenties, and found out that Fiora and Valenti were registered in separate wings of the hotel. Yeah, I know. It shouldn't have mattered.

But it did.

I opened a bottle of room-service wine and paced for a while, trying to decide if I should be sane and sensible and take Harvey's advice about getting in the wind. I've never been one to take orders gracefully, but I couldn't think of a good reason to hang around Santa Fe. As Maggie had told me eight or ten times, she was a big girl, fully capable of opening her own doors, going home alone, and cutting off a man's balls without any more aid than her rusty pocketknife.

As for my own tangled personal life . . . there was little point in staying in Santa Fe. On the other hand, my eight weeks in the wind hadn't given me much peace of mind. The small progress I'd made toward accepting that which couldn't be changed had been wiped out by a single look at Fiora.

The wine was so *ordinaire* as to be invisible, but it was better than the taste in my mouth when I thought of Fiora and the past. We had been living together again, cautiously, growing day by day toward a better understanding of ourselves and each other. Yet when it came to the crunch, she hadn't trusted me. When trouble came calling, she did what any other God-fearing, law-abiding citizen would have done—she called in the FBI.

I believe in God, at least in *a* god, although I've never figured out what her name is. However, law-abiding is a god of another color entirely. Cops have their own priorities. Sometimes those priorities coincide with mine and sometimes they don't. In Fiora's case, they didn't. The FBI wanted to make an arrest.

I wanted to plant a tree.

It was the only way to make sure no one got hurt. That had been Fiora's rationale for calling in the Feds rather than letting me take care of her problem myself. I didn't like that rationale any better now than I had then.

Nothing new. Nothing had changed.

I prowled from bed to bathroom and back until the sound of my own footsteps irritated me; then I sat in the silent room, sipping mediocre wine and thinking about Fiora, the woman who had no faith in me.

It was the only way to make sure no one got hurt.

Well, nobody got hurt, pretty lady.

That suave son of a bitch who killed your brother, who drove nails through the back of my hands, who was perfectly prepared to blow both you and me into our next incarnations with a twelve-gauge shotgun . . . that bastard is still alive in an FBI counterintelligence safe house, being fed caviar and vodka while the Feds question him in relays. When they run out of fish eggs and patience, they'll swap Volker's ass for some Western operative who got caught with his hand in the wrong Russian cookie jar.

No one got hurt.

Yeah, pretty lady. No one got hurt.

I flipped on the television, hoping to drown out the past in the banalities of the eleven o'clock news. At the very least I hoped to stop searching the silence for the sound of Fiora's footsteps coming down the hallway, hesitating, and the husky catch in her voice as she called my name.

No one.

<u>e</u>LEVEN

I paid no attention to the flickering, colored shadows of the television set until I heard Georgia O'Keeffe's name. The TV must have been tuned to ABC's Albuquerque affiliate, because Ted Koppel was the man holding forth on the dreary state of the world. Apparently the producers of *Nightline* had decided they needed a bright little bit to break up the usual political posturing and had chosen to showcase the new O'Keeffe.

". . . and Joe Ballard of our Southwest Bureau has the story," Koppel said.

The picture on the screen cut to a tight close-up of the skull and the poppy. The lens pulled back slowly from the canvas and at the same time the sound came up, filling empty silence with the tinkling glasses and muted chatter of the Nickelaw Gallery party. The cameraman had been bored, but he was good. He caught the famous faces and the confident smiles of the wealthy art aficionados drinking champagne in the white-walled gallery. With one quick panning shot, he showed the surprise, then the pleasure, on a dozen faces as they responded to *Private Skull*.

It was an amazing tour de force. Viewed through the camera lens, the gallery party seemed more important, more electric, than it had actually been. Watching the filmed report was like watching a slickly produced sports telecast, the kind that turns the leisurely, sprawling game of baseball or the chaotic violence of a football scrimmage into a focused, quickly accessible choreography of force and counterforce. Television is the modern alchemist turning dross to solid gold.

Ballard narrated his story with an unerring grasp of drama, interspersing his words with sound and film bites of Nickelaw and Dr. Bradley describing the canvas and its importance in the hierarchy of American art. The bites were closely edited and reassembled out of order. All of them underlined the unstated conclusion that the canvas was the art find of the generation, perhaps of the century.

True to his instincts, Ballard leaned hard on the sexual subtext of the painting, O'Keeffe's ambivalence toward her aged husband, and paid off the emphasis with a film quote from Bradley. The quote hadn't been part of her prepared remarks, so it must have come from a later interview.

"Whether or not O'Keeffe was bisexual," Bradley said coolly, "isn't germane to my placing *Private Skull* within the body of her work. It is enough that she was under great stress from her marriage to

Stieglitz because her interests as a woman and an artist were diverging from his needs as an aging man of declining health."

The video cut to a brilliant blue-and-white panorama of the snowy plateau country at the edge of the Sangre de Cristos. Ballard picked up the voice-over narration.

"The newly discovered Georgia O'Keeffe masterpiece hung for decades in a small mud house in this poverty-stricken little village of Las Trampas."

Ballard wasn't a Westerner. It showed in his Anglicized pronunciation of the name of the little town; he flattened the *r* and made the *p* very distinct. But the cameraman salvaged the exotic flavor with a series of mood shots that conveyed the power and mystery of New Mexico's highlands. There was a nicely composed shot of Las Trampas strung out for two hundred yards along the narrow blacktop High Road. That shot was followed by quick studies of a small graveyard with white crosses and nosegays of plastic flowers.

"ABC has been granted an exclusive interview with Victoria Quinones, the woman who brought the masterpiece out of her home. Ms. Quinones, like the people of Las Trampas itself, is a very private woman. She granted an exclusive interview in the hope that it would satisfy the public's need to know the circumstances of the painting's discovery."

While Ballard spoke the screen showed a series of lingering portraits, Hispano and *indio* faces, villagers as stolid and impassive as the adobe walls of the brooding old church. The last face in the sequence was an elegant amalgamation of Indian and white and Spanish that reminded me of Maggie Tenorio, except that Maggie's face was all of a piece. The face on the screen seemed oddly blurred, as though heredity couldn't decide on which side of the racial question to tip the scale. The result was an off-center yet striking beauty that was almost eerie in its familiarity.

The dark-haired woman began speaking. That husky, whispering voice was unmistakable: Victoria Quinones.

"My aunt was a simple woman. Las Trampas and its people were her life. She did not understand the Anglo world. She did not want anything more than what she had. She simply liked the painting."

Quinones' voice was more accented than I remembered it from the tape. Perhaps the camera made her nervous, sending her back to the vowels and consonants of her childhood.

The scene on the television switched to a small courtyard in front of an old, sun-worn adobe house. The slanting light of late afternoon struck deep shadows from the round *viga* beams and gave the rough tan walls the texture of velvet.

Quinones, too, was a study in old southwest style, wearing the faded velveteen blouse, turquoise beads, and billowing ankle-length skirt that R. C. Gorman made familiar to a generation of art collectors. She wore her brown hair tied at the back of her neck with many turns of what could have been a rawhide thong. Her Anglo ancestors showed through in her thin nose and light brown eyes. The cheekbones could have been Indian or even Swedish—wide and high, setting off eyes whose lashes could have done with a bit of mascara. She probably would have fainted at the thought; she was as militantly unsophisticated in her makeup as Dr. Bradley.

The camera did a cutaway to Ballard, who looked out of place in his blue blazer and rep tie. Earnestly he asked Quinones, "Didn't your aunt realize that Georgia O'Keeffe paintings are now worth millions of dollars?"

"My aunt feared she had sinned in stealing the painting from the rubbish pile. When I first told her how valuable the painting was, she didn't believe me. When she did believe me, she made me promise not to tell. She was worried she would be named a thief. She had her home and her people and her church. That was enough."

It might have been enough for Auntie, but apparently her niece had bigger ideas. Reading between the lines, the old woman had hardly cooled before the painting was off the wall and into Nickelaw's hands. Quite a coup for Nickelaw, too. His galleries were noted for Native art, not for the fine arts of the conquering whites.

"Why did you sell the painting outright, rather than submitting it to auction where the price might be a great deal higher?" Ballard asked.

Quinones turned and looked out over the courtyard. The Minicam caught her profile, more European than *indio*. Her sentiments, however, were not.

"That painting belongs to the white world," she said, gesturing with hands that were almost as beautiful as Maggie's. "Las Trampas does not. The money from the painting will go to Indian artists who work in traditional ways with traditional materials. That is the art I love. That is the art that comes from the soul of this land. Indian land."

There was an insert of Quinones at work at a rudimentary potter's wheel. Finished pottery was displayed at the end of her worktable. The pottery's lines and designs hadn't changed in thousands of years. It was survival art, art gleaned from the cracks in the demands of a brutal, physically demanding life.

The camera ground on, showing rugs and sand paintings of the same primitive sort. All were beautifully made and meticulously authentic in their materials and designs. They were also static. They had none of the living tension and open-ended possibilities of the black soapstone bear, for the bear was the result of art's finding a new way to survive in a violently changing world. It was the synthesis of all cultures that called to me, not the bloodless preservation of any single one.

The scene on the television shifted to follow Quinones' gesture to the crystal hardness of the land beyond Las Trampas. The camera zoomed in on a skull, blurred, and then pulled back to reveal the O'Keeffe painting once more.

"So the art world has an astonishing new masterwork today, thanks to an Indian woman from New Mexico who long ago kept a temperamental artist from discarding a finished canvas," Ballard summarized. "And thanks to that same canvas, traditional Indian art will survive in the twentieth-century world. This is Joe Ballard reporting from Las Trampas, New Mexico."

The program cut back to Ted Koppel, half a continent away. "Thank you, Joe. And now—"

I hit the switch and sat in silence, trying to work up interest in another glass of uninteresting wine. In the back of my mind I heard footsteps coming down the hall toward my door. Light footsteps. They hesitated. Stopped. A soft tap on the door.

"Fiddler . . . ?"

For an instant the voice sounded like Fiora's.

I wasn't sure whether to be irked or relieved when I saw Maggie standing alone in the hallway. My reaction must have shown on my face.

"Come in."

"You're sure?" she asked dryly. "I mean, if you're expecting somebody else . . ."

I stepped back so that Maggie could enter. She walked in, shut the door, and eyed me rather warily. "Jesus, your ex sure knows all the buttons to push on you."

"If you want something to drink," I said, ignoring her remark, "there's a plastic glass in the bathroom. It's a good match for the wine."

Maggie didn't answer. I looked at her more closely, seeing her rather than the woman who wasn't there. Maggie's hand had a fine tremor as she touched my sleeve in a mute plea.

"Fiddler? Is it too late for you to take me home?"

"I don't know, Maggie. Is it?"

She took a deep breath. It didn't help. Her voice was as unsteady as her hands. "I'm afraid to go home alone."

I set down the untouched wine and picked up my parka. "Let's go."

"It may be harder than that. And it may be easier." Maggie hesitated, then spoke quickly. "The lock on my gate was open when I got home. I know I locked it. I'm positive I did. I went up the walk far enough to see that the front door was ajar. I thought I heard a noise inside, and then I thought of that little creep following me and I ran."

"Good for you," I said, meaning it. "Smartest thing you could do."

Maggie smiled shakily. "I wasn't thinking smart. I wasn't thinking at all." She took a ragged breath. "I guess I've finally just run out of nerve."

She let her breath out slowly, as though she were fighting for control. Maybe she was truly scared or maybe she'd taken Fiora's advice to heart.

Either way, the result was the same; I got the Detonics out of my bag and pulled on my vest.

The streets around Maggie's neighborhood were dead still: no Harvey, no stranger hunched down behind the wheel of a cold car, no nothing. I parked the Cobra in front of her little house and got out.

"Stay put," I said.

She didn't argue.

The front gate was still open. So was the front door. The Detonics was already drawn as I flattened against the wall and swung the door open with one hand. I pulled a glove off with my teeth and stuck my hand into the darkened room. The air inside was the same temperature as it was outside. The door had been ajar long enough for the heat inside the house to escape.

I let my breath out, kept my lungs empty, and listened for a minute. Nothing.

I found the light switch by feel, flipped it on, and waited. No hurried scuffling, no scrambling for cover, no sudden flight toward the back door. Keeping low, I stuck my head inside for a fast look.

The light in the room came from a pair of lamps that lay on the floor of what had once been a very pleasant combined living room and studio. Once, but no longer. A wrecking crew had been at work.

I crossed to the hallway, listening and turning on lights as I went. The house was cold and still. The kitchen and the two bedrooms were empty.

I went back outside to the Cobra. "Nobody's home now, but the place has been trashed."

Without a word, Maggie got out of the car and walked toward her front door. I followed her, more interested in her lack of surprise than in the mess inside.

Nothing had changed.

The prowlers hadn't been ordinary burglars. Ordinary burglars don't spend half an hour opening food in the kitchen and smearing everything around on the cabinets, counters, and floors. Somebody had been sending a message.

Maggie stood in the doorway of the house, surveying the wreckage. I stood next to her. Her face didn't give away anything.

I looked at the room. It took me a while to recognize a pile of wood as the remains of an easel. Next to it a canvas lay facedown on the tile floor, surrounded by tubes of paint and several dozen brushes that lay scattered and splintered like debris from a dying tree. Ruining the easel hadn't satisfied the wrecking crew. They had stomped several tubes of paint, bursting them open, spewing paint in all directions. Red, yellow, and orange footprints tracked across the floor. Furniture had been overturned, its upholstery ripped open and stuffing thrown about. A wall cabinet had once held stoneware dishes, which were now scattered in ragged chunks all over the place.

"Burglars?" Maggie's one word was both question and denial.

"Western Union. Can you read the message?"

Eyes closed, hugging herself, she said nothing.

I stepped around Maggie and picked up the overturned painting. It was a basin and range landscape, but it was unfinished. Now it never would be. Across its face someone had painted *You can't go back*.

"This mean anything to you?" I asked.

Maggie's eyes opened, focused on the painting, and then on nothing at all.

"I couldn't sleep last night," she said. "So I got up and started *Place of Power II*, painting it just the way I told you I should have painted it in the first place. I guess that one isn't going to work out either." She smiled bitterly. "*You can't go back*."

"And you don't want to go forward?"

She shrugged.

"Do you happen to know a little shit called Harvey Durham?" I asked.

Maggie's head snapped up in time for me to see raw fear in the instant before her expression shut down. She said not one word.

"Suit yourself." I turned around and headed toward the Cobra.

"I—Fiddler, wait!"

I waited.

"Where are you going?" she asked.

I didn't know I'd decided until I opened my mouth and said, "Back."

"To your hotel?"

"No. To California."

There was a long pause.

"Can I come with you as far as Palm Springs?"

t WELVE

Nighttime is for thinking, for remembering, for being haunted by the might-have-beens. You can cover a lot of ground during darkness. Too much, sometimes. Not nearly enough, most times.

Physical progress is no problem. Santa Fe to LA by car via Palm Springs is fourteen hours, nonstop, if your gas tank and your bladder are big enough. Just take I-25 straight south, hang a right on I-10, and go as long as you can. Next stop, the sands of Malibu. A thousand miles without a stop sign, a thousand miles of four-lane freedom, a thousand miles in overdrive with the cold wind slipping in through the seams of the driving curtains.

It always surprised me that this kind of individual freedom came from a military mind—General Eisenhower's, to be precise. He decided that in order to defend something the size of the United States, a commander had to be able to move his troops around quickly and efficiently. It was real nice of Ike to let us civilians use the system too. Narrow, winding country highways are quaint, but there's nothing like broad straight lines for making speed between two points.

Jimmy Carter, another ex-military type, tried to roll back progress in the name of fuel conservation, but the double nickel speed limit was an idea whose time never came west of the Mississippi. In the West we've worked out a more unstructured system—as fast as you care to go for as long as you think you can get away with it.

Between Ike and the peanut farmer, the surface of the interstates became a bit quirky, especially in the lonesome lands. I-10 is a tough, ruthless road, a cement garden path for long-haul rigs, those glistening double-trailer outfits with red, orange, blue, yellow, and green running lights on their cross-country farings and long CB antennas waving in the air like buggy whips.

Steinbeck's Mother Road, Route 66, may be only a disintegrating two-lane memory but there are still migrants headed west, folks down on their luck or folks who never had any luck in the first place or just plain folks who are pushing along the best way they know how. Mexican field hands drive a $500 Cadillac, going balls-out for the Salt River Valley to pick lettuce. An aging, overloaded sedan follows a U-Haul rental truck as a young couple has an Adventure in Moving. Old cars filled with hope and garbage bags full of clothes head west for a job in Lancaster or a retirement home in Sun City or a double-wide mobile home cemented to the desert floor somewhere east of Victorville.

We all shared the freedom of the highway, knew the lure of the limitless West. The straight-ahead joy of the Badlands and the openness of the Great Plateau were like a tonic to me, keeping me awake after Maggie had scrunched down into her seat and fallen into sleep or the kind of thoughts she didn't want to share.

That was fine with me. I didn't have any thoughts I felt like sharing either. When you can't go back and you can't go forward and you don't like the place you're in, you're in one hell of a fix. I didn't want to think about Fiora and me, but it was impossible not to do just that. Darkness is for remembering.

Fiora and I were lovers before we were married, while we were married, and after we were divorced. It should have worked. It came so goddamn close to working . . . but our own divergent natures kept getting in the way of our living together. The older we got, the more we pulled in opposite directions.

Fiora had always been and always would be the bright, ambitious woman for whom the Age of Feminism was created. Pomona College, Harvard Business School, sharpening at the London School of Economics and at the University of Tokyo: all on scholarship. The smart folks in the world of business and finance—and there are a lot of them—spotted Fiora early in the game. They devoted time and money to sanding off her small-town edges and putting a hard polish on the rest.

The process worked because Fiora wanted it to

work. Today she was plugged into an old-boy/old-girl network that was one of the most powerful in the world. She was rapidly becoming one of them.

Why and how she ever got involved with an auslander like me is simple. We were a lot younger then. It happened fast and it happened real hard and it has continued to happen on a regular basis ever since. We go along our separate paths—she being her orderly, savagely bright business self and me being my random, retrograde, fun-loving self—for months, even for years at a time. Then we collide and mesh and wonder how the hell we got along apart.

But sooner or later we ricochet in separate directions again and wonder what the hell went wrong this time and how anything so inevitable can still hurt so much.

A major part of the problem is that Fiora is in the money-shuffling pressure cooker twelve to eighteen hours a day, six to seven days a week. That's just how she is constituted. She needs a mate who can make a career of caring and sharing, because she doesn't have a hell of a lot of time to do either. Several Alan Alda clones auditioned for the part but couldn't keep up with her in the sack.

You see, that's the other part of Fiora: the uncivilized part that she has spent a lifetime trying to erase, the fey Scots part of her that sometimes dreams accurate dreams of violence and death, the part of her that comes to me like steel to an electromagnet, inevitably, time after time. Lots of people, including Fiora, are unnerved by the realization that there is something primitive, utterly irrational, and very powerful in her.

I'm not. I'm intrigued, enthralled, sometimes driven crazy. But put off? No way.

Unfortunately, I can't just spin on my thumb and wait for the odd hour or so when the elemental Fiora is let off the leash to play with her elemental mate. So I go out and about, looking at the world as it is, rather than as it should be, and doing my best to lend a hand or a boot or whatever else might be needed by people caught in the cracks between what ought to be and what is.

Minding other people's business can be damned hard on your health, which accounts for all of my scars and most of my worst arguments with Fiora. She says I'm afflicted by a disease that probably is hereditary. She calls it Uncle Jake's Syndrome, in honor of my mother's much younger brother. Jake was either a free spirit or a soot-black sheep, depending on who you talk to. Jake made a decent living importing Mexican agricultural products. Some agricultural products were more interesting than others. Marijuana, for instance, was far more compelling to him than zucchini.

It wasn't the money Jake loved, or even the dope itself. He smoked rarely and spent only as much money as was required to stay in business. The rest of the cash he stuffed in an old steamer trunk. What Jake really loved was the smuggler's life, the adrenaline life, the outlaw life.

I inherited Uncle Jake's Syndrome, but I didn't opt for the dope-smuggling life for the same reason that I didn't try to sell fortified wine on Skid Row. I couldn't swallow hard enough, long enough, to stay in business.

But that didn't clear up my case. Because the disease has serious, even life-threatening consequences —Jake died young, as Fiora well knows—people who suffer from Uncle Jake's Syndrome are very poor candidates for long-term relationships with anybody, much less with respectable women who stand a reasonable chance of someday becoming chairwoman and CEO of General Motors or the first female president of the Stock Exchange—or the U.S. of A.

We've tried, several times, to make it work. Fiora even gave up a senior partnership in a Beverly Hills venture capital operation to move to Newport Beach, looking for a middle ground where we could not only meet but live. We came close to finding it.

But close only counts in horseshoes and hand grenades.

I had always trusted Fiora's expertise when it came to investing my money, but when it came time for her to trust my expertise in pulling people out of deep holes, she couldn't run fast enough to the FBI.

I wondered how much help the FBI would be to her when Harvey came sniffing around. And he would. She had too many clients who had bought too much art from Olin Nickelaw. Maybe this time she would have enough trust to ask me for help.

And maybe next time Harvey's breath would smell like rose petals.

Memories. Like Fiora, I can't live with them and I can't get rid of them.

Finally sunrise came up in the rearview mirror, releasing me from night. The sky took on the color of a ripening lemon as the landscape began to separate from darkness. There were black lava dikes and volcanic plugs off to the south, and sandstone massifs rising like an anchored armada from the flat sea of the desert floor. High overhead an invisible jet drew a lacy contrail across the indigo sky, slanting southwest toward Phoenix, carrying a load of tourists to the land of eternal sun.

I looked over at Maggie. She was awake and about as talkative as the stone buttes. Neither of us spoke for eighty miles. Finally I pulled off the interstate at a little roadside settlement called Saguaro Sentinel. It consisted of a service station and Mini-mart, a diner with six stools and a grill, and two double-wide mobile homes surrounded by abandoned cars. But in the desert at the end of night, any place with gasoline looks inviting.

I parked under the canopy and turned off the engine. Maggie got out and started toward the restrooms and Mini-mart just across the concrete apron.

"Maggie."

She turned around quickly, startled by what she heard in my voice.

"I'm not a cop and I don't get off on slapping women," I said, "but if you don't tell me what kind of scam Nickelaw is running, I'll be more trouble than you've ever had."

tHIRTEEN

The pump jockey wandered out of the office wiping his hands on a blue grease rag. He was a somber Indian kid wearing a thin denim jacket, faded jeans, and grease-stained Wellingtons. The Cobra made as much sense to him as a UFO. I let him pump the gas but took care of the rest myself. As I worked under the hood, I heard Fiora's comment about the Cobra in the back of my mind and knew she was right—the car looked like shit.

By the time I'd checked and topped up the hydraulic fluid and the engine oil and tightened various hose clamps, Maggie was back with a paper sack full of something. She got into the front seat without looking at me.

The new tires squeaked impatiently on the concrete as we left the service station. I cleared the pipes a few times, enjoying their snarl through the underpass as we crossed back beneath the freeway to go westbound again. Then I slid back onto I-10 at a sedate 65 and drove three miles in third gear, letting everything breathe.

Maggie dug a package of Twinkies out of the bag, broke the wrapper, and gave me one. A balanced breakfast, sugar and grease.

"I know an IRS guy named Harvey Durham," Maggie said. "He's been nosing around for almost a year. I don't think he's very smart, though. He's still nosing."

"Maybe you should think again. He's acting like a dog with a new bone. He spent half an hour in my room last night, trying to convince me that it would be a good idea to leave town."

"Looks like he succeeded."

I ignored the dig. "Why does Harvey care where I am?"

In silence Maggie uncapped a plastic cup of black coffee and handed it over to me. I shoved the last bite of Twinkie in my mouth and took the cup, wondering if she was thinking how to tell the truth or the best way to present her lies.

"Why do you care?" she asked finally.

We could go on like this all day, answering questions with other questions until one of us got tired of the game. Meanwhile Harvey would go on sniffing around and dropping hints like bricks about my bookkeeper.

"Is Harvey using you to get at somebody else?" I asked.

Maggie glanced at me with quick surprise. "Who told you?"

"I know how cops work. Is it Nickelaw's ass Harvey wants?"

Her small smile was bitter. "Who else has enough money to matter?"

"What's the scam?"

Once more Maggie shook her head reflexively, as though she had been holding her secret for so long that she couldn't release her grip.

After a few miles Maggie spoke again, "What did you think of the O'Keeffe?"

"I'm a social critic, not an art critic."

"No, I really want to know."

"I liked it a hell of a lot better than the abstract you showed me in the gallery yesterday, and a hell of a lot less than the flowers."

"You were willing to pay ten thousand for the stone bear. Would you pay the same for the skull?"

"No."

"Why? Because it's a bad painting?"

"Ask Bradley whether it's a bad painting. I can only tell you I don't want to live in the same room with it. That's how I buy art. I can live with it or I can't."

Maggie smiled faintly. "You're right. You aren't an art critic. How much do you think the painting is worth?"

"Whatever anyone will pay for it," I said impatiently, "just like everything else in the world."

"The problem with art is that nobody except the buyer and the seller know precisely what the real price is."

Bingo.

"Especially the IRS?" I asked softly.

Maggie drew a deep breath and let it out in a sigh, as though she were weary of the secrets and glad at last to share them. "I thought it would take you longer to figure it out."

I hadn't figured it out, not until that moment. There are too many potential scams in a blue-sky and expert-opinion game like fine art. Forgery, for one. Money laundering, for another. But a tax scam explained more of what I'd seen last night than anything else.

On paper, the scam looks like charity. Purchase a work of art for cash, then donate it to your favorite museum. The government has decreed that such generosity is laudable and should be encouraged by allowing it as a tax deduction. So Uncle Sam underwrites part of the cost of your civic altruism. Depending on the year and your marginal tax rate, the government's share of your philanthropy is anywhere from 28 to 50 percent of the total.

In other words, you only have to inflate the reported cost of your donation two to four times to reduce the cost of your charity to nothing. Zero. Zip. *Nada*. Not one adulterated dime does your civic posturing cost you. The only catch is, you have to find an expert appraiser willing to blow the price of the donated item up as big as your ego.

"That's what the media circus was for," I said. "The IRS, not an auction. Valenti and Nickelaw were laying the groundwork for their case that the painting was worth twice what any sensible bidding would bring."

Maggie shrugged, not committing herself.

"How much is Nickelaw padding his appraisals?"

I asked. "Fifty percent? A hundred? More? Is he taking it out in trade or is he getting a cash kick-back?"

Maggie drank coffee. "I don't know that he's doing anything illegal. All I know is that Harvey's a real pain in the ass."

"You know more than that. Harvey wouldn't spend a whole year sniffing around you unless he thought you could help him nail Nickelaw."

Maggie looked out the windshield, unwilling to meet my glance. Her hand shook a little when she raised her plastic cup and made a pass at the scalding coffee with bloodless lips.

"How much do you know about Nickelaw's appraisals?" I asked. "Does he ask you for advice? Do you do appraisals for him?"

"Nothing, no, and no," Maggie said tightly. "If a piece of art says five thousand on the tag, I sell it for five thousand. That's my job. I'm a goddamn clerk. Olin's the expert on southwestern art. The IRS ought to know—he proved it in tax court five years ago."

"You mean this isn't the first time Nickelaw has tangled with the IRS?"

"They came at him over some Taos Masters he sold to a collector from Dallas. The IRS took the position that the appraised values were way too high. Olin took it all the way to tax court, and there wasn't a single reputable expert in southwestern art who wanted to disagree publicly with him. Good art is a matter of expert opinion. Olin's opinion carries a lot of clout in a very small field."

No wonder Harvey Durham wanted a piece of

Nickelaw's ass. Nickelaw had duped the government and then he had taken the IRS hotshots to tax court and rubbed their noses in it. Personal crusades have been launched for less. But even the CID of the IRS couldn't get Nickelaw without the testimony of an insider, somebody who knew exactly how the scam worked, somebody who could supply names, places, dates, documentation.

"Doesn't Nickelaw's 'expert opinion' ever leave a bad taste in your mouth?" I finally asked Maggie.

She gave me a Cheshire smile, plenty of teeth and a predatory gleam in her black eyes. I was willing to bet it was the same smile Nickelaw gave the IRS accountants on the way out of tax court. It was probably the same smile he gave Maggie after he smacked her in the face.

"Art is a business, not a holy calling," Maggie said flatly. "I call it the art of survival. People get rich off art all the time—collectors, dealers, sometimes even artists. Where's the big moral outrage in that?"

"Save it for the parish priest. What's your cut of Nickelaw's action?"

"Eight bucks an hour plus the chance to exhibit my work in his galleries."

It didn't sound like much. On the other hand, it was the gold ring on the carousel to an ambitious artist. Nickelaw knew it. He held that knowledge like a whip over Maggie's proud head.

You're good, but in this business, good is just another word for second-rate. You walk out, and it'll take me maybe five minutes to find someone just like you. You stay, and I'll put your stuff right out there with the best. Hear me?

Maggie had heard him. Next to what Nickelaw could do for her, Harvey didn't have any leverage. And even if he did, Nickelaw was more than ready to trash Maggie's apartment and leave a warning smeared across her painting.

An Allied moving van howled past us at 75, its turboed diesels screaming. The slipstream rocked the Cobra like a Piper Cub in the wake of a DC-10. Maggie looked at me. I looked at the road.

"I didn't ask for a goddamn testimonial from you," she said angrily, "so what the hell difference does it make to you how I earn my living or Olin earns his?"

"The IRS already tried to screw Nickelaw legally. That didn't work, but they didn't give up. There are other ways to screw a man than up front, and Harvey's trying them one by one. Right now he's looking for a twist on somebody with information, somebody like a trusted employee. Like you, Maggie."

Maggie grimaced.

I kept talking. "He'll settle for a guilty client, if he has to. Or a guilty client's bookkeeper." I squeezed the wheel, wishing it were Harvey's neck, and asked the question whose answer I really didn't want to hear. "How many of Nickelaw's clients have ties to Pacific Rim Investments?"

Maggie gave me a startled glance. "Five or six. Maybe more."

"Is Valenti one of them?"

She hesitated, then apparently decided that I could always find out the truth working from the other end. "Yes."

"I'll bet a lot of Nickelaw's clients have made generous donations to Valenti's Museum of Southwestern Art."

Maggie said nothing. She didn't have to. After all, there was no law against philanthropy.

"Small world, isn't it?" I asked sarcastically. "Everybody is one big happy incestuous family. Christ."

I was furious, even though I knew instinctively that Fiora wasn't involved in the scam. She could be ruthless as a falcon and clever as a mink, but she had a Scots rectitude about business that went all the way to the bone. Even Harvey would ultimately be forced to admit that—in a computer form letter, years after he had ruined Fiora's reputation, her career, and her life within the business community.

And I had no doubt Harvey would do just that on his way to ruining Nickelaw. There's nothing worse than a bureaucratic prick with a hard-on.

Neither Maggie nor I said anything more, which was fine with me. I knew too much as it was.

We crossed the Colorado River at Blythe in midafternoon. The low-desert temperature was in the 80s. I stopped long enough to stow the winter gear and the side curtains in the boot. Then I started driving. Hard.

West of Blythe, I-10 is flat and straight and virtually unpatrolled. Nobody lives out there but a handful of misfits, mystics, and miners. The Cobra was grateful for the chance to breathe hundred-mile-an-hour air. By the time I finished the run to Desert Center, the cylinders were hot and clean. Traffic thickened. Muttering, the Cobra settled in to breathing slow air again.

The sun was just sliding down behind Mount San Jacinto when we passed the city limit of Palm Springs. Maggie had been asleep or feigning it, wedged uncomfortably against the door. She stirred and straightened up.

"You going anywhere special in Palm Springs?" I asked.

She shook her head. "Just drop me at the Marriott. I have a friend here in town I can call."

I didn't bother to answer. Maggie had told me some of the truth since dawn, but I had a gut hunch she had left out more truth than she had told.

I pulled to the curb on Palm Canyon in front of the ersatz Moorish hotel a few minutes before five. Maggie got out and stretched slowly, trying to get rid of the cramps in her legs. Then she grabbed her small traveling bag from behind the seat and closed the door.

"So long, Fiddler," she said. "Thanks for the ride."

"Maggie."

Her head snapped around toward me.

"If you tell me the truth, I can help you."

She smiled oddly and shook her head. "Not this time, Fiddler. You've got Fiora on your mind. If it came to a choice between her and me . . ." Maggie watched me closely, then nodded. "That's what I thought. See you around, cowboy."

She turned and walked across the sidewalk to the front door without looking back.

When the door closed behind her, I let out the

clutch and drove down the street. At the end of the block, I made a right and stowed the Cobra in a loading zone.

The side door of the Marriott opened onto a crowded lobby. Several airport vans jammed with tourists and conventioneers had just arrived. They were all trying to check in at the same time.

I found a spot behind some plastic foliage and searched the crowd for Maggie. I didn't see her immediately, but then I caught a glimpse of her long black hair. The view cleared as the crowd shifted for a few seconds, flowing apart and then together once more as a bellman trundled a loaded baggage wagon through the lobby.

It wasn't much of a look, but it was enough. Apparently Maggie's "friend" had come in on an early flight and had been waiting for her arrival. Arm in arm, leaning comfortably against each other, Maggie and Dr. Lillian Bradley strolled toward the bank of elevators.

fOURTEEN

Thinking over all the variations and permutations of Maggie-Bradley-Nickelaw-Harvey kept me awake for the rest of the drive home. The possibilities ranged from an innocent lovers' reunion to something a hell of a lot more ambitious than a bit of genteel fiddling on the tax returns of the rich and shameless.

The most likely possibility was also the most difficult to make fly—collusion among the first three to defraud the fourth. Assuming that a tax swindle with a kickback sweetener was the goal, there still wasn't enough money in the deal for everyone; certainly not for Dr. Bradley, whose reputation had to be worth considerably more to her than whatever Nickelaw paid her as an "expert consultant" on the O'Keeffe.

The only way there might be enough money in the deal to tempt Bradley would be if the O'Keeffe were a fake rather than a genuine discovery. That was possible, of course, but not very likely. *Private Skull* had been through the laboratory-certification mill and had come out smelling like two million roses. The fact that an art hustler and a billionaire were the major beneficiaries of the new O'Keeffe was unfortunate, but nobody over the age of six believes that life is fair.

Besides, if you went with the O'Keeffe-as-fraud idea, then you had to believe that Nickelaw was dumb enough to take on a scam of that magnitude while the CID of the IRS was looking over his shoulder. Even the silent blonde wasn't dumb enough to try that stunt, and she didn't seem to have the brains of the average orchid.

Which brought me back to tax fraud and the ineluctable fact that there wasn't enough money to pay off the good Dr. Bradley. Unless Nickelaw had used Maggie's lovely body to make up the difference?

I had a hard time making that one fly, if only because there was no longer any need for the sexual antics. The O'Keeffe had been appraised by the marketplace at two million dollars. The deal, whatever the deal was, had been cut and the players paid off. There was no reason for Maggie to get into bed again, except for the best reason of all. She wanted to. Which meant . . . nothing useful in terms of fraud.

I was still chasing smaller and smaller possibilities in tighter and tighter circles when I pulled into the driveway at Crystal Cove. When I switched off the engine, all the physical sensations I had been ignoring hit me. As is the case with every competition-bred 1960s sportster, the Cobra rides like a lame mule at a full gallop; it doesn't make allowances for crazy Anglos who use it as a touring car. I climbed out of the seat feeling as though I'd been worked over with a rubber hose for seven of the last fourteen hours.

Kwame Nkrumah, my neighbor's Rhodesian Ridgeback, was dancing in place at the end of the driveway, wiggling and woofing softly with delight at my return. It's always nice to know somebody's glad to see you, even if he's a four-legged predator the size of a small pony. Kwame's owner purchased him as a guard dog, not as a companion; sentry duty makes for a long, solitary life for a hound. Sometimes I think I may be the only man in the world who really understands the loneliness that Kwame experiences. He greeted me as though I were a brother. I greeted him the same way.

We tussled for a couple of minutes and then he danced beside me while I unloaded my traveling bags and buttoned up the Cobra. I thought about breaking the rules and inviting him in for the company both of us wanted, but I refrained. Kwame's job was to prowl. The fact that he had adopted my house, my yard, and myself as part of his territory was a gift it wouldn't be fair to exploit.

"Sorry, boy."

Kwame took it like the gentleman he was, giving me an understanding look and a lick from a tongue the size of a Christmas stocking.

I had a bowl of bean soup from the freezer, half a package of crackers from the cupboard, and two glasses of Merlot from the Alexander Valley. My own mattress felt like home, except that my reflexes kept expecting to feel a comfortable weight on the other side of the bed, a comfortable warmth, another person breathing in the darkness.

So? Life is tough all over.

After a while I fell asleep.

Eleven hours later I heard someone outside my door. I woke up fast and hard, then realized that it was Luz Pico, which meant that it must be cleaning day. When nobody is home Luz strips floors or paints trim or overhauls the oven or the freezer. There's always something to do in a sixty-year-old cottage on a clay bluff above the surf line. If the house doesn't need her touch, she tends to the koi and the hummingbird feeder; I suspect she scratches Kwame's big ears, too.

Luz Pico is a slender Chicana who wears designer jeans and drives a Cadillac. Her lineage goes back to the Spanish soldiers who came north with Father Serra in the eighteenth century. But unlike some of the Hispanics of New Mexico, Luz still stays in touch with Old Mexico. That's where she gets a lot of her staff for her housecleaning business. The girls are from the poorest villages of the interior. Luz teaches them about Pampers and espresso machines, and she teaches her customers about six o'clock mass, minimum-wage laws, and employee benefits.

"Fiddler?" Luz called softly.

"*Buenos días, mi corazón,*" I said. "*¿Cómo estas?*"

"Twenty minutes, then we wash you with the sheets."

I groaned.

Luz ignored me. In rapid Spanish she instructed her staff to bide their time by feeding the humming-birds and watering the flowers.

"And don't forget the tree on the hill," she added.

That got my attention. There are a half dozen eucalyptus and a star pine on the lot, but they have all taken care of themselves for the last fifty years or so. I once had a lemon tree in a whiskey barrel on the corner of the deck, but the tree had died awhile back, root-bound and strangled. Like the koi in their pond at the back of the house, the tree had outgrown its space.

In fact, I'd been digging the koi a new pond when my life came apart and I got on the road. Maybe it was time I got off my ass and finished what I'd started. If nothing else, I could use the exercise.

Five minutes later I was dressed and headed up the little backyard slope to look at the hole. Luz had beaten me to it. There wasn't a hole any more. There was a lemon tree. It was one of the happiest living things I'd ever seen—lustrous dark-green leaves, smooth bark, branches heavy with fruit in all stages, and flowers whose perfume must have been perfected by God in Eden.

Luz's family has owned citrus groves at the mouth of Santa Ana Canyon for a hundred years. Much of the land has been sold off and paved over but the family *estancia* still stands at the east edge of Yorba Linda, in the middle of the most beautifully tended five-acre citrus grove in the state. The lemon tree must have come from there.

"Thank you, Luz. It's a beautiful tree. It will keep me in lemonade all year around."

"Do not thank me. Your wife picked it out and planted it herself."

"Ex-wife."

Luz shrugged as only she can.

I stroked a glossy green lemon leaf, cupped a ripening fruit in my hand, and tested the needle point on an inch-long thorn.

Fiora is nothing if not a complex woman.

"Guess I'd better get to work on a new koi pond," I said.

"The old pond has been expanded. It is so deep now that the raccoons can't catch the koi if you forget to put the screen over at night. My brother wanted to put in a waterfall, but Fiora said you preferred silence because it was easier to hear unexpected guests coming."

That stopped me. I'd never said anything like that to Fiora, but it was true. So I thanked Luz again and went back to the house. I traded my digging clothes for running clothes. Five miles later I didn't know any more than I had before, but my irritability index was low enough so I could sort through two months of mail without setting a match to the whole thing.

My Pacific Rim Investments address gets all the bills, as well as the fancy, personalized, computer-generated invitations to spend three days in a new resort, accept the gift of a television set, and listen to hours of the hardest kind of hard real estate sell. All the stuff the mailman brings to the Crystal Cove address is of the "Dear Resident" or "Postal Patron" variety.

The junk mail filled two trash bags. As though in commentary on my tenuous attachment to the real world, there were only two meaningful pieces of mail. In one, the State of California once again informed me that my private investigator's license had expired. I hadn't renewed it in years, but the state keeps trying to convince me that I need a special license to ask unpopular questions.

A second letter was more meaningful. It informed me that my concealed weapons permit would soon expire. I wasn't worried; the term of the county sheriff who had issued the permit still had a year to run. But it did remind me that I wanted to add a new pistol to the list of weapons I was authorized to conceal.

For years I've carried a short-barreled Detonics Combat Master. It's small and easy to hide. But I'd discovered a major drawback to the gun one morning when I pointed its short barrel at a very tough, shrewd man who was using Fiora as a shield.

Since then I'd awakened in a cold sweat more than once, remembering in cruel detail how it felt not to be certain that I could hit the very small target of his left eye at a range greater than ten yards.

I'd bluffed the matter through at the time, but my subconscious had just decided that I didn't want to run that kind of bluff again. Ever.

Before noon I walked into my favorite firearms store, a survivalist redoubt in the heart of Garden Grove. The clerk was a squared-away youngster with a mustache the color and size of a well-fed Norwegian rat. He stood unsmiling behind the long glass counter, arms folded across his chest.

"How are you this morning?" he asked.

His inquiry was polite and his eyes were skeptical. I didn't look like I belonged.

"Show me the most accurate handgun you have," I said.

He studied me for a second, trying to figure out whether I was a timid householder looking for stainless steel courage or some kind of freelance hit man. Whatever he decided, he kept it to himself. He turned, walked a few steps, and disappeared into the back room. A few moments later he returned with a flat leather pouch the size of a Britannica volume. He set it on the counter, unzipped it, and laid it open on the glass. Inside was a cold gray 1911-style semiautomatic with an overlength barrel that stuck out the front of the slide.

"Detonics Scoremaster. Six-inch barrel. It'll reach out a hundred yards, if you think you've got the nerves to hold it steady. But I only have it in Four-fifty-one Magnum. That's a little exotic for most shooters."

"How much?"

"Seventeen hundred and fifty."

I dropped the AMEX card on the glass countertop.

For an extra hundred, cash, he waived the fifteen-day waiting period on handguns.

Any new firearm, particularly a heavy semiautomatic pistol, takes a little getting used to. I ran forty rounds through it at the firing range in Fountain Valley, zeroing in the sights and adjusting to the nine-pound hammer recoil of the .451-caliber load. When I was finished, I had one full magazine and a couple of spares from the box of factory loads the survivalist had sold me.

By the time I pulled into the driveway in Crystal Cove, I was getting used to the way the pistol dug into the small of my back when I wore the holster. That long barrel was going to be a pain in the ass— literally—but ain't nothing in this world comes free, as Jake used to point out.

Funny thing, the subconscious mind. When the Cobra growled down the road into Crystal Cove, I wasn't particularly surprised by the fact that there was a white Porsche parked near my garage and two people standing at the edge of my property, watched by my four-footed unwelcoming committee, Kwame Nkrumah.

At the sound of the Cobra, Nickelaw and the drop-dead blonde turned toward me as though they were connected to the same central nervous system.

fIFTEEN

Like Nickelaw, the Porsche was a slick, trick-looking machine. There was a whale tail and fiberglass ground effects, louvering cut nicely into the front and rear fenders for cooling on the brakes and in the aircraft-carrier deck of the whale tail for the turbo, big fat Pirellis front and back, and *DS 935 by Dage Design* in flowing script on the back end. A hybrid street racer based on the Can-Am Porsche. A hundred and twenty-five grand on the hoof, maybe more.

The boy had expensive taste in cars.

I walked up to Kwame carrying rolled targets, a cleaning kit, a half-full box of ammunition, and the .451 in my right hand, muzzle pointed toward the ground and slide locked back in the open position.

Kwame looked over at me as I approached.

"Good dog."

His tail twitched. He'd rather have been a bad dog.

Nickelaw watched me without moving. "Does your dog bite?"

"He's not my dog."

Nickelaw didn't smile. I guess he didn't like old movies.

"Call him off," Nickelaw said. "Vikki is afraid of dogs."

I looked at the blonde. Her eyes were an odd amber-green in the full sunlight. She looked at me without blinking. She was about as nervous as a cement slab, but I told Kwame that he could relax. Immediately Vikki started off across the small lawn toward the side door of my house. Without hesitation she tried the handle, found everything unlocked, and walked inside.

"It's a long drive," Nickelaw said. "She had to pee."

After a few minutes of silence he went up to Kwame and held out his hand to be sniffed. Kwame obliged, but when the hand tried to pat his broad head, the dog ducked.

"Sullen bastard," Nickelaw said, turning back to me.

I assume he meant the dog.

"Where'd you find the Cobra?" he asked.

"Under a cabbage leaf."

He stared at the Cobra's sleek curves and deep blue paint for a few more silent minutes before he said, "Those were the good old days."

"Yeah. Back when the gasoline had lead and the Arabs had sand."

He smiled tightly.

"Sure you don't want to go inside and help Vikki take a look around?" I asked as I crossed the yard and dumped the cleaning kit, ammunition, targets, and gun on the picnic table. I kept the magazine in my hip pocket.

"Is that a side-oiler Four-twenty-seven?" Nickelaw asked, looking at the Cobra.

"Yes."

"That was the important Cobra," he said, looking away from me to the car. "The fastest straight-line production car ever made. It would take some work to put it in Concourse shape, but let me know if you ever want to sell it."

"I didn't know you peddled used cars too."

His smile was as thin as his black pegged jeans. "Automobiles are an important contemporary art form, just like paintings. They can also be a good investment. The Cobra cost maybe ten grand new. I know a collector with a fully documented S/C Cobra like yours. It has twenty-three miles on the odometer and has been in inert-gas storage since the day he bought it. He just turned down a million dollars for it, cash. That's a damn good return over twenty years."

"There's not much collector value left in my Cobra. It's carrying close to a hundred and fifty thousand miles on the odometer."

"Too bad."

"Cars like the Cobra are meant to be driven, not sacked up in plastic bags full of dead gas."

Nickelaw's ruff went up before he remembered that he was trying to be polite. "I keep forgetting you aren't a collector. You don't understand the psychic obsession certain things hold for collectors. Except, perhaps, for the bear? Are you still interested in owning that piece?''

I glanced at Kwame, who now lay at my feet. He reminded me of the bear's muscular grace, but Kwame's muzzle had a faint dusting of gray. Flesh ages much more quickly than soapstone.

"I'm still interested," I said.

The side door opened and closed. I watched Vikki walk toward Nickelaw. Her expressionless face said she hadn't found what, or who, she was looking for.

"I'd like to give you the bear," Nickelaw said to me.

"Why?"

"Because you're going to do me a favor."

"I don't do ten-thousand-dollar favors. They're the kind that come with life sentences."

"Oh, I don't want anybody killed. I just want to know where Maggie is."

"I can tell you where she isn't. She isn't here. Vikki can vouch for that."

Something in my voice got to Kwame. He shifted subtly, still lying down but no longer relaxed. His eyes followed Vikki when she walked toward me.

"Maggie left Santa Fe with you," Nickelaw said, "but she isn't here with you now."

"Then she must be somewhere between here and there." My tone told him how much I didn't care.

Nickelaw's mouth flattened and his eyes narrowed, changing his face from handsome to snake-mean. Vikki wasn't interested in the transformation. She turned away and wandered over to the picnic table. She picked up the pistol with confidence, checked that the chamber was empty, then sighted out to sea with it. After a few moments she looked at me.

"Do you mind?" she asked.

"Yes."

"But I've never held a D-Mag," she said softly, looking up at me with her strange, empty eyes.

She held the pistol properly, with muzzle toward the ground. Then she smiled and at the same time slipped the safety. The slide racked back into its closed position with a smart, well-oiled snap. I met Vikki's sweet, dangerous, vacant gaze until she turned and put the gun back on the table.

What a pair. Nickelaw liked hot cars. Vikki was a gun freak.

Belatedly I realized it was the first time I had heard her speak. She had a sexy, breathless voice. Something about it reminded me of someone else.

"Why are you bothering to protect that Indian bitch?" Nickelaw asked. "She won't thank you for it the way you expect to be thanked. She was raped when she thirteen. She hasn't let a man touch her since."

"Was there anything else," I asked, "or were you two just leaving?"

Nickelaw's skin darkened beneath his careful tan. He didn't say anything, but Kwame's head came up and his whole body hummed with anticipation.

"I could make a lot of trouble for you," Nickelaw said.

"I doubt it. You're used to dealing with people who can't wait to please you, but I'm not looking for the beautiful man's approval. I don't need an art historian to authenticate my paintings. I don't need a media show to validate my taste. And I sure as hell don't need to make phony museum donations to reduce my annual tax bill."

Nickelaw's face went pale. It could have been anger or fear or both. He took a quick step toward me.

Kwame came to his feet like the muscular black predator he was.

"Listen, cowboy," Nickelaw said in a cold, low voice. "Artistic reputations are very valuable and very easily damaged. You impugn my business practices like that in public, and I'll haul your laid-back ass into the nearest courtroom on a slander charge."

Kwame's head followed every motion Nickelaw made.

"If you like that dog," he continued flatly, "you make goddamned sure he doesn't move toward me. I'll kill him."

I didn't know if Nickelaw would succeed in carrying out his threat, but there was no doubt that he was ready to try. He had shifted his stance slightly until he stood loose-limbed, balancing his weight, positioning himself for what would probably be a round kick. He kept his eyes on Kwame and waited.

There was a confidence and cool readiness in Nickelaw's body that said more than any words could have. He might have been pretty, but he was also deadly.

Kwame had sensed the challenge instantly. He made no sound. His lips slid back in a silent snarl as he raised himself up into a crouch as though by magic. Unblinkingly he watched Nickelaw.

The dog's focus was so intense I wasn't sure I could call Kwame off if I wanted to, but it would have been criminal to send him against Nickelaw for no better reason than the hope of teaching the man some manners. A well-trained *judoka* is a very quick, very graceful killing machine.

"Kwame," I said quietly. "No."

The dog's teeth disappeared and his stance relaxed slightly, but he still watched Nickelaw with the intensity of a hungry predator.

Nickelaw looked at me in exactly the same way. It was only fair. That was the way I was watching him.

"You're smarter than I thought, cowboy. Don't get in my way again. In fact, don't even let me see you again. Vikki, get in the car."

Vikki made a wide circle around us and walked quickly toward the Porsche. Nickelaw backed away for the first ten steps, then turned and strode to the car. Vikki was in the driver's seat by the time he got in. She fired up the engine, revving hard. The blower whistled sharply as she backed onto the dirt verge, slipped into first, and started forward.

When the rear wheels were pointed at the Cobra, Vikki rapped the accelerator hard. The turboed six-cylinder engine coughed, then howled. Several hundred horsepower poured into the drive train, making the ten-inch-wide back tires spin as though they were on ice. A rooster tail of gravel and dirt shot across the driveway, sending a handful of pebbles pinging off the rounded aluminum rump of the Cobra. The Porsche stripped rubber and vanished.

There was a day when I would have put eight rounds through the whale tail of the fancy customized Porsche without a second's hesitation. The day would have been today, if I had thought it would do any good. But I knew it wouldn't. Making Swiss cheese of Nickelaw's toy wouldn't prove anything except that I was as thick in the head as the drop-dead blonde.

Maybe it's just that Kwame and I are both getting a little gray around the muzzle. And maybe it's as simple as the certainty that when I take my pound of revenge, I'm not going to settle for a handful of fiberglass whale tail.

SIXTEEN

Benny has access to more data banks than the federal government. What would take anyone else hours, days, or weeks to perform, Benny does in minutes. Best of all, he never asks embarrassing questions about my right to know.

I pulled into the alley behind Benny's West Newport duplex in a cloud of black smoke. The 2002tii hadn't been driven while I was gone and was cranky as a result.

Before I could knock, Benny opened the door of his workshop. I started to say hello.

"You should stop running aviation fuel through that engine," Benny said curtly. "Sounds like Chinese bloody New Year."

"It has something to do with the Protestant work ethic. German cars don't like sitting around doing nothing."

Benny spun the wheels of his chair in opposite

directions, turning in place, and went back into the shop without so much as a civil word to me. I tucked the sheepskin-lined case holding the Detonics under my arm and followed.

"Gosh, it's nice to see you too," I said when I caught up with him.

Benny opened a drawer and began rummaging through electronics detritus as though he were alone.

"You're stepping on my lines," I said after a while. "I'm the one who's supposed to be mad."

Benny grunted but didn't look up. He's really a sensitive soul, down underneath his wild black growth of beard. He wanted to be coaxed. The question was, what lure would be best? I looked around the workshop for inspiration.

The place had been gutted, rewired for the twenty-first century, and customized with bins and finicky little drawers for the thousands of electronic parts that go into Benny's equipment. Everything is set up for a man in a wheelchair, a man who prefers to live by himself and who makes enough money to do just about anything he wants. Benny has owned the house since the days when West Newport duplexes were considered cheap investments. Since then, Gold Coast real estate prices have gone ballistic. Benny turned down half-million-dollar offers on his place simply because he couldn't be bothered to move.

Which reminded me of a sure-fire lure. . . .

"How's the baby prince from the Banana Republic?" I asked.

Benny scratched his beard irritably.

A reaction. Progress.

"What was that little twit's name, anyway?" I continued, sliding the lure by him again.

"Hector."

An answer. Surly, but an answer nonetheless. I waited for more, knowing that Hector—a young Central American who had bought the duplex next door to Benny's six months before—wasn't one of Benny's favorite people. Supposedly Hector was attending UC Irvine, but he never seemed to get around to studying. What he did get around to was turning his house into a mink-lined party pad and entertaining large, loud groups of friends.

Just before I took off, Hector had ambled over and offered to buy Benny's house. Well, "offered" is the wrong word. "Demanded" is closer to the truth. Hector was willing to pay a fair price because he wanted to demolish Benny's place and install a tennis court on the lot.

"Yeah," I said, finally. "Hector. How'd it turn out with the young Napoleon, anyway?"

Benny resisted the lure for a good long time, maybe thirty seconds. But I could see he was weakening, so I said nothing.

"Miserable little wanker turned out to be the son of the defense minister of one of those miserable little republics down there," Benny finally muttered.

"Be damned," I said.

"Took me a week to track that little fact down, during which time he held one continual party, sort of a lease-breaker to convince me I didn't want to live here any more."

I looked around the workshop. "I don't see any packing crates."

Benny wheeled away a few feet, opened a drawer, and poked at the contents. He wasn't really looking into the drawer, though. He was just making me wait.

"Once I found out who Hector was, I called an old friend, a guy who's in Beirut now," Benny said after a minute. "His passport says he's a Canadian, but when I knew him he was in the U.S. State Department."

Benny is a former New Zealander who was once the Ice Cream King of Saigon. He knows people who were accredited to the U.S. Embassy as "agricultural attachés" or "cultural exchange officers." Nowadays they are "political secretaries" or "communications liaison officers" in Beirut or Prague, or discreet members of the import-export community, but the work they do is the same.

"And?" I asked.

"He called an old friend who works as an international consultant in Miami. The consultant called an old friend who used to be in the arms business. The munitions bloke called somebody in the presidential palace. The Chief of Staff of all the armed forces called Hector and told him to knock that shit off or he'd be sent to the family's *finca* for the next three years to pull weeds. Hector called me and announced that he didn't need a tennis court. Seems he's taken up Ping-Pong."

While I laughed, Benny wheeled over to one of his seventeen computer terminals and checked the screen. He made a pleased noise and began tap-tap-

tapping on the keyboard. With his glossy black hair and beard flying about his heavily developed shoulders and torso, he looked like a cross between Rasputin and Mr. Universe.

"It's nice to be home, thanks," I said, getting myself a cold Corona from the refrigerator at the back of the room. "Want one?"

Benny grunted an affirmative. I opened the Coronas, set one on the table in front of him, and looked over his shoulder. An entry was coming onto the screen, one slow character at a time, like Chinese water torture: drop . . . drop . . . drop. . . .

"Now I've got you, you son of a bitch," Benny said in a voice that reminded me of Kwame's lips curling back to reveal gleaming teeth. "Bleeding Soviets won't ever catch up, *glasnost* or no."

I squinted over Benny's shoulder at the screen. The entry looked like a typical database inquiry. "Are you logged onto a Soviet computer?"

He shook his head. "I'm an imposter terminal on the International Scientific Database Network, a little venture in global cooperation that's headquartered in Geneva. It allows access to all unclassified scientific and engineering data bases in the U.S. and the Soviet Union, sort of a public library for technicians on both sides of the Iron Curtain."

I drank some of the Corona and cleared a spot on a workbench for the Detonics case.

"I've been monitoring a set of queries from the Metallurgical Institute in Moscow for about a week now, looking for patterns," he continued, watching the screen intently.

"Naughty, naughty, spying on library patrons like that. Haven't you heard? The Cold War's over."

"And I'm Mike Gorbachev's identical twin sister. The Cold War will never be over, boyo, not completely. This wanker I'm watching has been logged on for almost an hour. He's searching U.S. engineering data bases for information on a metallurgical process involving expended uranium metal."

"At least he's not trying to find out how to build bigger and better bombs."

Benny made a rich sound of disgust. "Boyo, there's only one known use for expended uranium: armor-piercing projectiles. This young live wire is trying to figure out how American defense contractors fabricate antitank ammo for the minigun on the Cheyenne helicopter gunship." Benny smiled thinly. "He knows I'm watching, though. He just queried me, asking if I had any recommendations. I told him to fold it until it was all corners and shove it to Siberia."

"You're hopeless."

"Thank you."

Benny pushed away from the console, took off his half glasses, and rubbed his eyes. Then he rolled over and unzipped the leather case I had left on the workbench.

"You talked to Fiora yet?" he asked.

"I don't know where she is."

"You're a bloody stupid bastard, aren't you."

There was no question in Benny's voice. He is enormously fond of my ex-wife. He would kill for her if she asked him. He'll even protect her from me at times.

Benny looked into the case, studied the gun, then took it out of its fleece nest. He looked at me, waiting.

"I talked to her in Santa Fe," I said. "She was hanging around with something called Roger Valenti."

In some ways Benny knows me better than I know myself. That makes life damned uncomfortable for me at times. This was one of them. His smile was as hard and shrewd as his eyes. He was enjoying the jealousy I had no intention of admitting even to myself.

"That sort of thing happens when you go off and sulk for months at a time," he pointed out. "Valenti's a decent enough sort, for a billionaire."

"Do I really hear you sticking up for the man who owns half the undeveloped coastline in Southern California? I thought you were violently opposed to plutocrats."

"Only when they get in my way. Valenti hasn't." As Benny spoke he field-stripped the pistol and set the pieces out on the clean cloth that had been inside the case. "You have, though—gotten in my way. You almost drove Fiora bonkers these past months."

I took a long pull of beer, trying to damp down the anger that rose in me every time I thought of what Fiora had done. "She knew what would happen when she shoved Innes between Volker and me."

"She was just trying to protect something she loved. You."

Benny eyed the disassembled parts, looking at the

edges of the machined metal and staring down the barrel at the dizzying pattern of lands and grooves.

A long swallow finished my beer, but it wasn't enough to put out the fire. I rapped the bottle on the table.

"Christ knows I need all the help I can get in a fight," I said calmly. "Right?"

Benny's blunt, deft fingers tugged at his shaggy beard. It was the second time in as many minutes that he had done that, which meant he was genuinely angry.

Bingo. That made two of us.

"She blames herself that Volker ever met you," Benny said, spacing his words carefully and talking slowly, as though he were speaking to an especially dim child. "It cuts her up inside every time she sees those scars on your hands." He looked at me. "Before she called in the FBI, *she dreamed you were dead.*"

I started to say something, but no words came.

Fiora's Scots bloodlines have some odd twists and turns in them. She is connected to people she loves in some uncanny and uncomfortable ways. She was in the States, yet she knew before I did that Jake had been killed in Mexico and I had survived. She was miles away, yet she knew that her twin brother was dead the instant a bullet took the back of his head off. She knows when I'm in danger before I do.

It hasn't made our life together any easier.

"What would you have done in her shoes?" Benny demanded. "Think about it, Fiddler. Think about it real hard. Then go apologize for being such a bloody horse's arse."

My empty beer bottle made a satisfying sound when it hit the bottom of the metal wastebasket. I walked over to the refrigerator, got another beer, and snapped off the lid with the edge of the counter.

"God save me from sodding idiots," Benny muttered to himself as he started reassembling the pistol.

"I was going to ask you to run a make on someone," I said. "I changed my mind. Fiora can have it done."

Benny's eyes narrowed as he spun to face me. "Did Fiora ask you to do something for her?"

"No."

He rolled over and took the beer out of my hands. "One's your limit. You're driving."

He drank a few swallows, belched thoughtfully, and either smiled or snarled. With that much beard it's hard to tell.

"Who's the target?" he asked.

I wouldn't get a second invitation, but I was ready to let this one go by. The only one who can pull my cork faster than Benny is Fiora.

And the only one I love more than Benny is Fiora.

"His name is Olin Nickelaw," I said finally. "The IRS wants him bad. He beat them in tax court. Now they're playing hardball. They're twisting everyone who has ever done business with him, trying to find somebody who can prove he's dirty."

"So?"

"So Fiora happens to have several clients who

have bought investment art from Nickelaw and then donated it to various museums. Sooner or later—and I'd bet sooner—the IRS boys are going to go to work on Fiora. It would be real nice if she could throw them a rancid bone called Olin Nickelaw."

"How do you spell it, and do you have a DOB?"

I spelled Nickelaw's name. "I can only guess at his birth date."

Benny wheeled over to another computer, typed like a madman, and then came back to me.

"The rest of it," he demanded.

This time I wasn't tempted to pass. It felt too good to be home. I gave Benny the other pertinent names and told him the background. He took notes on the screen, scratching his beard like Kwame in flea season, designing a computer probe in his agile, devious mind. After a few minutes he closed the file, went back to the workbench, and reassembled the Detonics. Then he cruised the workshop's aisles, opening and closing drawers until he found a tube of lubricant.

"It's a scam," Benny said. "The only question is, who's scamming whom?" He locked the slide back on the gun and applied a light coating of oil to the action. "But at least one thing is beginning to make sense."

I made an appropriate noise.

"Fiora called me this morning, wanting to know whether I had any friends at the IRS." Benny wiped down the gun, making it gleam. "Seems she got a letter this morning from the district director of the regional enforcement office, some piss-ant bureaucrat. It was formal notification of a pending audit of your tax return by the CID.''

"Harvey's a slow learner," I said, taking back my gun, working it: clean, smooth, solid. "Guess I'll have to go back to Santa Fe and say it to him all over again, slowly."

"Not with that piece," Benny said, nodding at the Detonics.

"Something wrong with it?"

"Nothing mechanical. It's a sweet, clean weapon. Well made, well assembled, and beautifully finished."

"Then what's the problem?"

"Problems. There are two."

I waited, knowing Benny would tell me eventually.

"The Four-fifty-one Magnum uses a cut-down Three-oh-eight Winchester cartridge, right?" he asked.

I shrugged. "I didn't read the fine print on the box. All I know is that the gun can be accurate up to a hundred yards."

"Good stopping power, too," Benny said. "But you'll have to find somebody to do your custom reloading, or do it yourself."

"Or have a friend I trust with my life, who makes the loads better than I ever could."

Benny grimaced and chewed on a straggly end of his mustache. "Yeah, yeah, I'll keep you in loads."

He puts up with a lot from me, and we both know why. The trouble with being a practitioner of esoteric electronic and military arts is that so few people can appreciate the artistry of what you do. I appreciated what I could of Benny's skills and simply admired the rest.

"But there's still the other problem," he continued. "That's a signature gun. You may as well etch your initials on each slug. Somebody turns up with a Four-fifty-one Detonics round in him, and the list of suspects will be narrowed to about ten people."

"No problem. Any slugs I leave behind, I'll be glad to talk about to a judge."

Benny shrugged. "I'd rather not spend the time in court, but it's your choice. Just do me a favor, mate."

"Sure."

"Don't throw away the other pistol. You never know when you might want to settle out of court."

"Like with the CID of the IRS?"

Benny shook his head. "They aren't interested in settling. Not with you. It's Fiora they're after. They slapped an audit on every one of her clients, everybody she's ever advised, everybody who has ever been associated with her."

That was the worst kind of news, but Benny wasn't finished talking yet.

"I spent an hour in a data base that tracks the proceedings of the Tax Court and the IRS Appeals Division. There's no statute of limitations on the code section they're using. It involves financial advisers suspected of perpetrating fraud. They'll probably start subpoenaing all her clients."

"They'll ruin her."

Benny nodded. Then he did an odd thing; he hesitated. His fingers fiddled with the tips of his long mustache, then smoothed everything back in place.

He looked up, pinning me with those intense black eyes of his.

"She needs you, Fiddler."

"She needs a good tax lawyer more."

"Help her."

"That sounds like an order."

He opened his hands as though to show me he was unarmed. I didn't believe him.

"And if I don't?" I asked.

"Then I will."

There are critical moments when the right or wrong word can irrevocably change a relationship. The idea of Benny and Fiora together wasn't fanciful. It wasn't even farfetched. It was simply something I had never allowed myself to think about.

"She needs you," Benny said.

"Sure, like a fish needs a bicycle; isn't that the saying?"

Benny made a rich, rude noise.

"Modern women don't need anything or anyone," I said evenly, trying to keep a lid on my anger. "They're self-sufficient. It's an article of faith, like virgin birth or life after death. Never get in the way of anyone's religion, Benny. They'll gut you and praise God for the opportunity."

"You think Fiora's praising God right now?"

I remembered the shadows within her eyes and the dark circles beneath. I didn't say anything.

"How about you, mate?" he prodded. "You going to tell me you're spending a lot of time on your knees thanking God?" He made another rude noise, answering his own rhetorical question. "You two do better together than you do apart. Work something out, Fiddler. Something we all can live with. Do it soon.''

"That's going to be tough. I don't even know where she is.''

"Try Valenti's great turd of a museum at ten tomorrow. And go in on tippy-toes, boyo. She's in more trouble than she knows.''

I turned to go but stopped when I got to the door. I dug out the tiny box I'd been carrying and lobbed it at Benny. The Indian ring was heavy enough to make that little package fly. Benny snagged it one-handed, looked at the box, then looked at me.

"What's this for?'' he asked.

"The pure hell of it.''

When I left, Benny was eyeing the box like a bomb tech looking at a ticking package.

SEVENTEEN

I dreamed about wheels within wheels within wheels, all spinning along at different speeds and in different orbits, out of true and wobbling wildly. I dreamed that the New Age Navajo mechanic from Santa Fe and I were jugglers spinning plates on sticks in the circus. He was the perfectionist, trying to get each plate perfectly balanced. I was the pragmatist, trying to keep them all spinning. Every time I finally got them all going at once, he would come along and try to straighten them out.

Throughout the dream, Georgia O'Keeffe peered down at us from high atop the Black Place, disapproval in her dark, fierce eyes, eyes that also belonged to Maggie Tenorio. Both of them hated the skull. One of them hated the poppy. I forget which one, although it seemed important at the time. Harvey was in there somewhere: I didn't see him, but I smelled him. Fiora was there too, unseen, a pure rill of alto weeping down the scales.

Not surprisingly, I was awake before six. I did my usual morning workout, then did it all over again. Nothing helped. I was as edgy when I finished as when I started, and I still had time to kill before I went to the museum. I washed and hulled a basket of early strawberries, made coffee, and hid from reality in the pages of the *Los Angeles Times*.

The only story worth reading was right there at the bottom of the front page, under a two-line headline: NEW O'KEEFFE PURCHASED BY VALENTI'S MUSEUM OF SOUTHWEST ART. The kicker headline got my attention: *Record $3.6 Million Price.*

> In one of the most important art transactions this year, the newly discovered Georgia O'Keeffe canvas unveiled last week in Santa Fe has been purchased by a Southern California art patron.
>
> Roger Valenti, multimillionaire land developer and art collector, is reported to have concluded negotiations with the present owner this week in New Mexico. Valenti, chairman of the board of the new Museum of Southwest Art, is expected to donate the painting to the museum in time for its formal opening next month.

The byline on the piece belonged to the *Times'* second-string art critic, George Driscoll. There were several paragraphs of background, then fresh material.

> Reports of the acquisition swept through the art world yesterday, delighting local art enthusiasts and irritating several East Coast patrons who had expressed interest in obtaining the work. A spirited bidding war reportedly had been under way for at

least forty-eight hours before the Newport Beach developer won out.

"The MOSA owned no major O'Keeffe work," said one source close to the museum board. "It was imperative that we obtain this one in order to secure our place as one of the major foci of art in the Sun Belt. The competition for the canvas was intense, especially from East Coast interests. We are delighted to have acquired the painting."

Other reaction was less enthusiastic. "We didn't need the canvas as much as the West Coast interests did," said Arthur Desmond, curator of American paintings at the Whitney Museum, one of the unsuccessful bidders in the informal auction. "We dropped out when that became apparent. Their bidding had nothing to do with art."

I hunted through the paper for the continuation of the story and found it under a three-column photo of the skull taken the night of its unveiling in Santa Fe. The photo had been tightly cropped, but in one corner Olin Nickelaw smiled broadly. I wondered why he hadn't been smiling the previous afternoon in Crystal Cove. He certainly hadn't acted like a man who had just pulled off the art coup of the decade. Three point six million was a price for the record books.

O'Keeffe, the most admired American woman painter in history, gained early recognition when her works were shown at the New York gallery of Albert Stieglitz, a leading proponent of modernist painting. But O'Keeffe later became associated with Southwest themes and images. She lived most of the last fifty years of her life in northwestern New Mexico, where this previously unknown painting was discovered earlier this year.

The painting, which depicts a skull of uncertain

origin, is believed to be the first expression of what
would later become a dominant motif in O'Keeffe's
work. The painting will join an extensive collection
of other Southwest art, much of it donated by Valenti, in the almost-completed museum complex on
Upper Newport Bay.

Valenti, who was reported to be in Washington on
a business trip, could not be reached for comment.
His personal spokesman refused to confirm the
transaction, although he did acknowledge that the
developer would participate in a news conference
scheduled for 10 a.m. at the museum today.

The time had a familiar ring to it. I wondered
what Fiora would be doing there, holding the great
art patron's hand? If so, she sure as shit didn't need
me around. *Benny, what the hell are you up to?*

There was no answer, so I kept reading.

Other sources familiar with the transaction revealed, however, that Valenti paid $3.6 million for
the painting. If confirmed, the price would be a
clear record for an O'Keeffe work and would become a new benchmark for paintings by contemporary American artists working outside of New York.

The painting was discovered recently in a New
Mexico village by Olin Nickelaw, a Santa Fe art
dealer. Nickelaw was reported to be in Southern
California for an announcement of the deal, accord-
ing to the manager of his Beverly Hills gallery.

There was a sidebar story with Southern California art patrons and business leaders gloating over
the acquisition, while art historians from both USC
and UCLA talked up the importance of the work.

One of the quotes intrigued me, probably because
I was in a surly mood. Dr. Donald Starwood of the
LA County Museum was quoted as saying he was

"really looking forward to a close examination of the work, whose provenance is extraordinary."

I filed the name for future reference, folded up the *Times*, and wondered whether the *New York Times* and the *Washington Post* would take a more jaundiced view of the entire O'Keeffe affair, now that their civic pride had been wounded. Probably. If there were any possible dirt on the O'Keeffe, it would be in tomorrow's East Coast papers.

I checked my watch. Plenty of time until ten. Too damn much time.

I thought about tinkering with the 2002, whose problem was aviation gas or the fuel system or both. The thought of taking apart the engine to find out which didn't rivet me. I was in no mood to fuss with a temperamental Teutonic machine. Germans are great engineers but too intolerant: disassembly, repair, and reassembly of German engines aren't jobs, they are ceremonies, separate and distinct, with individual rituals and proprieties to be observed at every step. Don't ever buy a German car unless you have an ordained mechanic on hand. I do, and I was damned grateful to drop the mess in his lap.

The shop kid from Autobahn West drove me back home. I loaded some gear in the Cobra and drove up the Coast Highway toward one of the most expensive sloughs on the North American continent.

California's coastline is indented at a half dozen places by shallow estuaries, which are more like brackish tidal flats than navigable harbors. Newport Bay was one of those estuaries until about fifty years ago, when an aggressive set of city leaders pushed a pork-barrel dredging project through Con-

gress. The Army Corps of Engineers cleaned out a
network of channels and dumped what they
dredged on a few low tidal islands, creating both a
small craft harbor and some really expensive piles of
mud.

Ten thousand pleasure boats from ten to a hundred and ten feet long now call Newport Harbor
their home port. Fifty thousand people live on what
used to be tidal flats and sand bars. The surrounding
waters are among the most polluted in Southern
California, but don't tell that to the people who pay
for building lots by the front inch. If it costs that
much, it has to be paradise.

Like the rest of Orange County, Newport Beach
has a civic stepchild complex that seems to be as-
suaged only by periodic extravagant gestures such as
the Museum of Southwest Art. More and bigger are
good and better. Valenti's MOSA complex was no
exception. Laid out along a quarter mile of bluff
overlooking the bay, the main building and gardens
were inspired by the Getty Museum in Malibu, designed by a famous Italian architect, constructed by
the largest subdivider in America, and paid for by
the most intense marketing campaign since New
Coke.

The result is a glass and steel ego statement that
cost thirty million bucks and occupies the last of the
unbuilt land on the bluffs overlooking Newport Bay.
The MOSA's grounds are kept like putting greens
with a huge fountain and reflecting pool to break up
all that grass. Some people love the MOSA's architecture, and some think the bluffs looked better covered with sea gull guano.

Most of the local controversy about MOSA grows
out of resentment toward Roger Valenti, who is the
controlling force behind the biggest coastal land development firm in California. Valenti managed to hit
the interest markets and the curve of demand for
housing at just the right time. He put together the
leveraged buyout of a major chunk of California
coastline and interior rangeland. Twisting arms and
dodging brickbats, Valenti managed to accumulate
the requisite government approvals and launch a
three-thousand-acre development worth, literally,
billions.

In the process Valenti became outrageously
wealthy. He doesn't make the *Fortune* list of the
hundred richest men in America, but he's not far
out of the running. To a lot of people Valenti sym-
bolizes success, money, power, and the kind of com-
mercialism that adds shine to the concept of crass.
These people particularly resent the fact that Valenti
tied the MOSA's civic-financed complex directly and
indirectly into his high-ticket residential and commercial developments, thereby doubling the worth
of his own holdings.

Valenti could afford the O'Keeffe at twice the stu-
pendous price. The painting's prestige would be
worth millions to the Plaza de Bellas Artes shopping
center and the four high-rise office buildings that
were affiliated with the museum where *Private Skull*
would reside. Besides, Uncle Sugar would be footing
half the bill, maybe more, if Valenti had taken the
trouble to cut an under-the-table deal with Olin
Nickelaw—and from the size of the final purchase
price, I could only assume some major inflation had

taken place. That would be one shrewd transaction; but then, Valenti had proven himself to be one shrewd son of a bitch.

None of those thoughts exactly put a smile on my face as I pulled into the plaza parking lot a few minutes after nine thirty. The marine layer was just beginning to burn off. The gulls and terns wintering in the upper bay were on the move, swirling gracefully around the dumpsters behind the swank restaurants of the plaza. Despite all the development, Upper Newport Bay probably supports twice its original wintertime population of feathered foragers. The birds all live off the dumpsters filled with half-eaten sourdough rolls and cold linguini with marinara sauce.

I put the beat-up, faded cover over the Cobra, disguising its telltale lines and color. Binoculars around my neck, I joined a handful of lazy ornithologists who preferred to look down on the bird life of the marsh from above rather than trudge on much-traveled paths through the marsh itself.

There was no one closer to me than fifty yards. I went to the edge of the parking lot, used a bush to break up my silhouette, and lifted the glasses. Across the small arroyo from me was MOSA's parking structure. The day shift was just arriving—a few curatorial types in a sensible yet stylish Volkswagen Jetta, three car-pooling secretaries in a Corolla, and a member of middle management in a silver 325 Bimmer.

No wonder Detroit is screaming. Nobody on the West Coast, not even the hired help, drives American cars.

From the street side, the museum looked largely finished. Crews of Mexican landscapers were manicuring the freshly laid sod and shoving in trees that were already twenty feet tall. Beyond the building earthmovers and other massive machinery growled and groaned, sculpting the outlying grounds in preparation for the opening ceremonies, of which the O'Keeffe would undoubtedly now be the centerpiece.

A security guard checked the grounds in an electric golf cart. He was a lifeguard type, tanned and well built, squared away in his blue uniform, which was hung with shiny, official-looking badges and buttons and nameplate. The guard was crisply laundered, recently polished, and fundamentally bored. The building was largely empty of treasure at this point and he knew it.

Yawning widely, he pulled up to the little security office beside the entrance to the parking structure. He stretched, removed his uniform jacket, and stowed it in the compartment beneath the seat. He went inside the guard shack and didn't come out.

I looked at my watch. Quarter to ten.

Traffic began to pick up around me as plaza employees and early customers arrived. At nine fifty the first television crew appeared at the museum, driving a gray Suburban with its ack-ack-style transmitter antenna lashed in traveling position on the left rear corner of the roof. The rig disappeared into the parking structure, then reappeared in the sunlight on the second level. A reporter in a blue blazer and a cameraman in jeans got out and went toward the museum. Two more technicians came out of the vehicle, ran the antenna up on its power mast, and pointed the twin barrels toward Burbank, where the electronic pulses would be stored for later replay to LA Basin audiences.

A rig from a competing station arrived a few minutes later and set up next to the first. The crews greeted each other like old rivals. Shortly afterward the guard left the little office at the entrance to the parking structure and headed for the main building.

I was getting ready to head over to the museum myself when a Plymouth four-door sedan rolled in off the Back Bay Road and onto the museum grounds. I ran the zoom glasses up to eighteen power and refocused as the sedan pulled into the parking structure. The sun shone through the open sides of the lower parking level brightly enough that I could follow the car as it made a complete circuit to the top, then backed into a space immediately adjacent to the elevator.

The sedan was parked nose out, giving the driver a view of the entire building without being obvious about the surveillance. The driver was cautious, professional . . . and an IRS agent.

I watched Harvey Durham for a few more minutes. He sat with his window down, smoking the end of one cigarette and lighting another. He was bored, not nervous. Whatever he was doing he had done a thousand times before.

At five minutes before ten I was still watching Harvey so closely that I almost missed the glistening silver four-door BMW's arrival. The car had a shiny, untouched, absolutely new look, like a salmon just hooked up from the cold depths of the ocean. The car pulled smartly up to the entrance of the parking structure and hesitated long enough for the driver's golden hair to catch the sunlight. I stared, knowing without really being able to see, that the driver was Fiora.

Abruptly I realized that I was so furious my hands were trying to squeeze the binoculars to paste. The reaction was pure jealousy: I'd barely been out of Fiora's life two months and already she had replaced the red 635 BMW coupe I'd bought her for Christmas the year before.

The new BMW suited Fiora. It moved like a silver bullet, hard and practical but with a marvelous predatory grace. The car gleamed through the lower part of the parking structure, circled the building once, then pulled into a vacant space and parked. Fiora got out and walked quickly to Harvey's car. Every line of her body told me she didn't like what she was doing.

I ripped the cover off the Cobra, started the engine, and headed for the parking structure.

Tippy-toes, huh? Right you are, Benny. I'm going to tiptoe all over that rancid son of a bitch.

eIGHTEEN

$\mathbf{A}$ quick circle around the parking structure told me there were no more security guards on the site. I parked the Cobra and walked in past the empty security office.

The guard's electric cart was still sitting by the office, the blue jacket was still in the compartment underneath the seat, and so was a baseball cap with a museum security logo on the front. The jacket was too small in the arms and shoulders, but my jeans nearly matched the uniform blue. The key for the golf cart was in the dashboard ignition. One twist and I became a guard on patrol. I pushed on the foot pedal and fell into line behind a Dodge Omni with press-photographer plates.

There were fifty or sixty cars on the first parking level and more pulling in all the time. I hummed along quietly, passing a row behind the Plymouth. Out of the corner of my eye I could see Harvey and

Fiora in the car. He was slouched with his back against the door, watching her while he talked. She faced the windshield. I couldn't see her expression but her shoulders were rigid.

Harvey had parked in a position that gave him a clear view of all approaches . . . except one. I drove the cart up the ramp to the rooftop level and got out. There were three television crews in place now, killing time by lagging quarters against the waist-high balustrade. None of the men did more than glance at me.

The elevator car was on the roof level. The door slid open instantly when I punched the button. The drop to the lower level was only eight or nine feet, but the elevator ground along like a burro carrying a load of sheet steel up a hill. When the elevator finally stopped, the doors slid open without a sound.

I crouched and took a quick, low look to the left. All I could see was the front three feet of Harvey's Plymouth. The wall of the elevator shaft screened me from his line of sight. I eased out of the elevator and stood with my back to the wall until the doors slid shut.

The parking structure was so quiet that I could hear Fiora's voice. She had rolled down the window to dilute Harvey's cigarette smoke or his feral odor. Her words were clear, low, calm, coming from no more than eight feet away.

"What makes you think I know where the Tenorio woman is?" Fiora asked.

Her tone was a combination of impatience and adult restraint, as though she had become tired of the conversation but knew she had no choice except to pursue it. She uses that tone on people she doesn't like. It's designed to make them feel six years old.

"You know, baby."

Harvey had a fine, condescending edge to his voice that could only be described as sexual. He knew Fiora didn't like being close to him, and he knew he liked being close to her. But what really got him off was the power: his tone let her know she had to take whatever he smeared all over her and then say thank you when he was done.

"I hardly know the woman. The last time I saw her was in Santa Fe, at the Nickelaw Gallery party. I didn't even know she was in Southern California. If, as you say, she *is* here."

Fiora's cool, controlled voice doubted that Harvey would know how to find his butt with both hands and a rearview mirror.

"Well, then, you'd better get off your high-class ass and start looking for her," Harvey drawled. "I might be able to help you out of this bind you're in, but I sure as hell can't do anything for you unless you can do something for me . . . if you get what I mean."

"If I get what you mean," Fiora said slowly, thoughtfully. "No, Mr. Durham, I'm not sure that I do."

"C'mon, baby, a smart girl like you knows what a man like me wants."

"A smart girl wouldn't know any men like you."

Fiora's voice was cool and flat and 100-percent-platinum bitch. I couldn't believe what I was hearing. She was taunting a man who could ruin her with a half dozen phone calls, a man who played games the likes of which she couldn't even begin to imagine. She was in so far over her head it would take her a week to hit bottom after she drowned.

And she would drown. Harvey would make sure of it.

"Let me guess," Fiora murmured. "I suppose a garden-variety blow job is what you had in mind?"

"Huh?" Harvey sounded like he'd nearly swallowed his tongue.

"No, probably not," Fiora continued in cool, derisive tones, talking right over him. "That might reveal your gonadal insufficiency."

"What?"

"Watch my lips. I'm talking dirty to you. I thought that was the most your heart could take."

I would have paid a thousand bucks for one look at Harvey's face, but I didn't dare poke my head around the corner.

"Listen, you—" he began.

"I have," Fiora interrupted. "I didn't hear anything useful. If you want Ms. Tenorio so badly, why don't you rattle Olin Nickelaw's cage? He knows her much better than I do. Do you understand me yet? In words that even you might comprehend, you're pissing on the wrong fire hydrant."

"You're a real gold-plated bitch," Harvey said, discovery and anger warring in his voice, pulling it into hoarseness. "You don't know how much trouble you're in. You've got your fancy car and your sexy silk dress and your big fat expense account, and you think you're untouchable. But you ain't, baby. I'm

going to touch you in ways you won't forget. I'm
going to be all over you like stink on shit."

"Thank you. I was wondering where the smell
came from."

Oh, God, Fiora. For once just shut up.

A badly muffled Suzuki Samurai pulled into the
parking structure, its motor noise filling the concrete
box and blotting out both Fiora's and Harvey's
voices. Using the noise for cover, I dropped low and
stole a quick look around the corner.

The right front fender and passenger door
shielded me perfectly from Harvey's line of sight. I
could see blond hair—the back of Fiora's head. She
was half turned and pressed against the door, trying
to stay as far away from Harvey as the dimensions of
the front seat would allow.

I eased forward, belly-crawling along the right
side of the car as the noisy Samurai came down the
aisle past the Plymouth. I slid around the right tail-
light, moved along the back bumper, and got to my
knees. Nobody but me heard the steel whisper of
the new Detonics sliding out of its holster in the
small of my back.

The Samurai parked and shut down. I could hear
Fiora's voice once more.

". . . didn't say I was refusing to cooperate. I
simply said I don't know where Maggie Tenorio is.
Why should I? She's a sales clerk, not the owner of
the gallery."

"Then you find out where she is. You were the
go-between on the O'Keeffe. Find out where it is!"

Where it *is? What* it?

I held my breath, trying to catch every word. As

though she had read my mind, Fiora asked the right question.

"Are you saying that the O'Keeffe canvas is missing?"

"Yeah, just like Tenorio is missing," Harvey snarled. "They're probably in the same place. And you're going to find both of them for me or I'll send letters to every client you ever had or ever wanted. Hear me, bitch? I'll ruin you!"

"I'm an investment counselor, not a detective." Fiora's voice was quiet but taut with the same tension that had drawn her shoulders into a rigid line.

"You sure are, baby. And the O'Keeffe is probably on the way to one of your fat-cat clients. Hell, it might even be in Valenti's closet. He's such a smart son of a bitch writing off millions in taxes with his goddamn museum. That's where you come in. You've got your hands in the pants of some of the richest men in California. You advise them. You know where they're hiding their money. You know what they like in their government-subsidized art collections. I think one of those men has the O'Keeffe. You find out which one. And do it fast, baby. I'm not a patient man."

There was a silence, followed by Fiora's long sigh. "Look, Agent Durham. My clients work within the law or they find someone else to handle their affairs. Are you sure the O'Keeffe is missing?"

"Watch *my* lips. The O'Keeffe is missing, and if you don't come up with that list for me, you're going to end up keeping books for the federal prison commissary at Pleasanton. Some of those ol' bull dykes up there would love to see a sweet piece like you come through the gates.''

Harvey's voice was as dirty as his smell. It made my skin crawl. He chuckled low in his throat. Intimidation was part of his job, and he was a man who enjoyed his work.

''You know how those big lizzies like to get it on, don't you? Coke bottles, that's how, the two-liter size. Be a tight fit on you . . . at first.''

I had heard more than enough. I duck-walked forward a few feet until I was even with the back door of the Plymouth. The driving mirror stared at me like a big glass eye. In it I could see the side of Harvey's head. He was still watching Fiora.

Then he was watching me. His eyes looked at me for a half second without real recognition before they got big. The message was still on its way from his eyes to his brain when I stood up and poked the tip of the big Detonics' barrel into his ear.

''Don't,'' I said.

He didn't.

Fiora turned to face me. The surprise registered in her eyes too.

''Hands through the wheel,'' I said. When Harvey hesitated, I jabbed the muzzle a little farther into his ear, reinforcing the tactile impression of cold steel. ''That's a Four-fifty-one Detonics Magnum nibbling on your ear. The sales clerk told me this gun has a real touchy trigger. Don't piss me off, pal.''

Slowly Harvey's hands appeared and gripped the wheel as though he were preparing to drive away.

''*Through* the wheel,'' I said. ''Pretend you're going to give the the steering column a blow job.''

After another brief hesitation, Harvey stuck both arms through the spokes of the steering wheel and laid his cheek against it. I relieved a little of the pressure on his mastoid bone.

"You're making a real mistake, asshole," Harvey said. "Assaulting a federal officer at gunpoint is worth at least a dime. In fact—"

"Shut up."

He did.

With my right hand I pulled off the security guard's cap and tossed it on the concrete floor. Fiora was still looking at me, her eyes dark with surprise. I pointed at the lock on the rear door beside me. She glanced at Harvey as though she were unwilling to approach him. Finally she leaned over and stretched toward the back door. The door lock made a little thump as she released it.

I reached back and pulled the door handle. It popped open. Harvey twitched. I tapped him sharply, imprinting the nerves on the side of his face with the cold reality of the big muzzle. He got the message and froze. I stepped aside quickly and slid into the back seat.

As I moved, Harvey was out from under the gun for a second. He knew it and I knew it. But we both also knew it would take him more than a second to disentangle his arms from the embrace of the steering wheel.

I sat in the back seat and closed the door.

"Where is it?" I asked, resting the muzzle of my gun against his atlas vertebra.

"Right side, belt."

He wore a light jacket. I nodded to Fiora. Wordlessly she pulled his jacket back, unsnapped the keeper, and unholstered his Magnum. I took it from her and laid it on the back seat beside me. Harvey twitched again.

"Fleas?" I asked.

Harvey didn't answer.

I glanced at Fiora. Her face was pale, but anger had begun to replace fear and surprise. I touched my index finger to my lips as warning.

"Did you get it all?" I asked her calmly.

For an instant she looked confused, but Harvey's face was turned away. He couldn't see her expression. I nodded encouragingly. She caught on fast.

"Yes," Fiora said. "All of it."

Harvey started to sweat.

"That's right, Special Agent Durham of the IRS CID. Ms. Flynn is wearing a body bug. Smile, buddy. You're on *Candid Camera*."

"I'm just doing my job, twisting an informant. Nothing wrong with that."

"Save it for the six o'clock news. Maybe your sexist patter works on a hooker from Watts, but you're in the big leagues now. You're leaning on a very powerful Pacific Rim business executive who just happens to be a woman. Know something, Harvey? Whatever passes for your balls are in her tiny leather purse."

From the corner of my eye I saw Fiora shoot me a glance as hard as old green Coke bottles. Without a word she got out of the car, shut the door quietly, and stood beside the elevator, arms crossed in front of her, inspecting the toes of her lizard pumps and breathing the fresh air.

The Detonics was like a tuning fork passing on to me the vibrations of Harvey's rigid neck and shoulder muscles.

"Know something else, Harvey? The lady is well and truly pissed. I'd advise you to think of something that would make her happy again. Fast."

For a moment longer Harvey sat rigidly, fighting his own unhappy realization of the inevitable. Abruptly the flesh beneath the muzzle of the gun went slack.

"I suppose you have a suggestion," he said, his voice tired.

"Yeah. I think you should forget all about using Ms. Flynn as a snitch. While you're doing that, you should forget that you were going to roust her clients too. As a matter of fact, I think it would be a great idea if you forgot you ever knew her name. Go find another informant, Harvey. One who has never heard of Fiora Flynn."

Harvey didn't say anything for a few moments. His smell wasn't getting any better, so I bore down on the gun until he grunted.

"I'll take that as an unequivocal yes," I said.

This time his grunt was closer to English. Definitely a positive response.

I let Harvey straighten up and pull his arms back through the wheel while I picked up the Magnum from the seat, broke out the cylinder, and shook the cartridges onto the rear floor mats. I flicked my wrist, the heavy pistol snapped shut, and I dropped the gun onto the floor along with the bullets.

As I opened the door and stepped onto the cement, Harvey turned slowly in the driver's seat, stared at me for five seconds as though he were trying to memorize me, then turned away. He started the Plymouth and yanked the shifter into drive. The car jumped forward, its tires squeaking on the cold concrete. In a few seconds he was gone.

I looked across the now-vacant parking spot at Fiora. She was still studying the toes of her shoes. I shoved the new Detonics back in place under my down vest, put my hands in the hip pockets of my jeans, and walked over until I was beside her. She smelled clean and warm, like too many good memories.

A glance at the silver tail of her new car reminded me of all the reasons I had to be angry with her. The chrome logo sparkled: 750iL.

"What happened?" I asked. "Red BMWs weren't in this year?"

Fiora looked surprised at my choice of subjects.

"Somebody swiped my car out of valet parking at the Ritz Carlton," she said tightly. "He got about two blocks and hit a bridge abutment. The hotel was so upset they settled without a claim. I put it on the first car I liked."

I grunted.

"Thanks—" she began.

"You're welcome."

"—for screwing things up royally."

That surprised me. Fiora's eyes were clear and dark with the same anger that put red flags in her cheeks and made her hands shake slightly.

"Are you saying you enjoyed your tête-à-tête with Dogbreath Durham?" I asked.

"A few more minutes and I would have known where the leak was."

"The only leak is in your brain if you—"

She was talking over me now. "Only five people knew that the O'Keeffe was missing."

"—think that you could have learned anything more from Harvey than shit smells," I said, talking right over her. Just like old times.

"He would have—"

"He would have ground you up and fed you to the clams. You're playing way out of your depth. What the hell was Benny thinking of, letting you come here alone!"

"Letting me? *Letting me?* FYI, Fiddler, I'm a big girl. I don't check with a man before I—"

"Bullshit. You checked with Benny. He told me you would be here, and he told me you needed help. He was right. You rub up against something like Harvey, and you'll never get the stink off you the rest of your life."

"And you will?"

"I didn't smell that sweet to begin with, did I, pretty lady?"

The steel tips on Fiora's pumps clicked sharply on the concrete as she walked across to her car and opened the door. She tossed her bag into the front passenger seat, got in, and closed the door hard behind her. The big engine came to life with a throaty grumble. She backed out without looking in the mirror, then straightened and drove away. Her tires came so close that my toes tried to crawl up my shins.

nINETEEN

How the hell do you rescue a damsel in distress when the damsel refuses to admit she's in distress and keeps thumbing her nose at the foulmouthed dragon?

Maybe she ain't in distress. Did you ever think of that?

Yeah, I thought of that. I thought of that pretty carefully. Then I rejected it.

Fiora is a very bright, very tough woman, but there is a part of the human barnyard she simply doesn't understand. Harvey Durham squatted four square in the middle of that human manure pile.

It was a lot more than Harvey's rotten teeth or mean disposition. Police are human beings with badges, which means cops come in three varieties: good, bad, and indifferent. Usually you get all three mixed together. It's the badge that makes things tricky. The badge gives cops the full force and maj-

esty of society with which to be good, bad, and indifferent.

Harvey's badge made him dangerous, but even
that wasn't the full story. Harvey wasn't an ordinary
cop. He was an intelligence cop. Intelligence cops
are . . . different. They aren't interested in putting
people in jail or making cases that will stand up to
Supreme Court scrutiny. Intelligence cops want information, secret information, the kind of information that people pay for, kill for, die for.

There are all kinds of ways to ferret out secret information, but the cheapest and quickest way is to
find people who know the secret and threaten
them, twist them, wring them like a dishrag until
the secrets pour out like greasy water. That's what
Harvey had tried to do with Maggie. It hadn't
worked. Maggie had split from Santa Fe without
leaving so much as a change-of-address card behind.

At least Maggie had shown the good sense to get
in the wind. Now Harvey was trying to wring secrets
out of Fiora, who thought she was bulletproof. Fiora
hadn't the faintest idea what kind of bad luck an
intelligence cop could be. She had guts and good
instincts, but she had made one crucial error. She
thought she could tease a secret out of Harvey with
the steel needle of her own intellect.

Wrong.

Harvey doesn't give out secrets, he collects them
the same way he collects souls. You can't give an
intelligence cop like Harvey the correct time of day
without getting dirty in the process. Harvey works
like a recruiter for the KGB or the CIA. He starts
small, asking for such a little piece of information—

just a tiny taste—that you would foolish if you don't cooperate.

But he isn't really interested in that little taste you give him. He's after the compromise you make in speaking to him. He'll use that compromise against you. He'll embarrass you with your friends or your business associates or your clients. He'll pump up that tiny compromise until it looks like you gave away Fort Knox, motherhood, and the neutron bomb. He'll make you out to be a New Age mix of the Rosenbergs, Nixon, and Ollie North.

Unless, of course, you agree to continue to compromise yourself and your friends. Then you'll be okay. Really. You have Harvey's word on it. Cross his heart and hope to die.

You see, the intelligence cop isn't after information per se. He's after you. Why settle for a few facts when he can own the encyclopedia? You. And you'll continue to be his access to information until you run out of secrets or you die or until he retires or someone gets brave and wastes him.

There were two ways to deal with Harvey and have a chance of coming out intact. One was Maggie's way: vanish. The other method was the one I had used—reverse the twist, control the controller, put the boot on the other foot and shove it up his ass.

I couldn't tell whether Harvey was more concerned about the possibility of an internal-affairs complaint from a unisex civil-rights lawyer or my threat to put a D-Mag slug through his brain. It didn't really matter, so long as Harvey got lost and stayed that way.

Now all I had to do was convince Fiora. Unfortunately she was long gone. Maybe she would head back to Benny. I hoped so. Benny would set her straight once he found out the game she had been trying to play.

I shoved the guard's jacket into the designer trash can by the elevator, then had a better idea. I pulled the jacket out, wrapped it around the can, and zipped up the front. Between the uniformed trash can and the guard cart up on the roof, maybe even the stoned surfers on MOSA's security staff would wake up to the fact there was a strange, wonderful world taking place all around them.

Now if I could only figure out where I fit into that world. Life was simpler when distressed damsels realized that they needed a helping hand from time to time.

Hands shoved in my hip pockets, I stood near the elevator and watched a stready stream of journalists park their vehicles, get out, and head for the museum. The media didn't have any problem deciding how to deal with distress, whether of the male or female variety. They gathered like vultures. I wondered if any of them knew about the missing O'Keeffe.

I slid in behind a camera crew from one of LA's independent stations. They were lugging a stone-age camera and sound box. Next to the cutting-edge Minicam and microwave relay crews, these guys looked a bit scruffy. I must have fit right in, because the guard at the door didn't give me a second look when he waved everyone down the museum corridor toward a small auditorium.

A dozen cameras were already set up on one side of the stage. Thirty journalists and technicians milled around in the front rows. Even so, the atmosphere was more relaxed than it had been at the first unveiling of the O'Keeffe in Santa Fe. The media pressure had intensified, but the novelty called *Private Skull* was already wearing thin. The whole affair reeked of third-day leads patched onto yesterday's stories.

Though it was well past ten, the podium was still vacant. I found a seat in the fourth row between an anorexic young blonde and a fat rumpled man holding a stenographer's notebook and a tape recorder. The blond fence rail was in full stage makeup, the mark of an on-air television reporter. Her austere blue suit would play well on the East Coast but was too formal for the Gold Coast. She fussed nervously with her hair and her collar. She turned and gave me a smile that was as thin as her eyelashes.

"What time was this thing supposed to start?" she asked.

I looked at my watch. "Twenty minutes ago."

"That's what I thought." She tugged on her collar again. "I'm supposed to file on this and then cover that AIDS thing in Santa Ana at noon. Christ, why can't they get these damn things done on time." She twisted in her seat and signaled her cameraman. "Let's do the cutaways now, get them out of the way."

The cameraman, who was black and built like a nose tackle, shrugged, pulled the Minicam off its tripod, and came over. He snapped on the spot lamp. Hard white light poured over the reporter. He checked his focus and nodded. The blonde scribbled in her notebook, paused long enough to look attentively at the empty stage, then scribbled again as though the conference were under way.

"Blue smoke and mirrors," I remarked to the fat man.

He grimaced. "Pretty faces and photo opportunities and to hell with the truth."

The man wore a tan corduroy sports coat and a plaid shirt. His plastic-laminated press credential hung from a chain around his neck and rested on his belly. The credential identified him as George Driscoll, the *Times* art critic who had written the O'Keeffe rehash I had read over breakfast.

There was a concerted rustle and murmur from the crowd as Lillian Bradley made her way down the aisle and took a seat at the front of the auditorium. She was dressed in an efficient business suit and carried a leather briefcase. As she waited she dug out a sheaf of notes and went over them as though preparing herself to speak. There was a pallor to her skin that hadn't been noticeable in Santa Fe, and a grim line to her mouth, as though her head hurt.

"Is Bradley talking again today?" I asked the art critic.

"Hell, yes. She's joined the circus too. Everybody has. Why not one more?"

"I thought she was *the* expert on O'Keeffe."

"Once, maybe. Not now. She's on sabbatical from Yale, a has-been. She hasn't done any important work in at least a decade."

"You're saying this O'Keeffe isn't important work?"

"It's work for hire," the critic said disdainfully. "I don't know whether she's on the payroll, but I do know she wants to be."

"Nickelaw's?"

"Good God, no. Nickelaw is an unimportant middle-range art dealer. Lillian Bradley is after a curatorship at Valenti's museum. She'll probably tell him anything he wants to hear. Everybody knows for-hire academic critics are whores. They'll flatter anybody who might be good for a consulting fee or a private grant."

The for-hire newspaper critic had a full measure of the disdain that seems to come with the journalistic territory, but I didn't say anything about pots calling kettles names. I wanted Driscoll to keep talking. Like most reporters, he had a hell of a lot more interesting stuff in his head than ever made the columns of the paper.

"Is Valenti's ego that fragile?" I asked.

The critic laughed sharply. "You don't think that philanthropy is the same as altruism, do you? Roger Valenti is constructing a memorial to himself and enhancing the value of his commercial property, all at public expense. Lillian Bradley can't wait to help him."

I looked around the room. "I don't see any tombstones. Not even a self-congratulatory plaque."

"There will be." The critic shrugged. "Valenti isn't as bad as some of them, but he'll get his name in front of the public. All of them do. Armand Hammer and Norton Simon both drew up formal contracts when they 'gave away' their collections. The contracts are odes to self-aggrandizement, but museums on both coasts fought to get a piece of the action.''

''Does Valenti have a contract in exchange for the O'Keeffe?''

''If you're smart enough, and powerful enough, you don't need a contract. The O'Keeffe will be the centerpiece of an entire new wing—four galleries. Guess what name the directors decided on just last night?'' The critic snorted with derision, then laughed. ''The Roger Valenti Museum of Southwest Art. Not the Roger Valenti Wing—the Roger Valenti *Museum*. The other patrons are furious, but none of them contributed three point six million dollars.''

I wondered if one of the other patrons had been irate enough to ensure that the new wing lost its primary feather. Fiora should have been quizzing Valenti's rivals about the missing O'Keeffe, not teasing a foulmouthed dragon like Harvey. Maybe she was making the patron rounds right now. She had a good instinct for the kind of blood that got spilled in boardrooms.

The blond reporter next to me twitched and fiddled. The cameraman had finished recording her cutaways, so she had nothing better to do than pat her heavily moussed hairdo and twiddle with her pen and notebook. Off camera she looked fifteen years old and scared.

''Where's that painting?'' she said for the sixth time, intoning the words like a quiet prayer. ''Where's that damn painting?''

''I heard a rumor that somebody swiped it,'' I said.

She sat up like she had been goosed. "What? Really?"

I smiled and patted her arm. The bones were just beneath the skin, thin and brittle. "Wait and see."

She gave me a hostile look as I got up and left. Lillian Bradley was just across the aisle, still reviewing her notes.

"Dr. Bradley, I thought you went back east," I said, slipping into the seat behind her.

She glanced over her shoulder. Her expression said that she didn't recognize me.

"I was at the press showing in Santa Fe," I explained.

She turned in her seat, looked up at me again, and smiled professionally while she tried to place me. "I've been in Palm Springs," she said. "I just came up to help Mr. Valenti today."

"I didn't realize you worked for him."

"I've been retained as a consultant by the museum. The board wants to upgrade the fine arts side of their collection."

A nod and an interested look from me was all that was needed to keep Bradley talking.

"*Private Skull* is a spectacular beginning," she continued, her voice strengthening with enthusiasm. "But if the MOSA really wants to put together an important collection, they'll need to spend a great deal of money."

"They've got a leg up on it," I said. "But isn't three million plus change a lot to spend on something that's been lying around for so long? I'd be afraid the painting would turn out to be a fake."

Dr. Bradley's smile was both amused and weary.

"Believe me, that was the first thing everyone assumed. The painting has been examined exhaustively using a number of techniques—brush-stroke analysis, pigment analysis, X-ray analysis. I myself have studied the grounding, the canvas, and the subject matter, but other historians and technicians did the rest of the work."

The remembered pleasure of discovery transformed Bradley's face.

"The provenance of *Private Skull* is unorthodox, but the authenticity of the painting has been settled. It's undeniably O'Keeffe. Even more importantly, *Private Skull* portrays a personal watershed in the artist's own life. The painting is a once-in-a-lifetime find. I thank God that I lived long enough to see this canvas."

If Bradley knew anything off-color about the O'Keeffe, it didn't show. There was a sheen of real emotion in her eyes and her voice had become husky. The pleasure of having a part in the discovery of *Private Skull* radiated through her, taking years off her age.

"Too bad somebody stole it," I said quietly.

For a few seconds nothing happened. Then Bradley blinked and focused on me. The pulse beat that was visible in her neck quickened. She glanced around the auditorium and its crowd of increasingly impatient reporters. She looked at her wristwatch and realized that the press conference was late and getting later with each moment. She looked again at me.

"That's . . . impossible," Bradley said hoarsely. Then she lowered her voice so that none of the journalists would overhear. "Nobody said anything to me this morning. Are you sure?"

"Relatively. The media types don't know yet."

She blinked again. "Aren't you part of the media?"

I shook my head. "I'm a friend of Maggie's."

The pulse point in Bradley's throat began flickering like a strobe. Suddenly she was frightened.

"Oh, God, Maggie," Bradley whispered, closing her eyes. Then she opened them and watched me with cool hostility. "Why are you telling me this? What do you want from me?"

"I'm curious, that's all. I want to know who is doing what and with which and to whom. It's a congenital failure of mine."

Recognition came. "You must be Fiddler."

I nodded. "If you see Maggie, tell her she didn't run far enough. Harvey Durham is looking for her. So is Nickelaw."

Bradley stared at me for five or ten seconds, her eyes blank as her thoughts raced behind them. Then she stood up without a word, picked up her briefcase, and walked up the aisle toward the auditorium door. She didn't hesitate or look back.

The stopwatch in the back of my mind started counting. When sixty seconds had passed, I got up to follow her. Just as I reached the auditorium doors, a junior executive clone in a blue chalk-striped suit came from offstage and went to the podium.

"Ladies and gentlemen, the press conference has been canceled. Your organizations will be notified about rescheduling."

The room was silent for a few seconds before the reporters realized that the man had no intention of saying any more.

"Wait a minute," called a reporter. "What's going on here?"

"I am not authorized to answer any questions," the man said carefully.

With that he walked off the stage, his shoulders hunched against the angry barrage of questions.

The blond reporter waved to catch my eye. When she did, she gave me a gesture with open hands as though to say, Well . . . ?

I gave her a thumbs-up.

Instantly her face radiated the kind of smile that made me wish I had known her before she had starved off twenty-five pounds and sold her soul to Nielsen.

Before I left the auditorium, she was fighting her way backstage, notebook in one hand and a $3.6-million question doing push-ups on her tongue.

tWENTY

Lillian Bradley drove like a Yalie, tentative and out of sync with the hot steel racing past her on the freeway. She was in a blue Ford that had the clean anonymity of a rental car, but the color was just unorthodox enough to make it easy to track among the other vehicles.

Jamboree Road to the San Diego Freeway, northbound. Watch closely at the John Wayne Airport interchange and see a bright blue Ford make the transition to the eastbound Costa Mesa Freeway. Middle lane all the way through Malfunction Junction to the 91 eastbound. Then out through Santa Ana Canyon and the thinning traffic in Corona.

I might have rattled Bradley's cage, but she didn't appear to suspect she was being followed. She drove at a steady, modest speed through the small buildup of traffic at the 215 junction. It was the same for the knot of local traffic through downtown Riverside:

she ignored it. She passed up the Palm Springs shortcut through the badlands on Highway 60 and took the eastbound I-10 instead. For a while, my major problem was staying awake at the speed Bradley found comfortable—57 miles per hour.

Nothing in the scenery kept me awake either. The Los Angeles megalopolis has swallowed the Inland Empire. All the cities run together, creating an amorphous glob distinguished only by zip codes. At the edges of the sprawl, residential subdivisions exist cheek by jowel with a few declining citrus groves and cherry orchards and sagging chicken coops. As the local traffic thinned, I let Bradley range a mile or two ahead of me through Yucaipa and Beaumont.

The noontime sun was warm and pleasant, like a lullaby. Bradley's pace was two miles above the posted limit and thirteen below what most of the freeway traffic was doing. I had to stay in third to keep the Cobra from strangling on its own carbon.

Bradley signaled off at Highland Springs Avenue. There was nothing at that exit but gas and food, so I parked on the freeway shoulder a half mile short of the off-ramp and watched through binoculars while she pulled up to the full-service island at the Chevron station. She used the ladies' room and bought a cold soda while the attendant filled the tank with gas that would have cost 40 cents per gallon less if she'd pumped it herself. Five minutes later she got back on the freeway and staked out her spot in the sparse traffic.

I let Bradley go for a few minutes, then cleaned out the Cobra's pipes by running at 75 in third until I had the blue Ford in sight again. I slowed to 57 mph and settled into the groove once more, feeling the quiet exhilaration that always comes on that stretch of road when urban sprawl is behind me and the elemental desert is ahead.

The San Gorgonio Pass is the gateway to the Southwest. I-10 falls away down a gradual slope toward the embryonic rift valley, whose low point is marked by the dying Salton Sea. The gradient is deceptive; twice in ten miles Bradley's speed drifted all the way up to 62 before she discovered her recklessness and braked back to 57.

The wind was blowing like hell across the open desert, peeling a layer of grit from the land, softening all outlines with a glittering veil of mica dust. Even fighting the elements, it was grand to glide down into the shimmering crucible of the true desert on a brilliant spring afternoon. To some people the low desert is merely desolate. To me it is real in a way which no other landscape can be. The desert is the skull which always lives just beneath the gentle face of rain.

Bradley began signaling her intention to take Highway 111 about a mile early. I didn't want her to notice the distinctive profile of the Cobra so I lagged even farther behind, knowing that I would have to close up the interval once we were in Palm Springs traffic.

The blue Ford was a mile ahead of me when it disappeared around the hognose that's called Windy Point. Sixty seconds later I rounded the same curve.

There was nothing but empty highway in front of me.

For a second I couldn't believe it. There was no

damn place Bradley could be except on the highway, and she wasn't there. Then I remembered Aaron Sharp's Second Law of Surveillance: Everybody's got to be somewhere.

Lillian Bradley wasn't where she should be, so I started looking where she shouldn't be. I looked left and right and saw nothing but wind-roiled grit. I cut a wider arc on either side of the road and finally noticed the thin, rapidly dispersing rooster tail of dust thrown up by a car making its way up the outwash slope toward the base of Mount San Jacinto. At the head of the slope was a bench created by the same land fracture that had given birth to the pass itself. Above the bench rose the sheer gray massif of the ten-thousand-foot-high peak.

Foot off the accelerator, I coasted and looked for a way to get from where I was to where Bradley was. A minute later I drew abreast of a turnoff. The first hundred feet of road were paved. After that the surface became graded desert dirt, a gritty washboard of a road, but serviceable. Even the Cobra could make it, as long as I kept my eye out for big rocks.

Bradley was driving even more cautiously on the dirt, so I pulled over and waited for her to increase her lead. The DeLorme atlas from the Cobra's travel box showed the dirt road wandering up the outwash plain for another three miles to a group of buildings at the base of the mountain. When I got out and stretched, I could just make out the roofs of the buildings with the binoculars.

The wind was constant, flapping at my shirt and jeans, lifting my hair, ruffling my beard and mustache. My skin began to tighten and dry as the air stripped away moisture and left behind the taste of dust and sage and sun. It was the kind of day Aaron Sharp would have loved, as wild and uncurried as a mustang, the kind of day when the wind moaned your true name, your medicine name, the one you gave to no man lest he steal your soul; but the wind knew, and the desert stole your soul.

After a time I lowered the glasses, squinting against the wind. The Ford's windshield flashed back hard light as it crested the final rise before dropping out of sight.

Thirty seconds later I was following. The Cobra's springs rattled when the car dropped off the broken end of the paving onto the dirt surface. Within seconds a sheen of mica dust sparkled everywhere. I dropped to 15 miles per hour to minimize the flag of dirt I was raising.

When I was a mile short of the cluster of buildings, I started looking for a place to hide. The road dipped down and crossed a dry riverbed. The floor of the wash was a patchwork of hardpan and long stretches of gravel. About fifty yards to the north the wash made a sharp bend. The walls of the gully at that point were tall enough to hide a car, so I nosed the Cobra off to test the streambed with a front wheel. The tire sank no more than a few inches. I tried both front wheels. No problem.

I rolled quickly up the wash, trusting my momentum to pull me clear of occasional soft patches. Just around the bend there was a piece of hardpan a hundred feet long and thirty feet wide. I slid the car in tight against the gravel-studded gully wall and shut down. There was nothing to hear but the rattle of brush, nothing to see but the dry land, no mark of man but my own tire tracks rapidly being smoothed out by the wind.

Fifty yards away from the wash, toward San Jacinto, there was a boulder the size of a freight car. I hiked over and scrambled up one side. The rough surface of the rock was warm from the spring sun, but beneath that warmth the cold of winter was still locked within the granite. Lying on top of the boulder, I braced my elbows and cranked the binoculars up to 21 power.

The buildings looked as though they might once have belonged to a working ranch: small house and barn, a few old outbuildings and fences, and a shiny aluminum storage shed near the corral. The veil of wind-driven grit blurred the bases of the buildings but left everything else sharp. No matter what its origins, the place now appeared to be someone's well-kept weekend hideaway. A new coat of dark brown stucco had been recently applied to the original flat-roofed adobe ranch house. The front yard was planted with oleander and succulents. An ancient, magnificently graceful pepper tree shaded the house with dense curtains of lacy, pale green foliage.

Bradley's car was parked, empty, in front of the adobe house. There were no other vehicles in sight. I put the glasses down on the boulder, rolled over, and lay faceup in the sun for a few minutes, waiting.

Insight sometimes comes to those who wait; at least that's the theory behind passive surveillance.

It was after one o'clock. In the lee of the rock, the

THE ART OF SURVIVAL

air had a silky feeling. A commercial jet inbound for Los Angeles slid across the sky thirty thousand feet above me. He had been staged and sequenced the moment he was airborne in Amarillo or Phoenix or Houston. Now he was descending from thirty thousand feet, headed straight for Runway 25 Left at LAX.

I looked down toward Palm Springs. The city was obscured by dust. I realized I hadn't seen any outbound aircraft. Usually the sky around Palm Springs is alive with small aircraft coming and going. Not today. The wind had grounded everything smaller than a DC-10 and bigger than a hawk.

After counting to five hundred I rolled over and used the glasses again, wondering what was going on at the adobe house. Was Maggie there? Had she known about the missing O'Keeffe and not told Bradley? Had Maggie stolen the painting herself or did she know who had stolen it? Or would she be, like Bradley, stunned by the news of the theft?

Nothing new showed around the buildings when I checked again. I rolled over and watched the empty sky and counted some more before I raised the binoculars and watched the road and the country around me. Nothing creeping up from behind, nothing moving but the dry wind. I was dry too. I hadn't planned for a trip to the desert, but I always carry some cans of drinking water in the trunk kit for emergencies.

By the time fifteen more minutes passed, the idea of water became very appealing. Fifteen minutes after that, it became a fixation.

I checked the ranch once more, then walked back

to the Cobra's trunk, opened it, popped the top on a can, and enjoyed the taste of cool, clean water sliding down my throat. There was a package of beef jerky in the kit, but it would have made me more thirsty. I closed the trunk and headed back to my boulder.

As I scrambled out of the wash, a flicker of movement in the direction of the ranch caught my eye. I climbed my rock and had the glasses up in time to see a white Dage Porsche lunge over the rim between me and the house. The car was heading down the slope toward me, coming on hard.

I glassed the house again. Nothing moving, nothing new. I switched to the Porsche. It was roaring downhill fast, much too fast. The wind brought me the sound of twin turbos spooling up as the driver revved all the way to the red line in first, then in second, pouring way too much power into the wheels. The Porsche slewed to one side going around a gentle curve. The driver overcorrected, almost losing it the other way.

I ran back toward the Cobra and waited with the glasses up, wondering whether Nickelaw or Vikki was at the Porsche's wheel. Or Maggie. The fact that I liked the prickly Ms. Tenorio didn't mean she wasn't a crook.

The Porsche came down through the dry wash sideways, spewing so much dirt that I could barely make out the lines of the car itself, much less the identity of the driver. The car flashed up and out the other side of the wash going at least sixty miles an hour.

The spooling turbos and the mean snarl of the

car's exhaust came back to me above the keening wind. I could show myself and wreck the Cobra chasing the Porsche in order to discover who its incompetent driver was, or I could try doing it the easy way for once.

I climbed onto the boulder again and lay on my stomach, watching the white car slew and churn down the road toward 111. The engine sound faded, but I could clearly hear the squeal of tires when the Porsche made the left turn off the dirt road and onto the highway. The snarling sound became a thinning scream as the driver redlined through the gears. At the Windy Point hognose, the car disappeared.

By then the Porsche was several miles away and moving at what had to be more than a hundred miles an hour. If the wind caught the car wrong, somebody was going to decorate the landscape with $125,000 worth of wreckage and eight pints of blood.

I put the glasses down, expecting the car to merge with the westbound traffic on I-10. Instead, the white blur slowed, made the sweeping right-hand transition onto the freeway, and then began picking up speed at an incredible rate, going eastbound into the desert, racing away like a white bat out of hell.

Using the glasses again, I looked back at the house on the stone bench. Nothing had changed, but something had put the Porsche into flight. Bradley would know what.

I went to the Cobra and rolled delicately back onto the dirt road. When I got to the ranch, three black crows were scratching through the dusty floor of the corral. They jumped up onto steel fenceposts and jeered as I drove into the yard and shut off the engine. In ranch country, courtesy or curiosity usually brings somebody to the front door when a vehicle drives up. Nobody showed so much as one eye peering out the front window.

The sun had already begun to sink behind San Jacinto, pushing black velvet shadows out from sheer granite heights, throwing the ranch buildings into a kind of twilight. The wind swirled and cried around me as I pulled on my down vest to hide the gun in the small of my back. I went up the dusty concrete walk to the front door.

It was ajar, allowing the gritty wind inside. I reached back beneath my down vest and stepped to the right of the door.

"Hello the house," I called.

There was no response and probably no point in repeating the call. But I called again anyway.

"Dr. Bradley?"

Nothing answered but the wind.

I leaned to the side and pushed the door wide open. A distinctive scent curled out in greeting, unmistakable, unforgettable, a compound of smokeless gunpowder and animal death.

tWENTY-ONE

The living room of the ranch house had an artist's touch, or a professional decorator's. Navajo wall hangings, red chile *ristras,* and original oils on the walls complemented the handsome, hand-crafted wooden furniture. Everything was color-coordinated—even Lillian Bradley in her business suit, which had been ruined by blood.

You don't have to look for signs of life when someone's skull is wrecked. There is a boneless quality to the freshly dead that can't be faked. Bradley was no exception. Her body was sprawled in a chair, a blue steel revolver beneath her lifeless hand and a starkly white piece of notepaper on the table beside her.

I held my breath and made a quick check of the rest of the house. Nothing. Nobody home. No other bodies waiting to be discovered.

When I came back to the living room again, nothing had changed. Bradley's corpse was still sprawled in the chair with the back half of her skull splashed across the decor like an obscene Jackson Pollock. I could read the note without touching it: *I can't wait for death. The pain is too great.*

The words were scrawled awkwardly, as though she had been in a hurry and wrote under great strain. Understandable, considering what came next.

The stink of death welled up in the room despite the wind's attempts to blow through the house, cleansing it. I breathed through my mouth. It didn't help much. I looked at Bradley again, closely. What I saw was ugly, but that was no surprise. Violent death is always ugly.

The longer I looked, the less it seemed like suicide. Women seldom kill themselves with guns. Way too messy, as the sight in front of me proved. Women usually opt for pills or gas. But then, Bradley hadn't been a usual woman.

Was that all the violent end meant—a different artistic choice for a different woman? The art of death rather than the art of survival?

Or was there something else? Had my news about the O'Keeffe sent Bradley over the edge? If pain had driven her to suicide, what was the source of that pain? If Bradley had been helped into death, who profited?

There were no answers, simply questions and more questions asked in silence of an equally silent corpse.

I could do little more where I was, yet I couldn't force myself to leave. I kept looking at Bradley, wondering by what complex biological process the accumulated learning of a lifetime had been stored in what was now meaningless gore. I wondered what happened to that learning, to those sensory impressions and academic ratiocinations, and to the pain which her note said had made life unbearable.

There were no answers to those questions either, except the obvious one: life is transient, death is not, and sometimes the meaning of both is lost in the mess that's left behind. Dr. Bradley had left behind a bigger mess than most.

My stomach told me it was time to leave. When I got outside I stood on the porch, drew a deep breath through my nose, and forced the air out through my clenched teeth. A few repetitions and my stomach began to settle down. I knew I had to go back in there . . . but not now, not this instant. A few more breaths, a few more moments to savor the razor edge of desert air cutting into my soft tissues, telling me I was alive.

Dust gritted between my shoes and the cement walk. I did a circuit of the yard and saw nothing out of place. Beyond the yard the Dage's wide Pirellis had left distinctive tread marks in the dusty ruts other cars had carved out of the gravel driveway. The ruts led to a shady area in the lee of the barn. Had the car been put there to conceal an ambush or simply parked sensibly out of the sun and wind? The ground was baked so hard that the Dage had barely left scuff marks; footprints were out of the question.

I walked back to Bradley's car. It was as empty as it had looked from the boulder by the dry wash. The keys were in the ignition. I left them there and walked toward the house, retracing the path Bradley had taken to her own death. No sign of alarm here. She had arrived home, parked where she always parked, and gone into the house.

I hadn't touched anything yet, including the front door, so I didn't have to remove any prints. I went inside, resumed breathing through my mouth, and went to work. A cordovan briefcase and a small purse lay on the floor next to the ruined chair. Both the bag and the briefcase were open, as though Bradley had searched through them for a pen and paper.

The purse contained no makeup. Comb, toothpicks, mirror—and four bottles of medicine. Using my handkerchief I picked out the bottles one by one. All were from a New Haven pharmacy. Three of the medications were unfamiliar, but the fourth was codeine, ten grains: *Take as needed for pain.*

Bradley must have needed quite a few. The prescription for one hundred pills had been filled only two few weeks before, yet there were fewer than twenty pills left. Either her physician was Dr. Feelgood or she had something that made codeine addiction look attractive. That idea dovetailed with her suicide note: *I can't wait for death. The pain is too great.*

Then I remembered what Bradley had said to me in the auditorium, something about *Private Skull*— *I thank God that I lived long enough to see it.*

All right, given the pills and the note, suicide was possible, perhaps even probable, but Bradley hadn't looked like a woman considering her own death the afternoon I saw her put her arm around Maggie and smile.

The briefcase contained a thick, scholarly book on Picasso, in French, with several bookmarks in place. There was a copy of a slick art magazine. Stuck inside were photographic studies of *Private Skull*. There were several folders full of clippings and notes, one of which I had seen her studying in the museum.

The debris of a scholar's life. Nothing new in it for me. Nothing to suggest that things were other than they seemed. Bradley had been a woman in great pain, a woman in love, a woman who had arrived at a peak of personal and professional ecstasy; and she had killed herself at that peak.

Not a bad way to die.

Yet it bothered me. It's not quite human to kill yourself at the peak. Somewhere on the long slide down, maybe. At the bottom, surely. But at the top? When you die at the top, it's usually called murder.

I went back to the briefcase, handling papers by the corners only, careful not to leave prints. Along with the scholarly articles there was a thin manila folder. Inside was a set of printer's mockup sheets. Each bore a time stamp and job number from Desert Empire Printing, with an address and phone number in Palm Springs.

Using the handkerchief, I spread out the dummy sheets—letterhead, envelopes, business cards. They all had the same elegantly stylized logo and the words FINE ARTS SOUTHWEST, *Private Curatorial and Fine Art Consulting Services, Lillian Bradley, Ph.D., and Magdalena Tenorio, proprietors.* The business address was a post office box in Palm Springs. The phone number probably rang at some answering service.

Fine Arts Southwest.

It must have sounded like a piece of heaven to an aging East Coast art professor whose important work lay decades in the past. Private curators, private opinions, private money. They are the hottest thing in art. You just rent out your taste and expertise to rich schlubs who have neither. You pick out their art for them. You show them how to hang it, instruct them on how to appreciate it, tell them a couple of catchy anecdotes about the artist so they can wow their philistine friends.

It would have flown, too. Maggie would have been the classy shill, Dr. Bradley the brains. California would have been the happy hunting grounds, filled with insecure screenwriters holding fat development deals and nerdling software writers with six-figure salaries.

Bradley and Maggie would have joined the ranks of "experts" waiting to rent their services out to the nervous ranks of the nouveau riche. Koi experts will design your pond and stock it for you, too. Woodcarvers will make hand-crafted front doors at $10,000 to $30,000 each. Stained glass artisans will do tableaux of your life in more colors than Joseph's coat. Weavers will incorporate a portrait of your favorite pet into a tapestry for your dog house. Craftsmen will re-create your whims in brick, glass, nutty putty, or Bisquick. All it takes is money.

Service is a growth industry with a con man as CEO, and as often as not you get serviced the same way a bull services a cow.

Too many questions and no reliable answers. Bradley could be the con or the conned or both. The same went for Maggie. Nickelaw was no different.

As for Valenti . . . it would take a brave man or a fool to run a con on Valenti, but the world is full of brave fools.

I kept looking through the briefcase, hoping for something that would answer more questions than it raised. A leather date book lay next to the scholarly journal. Holding the date book by its edges, I let it fall open to the current week. Bradley's notation system was idiosyncratic but logical. She had held several meetings a day with prospective clients of Fine Arts Southwest. She and Maggie must have been charging for consultations already, because each meeting had been flagged with a reminder: *Bill three hours* or *Bill one hour*.

The museum appearance this morning in behalf of Roger Valenti was on the schedule. It was marked, *Bill full day, LB.* There was a notation for the following day, as well: *MT, AA 442, 312p,PS.*

MT was doubtless Maggie Tenorio, but the rest was elusive. AA? Alcoholics Anonymous? Nobody had a drinking problem that I knew of. PS was probably Palm Springs, but then again, it could have stood for anything from Post Script to Pink Sherry.

AA . . . American Airlines? That would fit with Palm Springs, and the rest could be flight information. I could also be as wrong as Bradley was dead.

I folded up the date book and put it back in the briefcase. A quick once-over of the rest of the house didn't tell me anything. Neither Maggie nor Bradley had left many marks on the place. It might just as well have been a hotel room. The master bedroom held two different sizes of clothing and the bathroom held two different colors of toothbrushes, but that was all. There were no half-finished letters or projects, nothing to indicate that the ranch house was more than a set that had been dressed for a canceled play.

Too many questions. Not enough answers.

I left the phone undisturbed in its cradle. There was no pressing reason to report Bradley's death and a lot of reasons not to. I left the front door the same way I had found it—ajar. The blowing dust had already obliterated the tracks that marked my arrival.

In the shadow of the mountain, the wind had developed a cold edge, like a knife blade. Down on the flats the wind was scouring the land. I got in the Cobra and drove toward the highway.

Less than halfway there I crested a small rise and nearly rammed head-on into Fiora's new car.

tWENTY-TWO

The big silver BMW swerved left. I cut hard the other way, looking for a soft spot among the rocks beside the road. The wind was kicking up clouds of road dust, but I got one quick glimpse of Fiora as we passed. The swoopy front end of Fiora's car missed taking a bite out of the left front fender of the Cobra by about two feet. At a combined speed of 60—30 apiece—two feet ain't much.

I braked hard and watched my rearview mirror, expecting to see red brake lights blossom in the dust cloud as Fiora stopped. Even if things had happened too fast for her to recognize me, she sure as hell knew what the Cobra looked like.

Fiora kept going as though I'd been a mirage.

For a second I was tempted to let her go. At best she would drive right into a gruesome suicide tableau. At worst she would become a material witness to a damned ugly murder. But neither was necessary. All I had to do was head her off.

Swearing, I downshifted into first and did a slalom turn, throwing a head-high rooster tail of loose desert dirt from the back wheels as I took off up the hill after Fiora. A hundred and fifty yards later the Cobra's nose was right up against the BMW's tail. There was no way Fiora could miss me in her rearview mirror.

She kept going.

I flashed the Cobra's headlights. Fiora ignored me. I honked. She increased her speed by ten miles an hour. We raced along for a hundred yards. Then the big fat back tires of the BMW kicked up a stone. There was nowhere to go on the narrow road, so I watched as the stone arced back and smacked hard into the Cobra's windshield with the sound of a pistol shot. The windshield exploded. Stinging kernels of safety glass hit my face and shoulder.

"Jesus Christ, woman!"

I leaned on the horn. Hard. Fiora glanced in the rearview mirror. Through the frame of the back window, I saw her lift her right hand from the wheel. She held her hand next to the mirror, where she knew I could see it against the windshield, and showed me an elegant middle finger.

I moved over to the right, as though to pass that way. As I expected, Fiora moved over to cut me off. I whipped the wheel hard left, waited a fraction of a second until I was straight, and then goosed the accelerator.

The Cobra's snarling sidepipes gave me away. Fiora heard them in the new position and moved to block the opening. She was too late. I had my nose in the tent. The aluminum hood of the Cobra was even with the BMW's back wheels. She couldn't cut me off without pranging her car and mine at the same time. I didn't think she would risk that.

I was wrong.

Fiora moved left, crowding me out into the boon-docks. At the last instant she drifted right about six inches, allowing me to avoid the chaparral. But it was close. I was as far to the left as I could go and still be on the road. My eyes met Fiora's in her sideview mirror. She didn't have to flip me off to tell me she wasn't going to give another inch. I could see determination in the flat line of her mouth.

The roiling dust cut forward visibility to maybe fifty yards, just enough that I could see the shoulder of the road flatten out ahead. I tucked one set of wheels on the graded berm and tested the traction. It wasn't great. Gently I fed gas and picked up a few feet on the BMW, bringing the Cobra's hood even with Fiora's door. I was too busy to look over and see her expression now; the footing was treacher-ous. I fluttered the throttle, trying to nurse more power to the wheels without spinning them in the loose sand.

An inch at a time I closed the gap. The undercar-riage of the Cobra rattled and banged. The 750 raced along as if on rails, as hard and relentless as Fiora's determination not to give in. We hit a loose patch and visibility went to shit. Suddenly a rock the size of a six-burner kitchen stove loomed out of the dust on the left.

Flip or fly.

I nailed the throttle. The tires spun, spun, caught, and the Cobra lunged forward. I don't know if Fiora saw the boulder. I do know that she hesitated maybe a quarter second, then kicked the accelerator and moved over to the left. She was too late. I was past her. The race was over and I had won.

Well, almost. I tried to cut back toward the center of the road to avoid the granite boulder. The Cobra's back end kicked in the loose dirt and the tires spun as though there were marbles beneath the dust. I cranked against the skid. Nothing happened. A little more. Still nothing—and then I saw that the left corner of Fiora's shiny new bumper had tapped the Cobra, trapped it, tipped the balance between forward momentum and sideways spin. I tried to correct again but it was too late. I was floating down the road sideways, caught on the bumper of a car driven by a woman who was intent on breaking me in half, and there wasn't one goddamn thing I could do about it.

Fiora recognized the situation at the last instant or I'd have been rolled up in the center of a ball of tinfoil and launched into the desert. She braked sharply and I did what I could, cutting the wheel hard, trying to whip the tail of the Cobra in an arc away from the big rock.

The laws of physics can't be amended that easily. Before the counterforce could take control, the left rear quarter of the Cobra smacked into the rock and I came to a savage stop. The sound of the hard metallic collision made my teeth ache. I looked over my right shoulder. The BMW's hood was about ten inches away. Through the clearing dust I saw the dome light come on as Fiora opened the door and got out slowly. She walked to the front of her car and looked at me. Her face was as white as Bradley's notepaper.

The wind caught Fiora's thick, tawny hair and blew it across her green eyes, hiding the shadows and the shock. She pushed her hair back with a hand that shook. Hair spilled and flew away again, pulled by the wind. Her lips trembled. She licked them and tried to speak. Nothing happened.

I watched her tongue and her trembling lips and her flying honey-colored hair. There was nothing I wanted to say to her and two things I wanted to do to her; one was against the law and the other didn't seem appropriate at the moment.

"Are y-you all right?" she asked.

I looked at her.

"F-Fiddler?"

"Yes. No. *Shit.* I'll live, no thanks to you."

Fiora hooked her upper teeth over her lower lip and bit. The gesture was totally unconscious and sexy as hell. She moved her head sharply, as though awakening from a trance. Then she leaned against the windshield's empty metal framework and shook. When it passed she took a deep breath and circled around to my left until she could see the damage to the Cobra.

For the moment, I didn't want to know, so I didn't look.

After a long time Fiora walked around until she was standing in front of me. She started to speak, bit her lip, and shook her head.

"Can it be driven?" I asked.

Fiora flinched. I didn't blame her. Even I didn't recognize the voice as mine. She said something to me. I couldn't hear her for the roaring in my ears. I waited for a moment.

"Can it be driven?" I asked again.

"I don't think so," Fiora said distinctly. "The front wheel . . ." Her voice faded. She cleared her throat. "The wheel is crooked, like maybe the axle is bent. There's oil leaking."

"Brake fluid," I corrected her.

She made a helpless gesture with her hands, telling me that there was no difference between oil and brake fluid right now. The Cobra was well and truly wrecked.

I stared past Fiora and back down the road toward the desert floor. The wind was gale force on the flats. The city had all but disappeared. Palm Springs Airport would be closed, no traffic in or out, probably not even commercial flights and certainly no charters.

"*Shit!*" I felt the top of the steering wheel bend when I struck it the third time. My hand hurt by then, so I quit. I came out from behind the steering wheel hard and fast. Fiora jumped when I landed next to her, but she was game. She didn't back up one inch.

I walked over to the edge of the road. A Spanish Dagger yucca was growing in the berm. I kicked it once, hard, trying to decide whether I could appease my rage by uprooting the cactus. The sharp point of one branch gouged the smooth leather of my boot. So much for sublimation.

I yanked my traveling kit from behind the Cobra's

seat and threw the satchel in the big BMW's back seat. When I slammed shut the door, a little black pigtail antenna peeking up from the molding over the back window caught my eye. I yanked open the driver's door. The interior smelled like new leather and Fiora's elusive perfume. The cellular phone was on the console between the two front seats. I got a dial tone instantly. While the number was ringing in Newport Beach, Fiora came over and stood beside the door. She held onto it with one hand and looked out across the desert.

Miraculously, Benny answered on the third ring.

"You know anybody with a flatbed wrecker?" I asked.

"Yeah."

"Can he keep zipped?"

"Yeah."

"My car is out of commission on a dirt road a mile west of Highway One-eleven just beyond Windy Point."

"A minute, mate."

I heard Benny lay the portable phone on the tray of his chair and push himself across the room. There was the sound of pages rustling.

"Right. I've got it in the Thomas Brothers, looks like a dirt road that goes up to some little—"

"That's it," I said, cutting him off. Cellular conversations go out over the open air and I was trying to remain vague. "Have your guy bring a crowbar too. A wheel has to be freed."

"Ouch."

"Shit happens," I said between my teeth.

Fiora flinched.

"You still on Apollo?" I asked.

I heard the key chatter of a terminal as Benny logged onto the airline reservation and schedule service.

"Ready," he said.

"Palm Springs to Albuquerque, soonest."

Key chatter, a grunt, more key chatter.

"No can do, mate. Palm Springs is shut down, zero-zero with blowing sand. No commercial service until further notice."

"That means no charters either. What about LA–Albuquerque?"

More keystrokes. Benny argued with himself over the proper codes and the correct routing while I listened to the wind and studied the uncluttered dashboard of the new BMW. The seat felt like an easy chair. Beneath the rich smell of new leather, I caught Fiora's scent again. It lingered where her body had touched the seat, where her hands gripped the wheel. Every breath I took told me the car was hers.

"Allowing three hours for you to get to LAX, there are no direct flights before midnight. The first flight that's even in the same time zone would be Continental to El Paso at eight thirty-five, but you'd have to wait until morning for a connection."

I tapped the leather-bound steering wheel with the edge of my hand and ran the numbers in my head. With the ignition key off, the speedometer was a ghost image in computer gray and orange. The numbers stopped at 160 mph/260 kph. I ran the numbers again. I liked them.

"Scratch the airlines. I'll take the Freeway Flyer."

"I thought you said it just ate a wheel."

"It did, but only because my ex punted me into a rock the size of a house."

"Bloody hell. You all right?"

"What do you think?"

"Bloody *bloody* hell," Benny muttered. "Take her car. It's faster than it looks."

"I already figured that out. I'll drop her at Hertz in Palm Springs, but if she can't get a car, send somebody to pick her up at the Greyhound station in LA. She should be in about suppertime." I hung up the phone and looked at Fiora. "Get in."

"I came here to see Lillian Bradley. That's what I'm going to do."

"You'll see more of her than you want. Her brains are spread across half the living room wall."

For a few seconds Fiora's expression didn't change. Then her eyes lost their sharp focus and tears welled up in them.

"Is that why you tried to . . . ?" she asked in a strained voice that faded before she could finish her question.

"Tried to save you from your own stubbornness? Yeah. But don't worry. I've made that mistake for the last time. Either get in or stay here and wait for the wrecker."

Fiora turned and walked around the front of the car. As she got in, I turned the key in the ignition and started the engine. The onboard computer flashed me all kinds of important messages and systems status reports as the V-12 came up to speed: SRS, ABS ASK, consumables, programmables, E-proms, and RAMs. It was like stepping into the cockpit of a spaceship, the kind we'll all be flying in fifty years. Fiora snapped her seatbelt into place and waited quietly. Her windblown hair made a curtain that hid her profile from me.

I pulled the shifter down into DRIVE, read the changes on the dashboard, and then released the brake. The BMW backed away from the wrecked Cobra. I found a wide spot and turned around.

"You want Hertz or Greyhound?" I asked.

"I'm going with you."

"Like hell."

She turned and looked at me. Her tears had left trails down her cheeks. Her eyes looked desolate, as though she felt she had just lost something enormously valuable, something she had never truly understood could be lost.

"I'm sorry, Fiddler. I'm very, very sorry, and it doesn't do a damn bit of good."

"Oh, for Christ's sake. . . . The Cobra's just a car."

She shook her head and more tears fell. "It's not the Cobra."

"Fine. It's not the Cobra. Do you want Hertz or Greyhound."

Fiora took a deep breath. "If you don't take me with you, I'll see that there's an APB on this car in every state from here to Florida."

Her lips might have trembled, but there was nothing uncertain in her voice. She would do just what she had said.

"Fuck it," I snarled. "Do what you want. You always do."

tWENTY-THREE

Fiora finally fell asleep around Vidal Junction, putting one of us out of our misery. U.S. 95 is straight and smooth where it crosses the Chemehuevi Valley. The BMW was like a rocket sled, straightening out the bends around Lobecks Pass. I drove at 120 mph while Fiora slept. I barked the tires making the 140-degree turn at Five Mile Station Road. By the time we got on I-40 eastbound, she was awake.

The little servomotor in her seat hummed as she adjusted the chair. She looked around, orienting herself. As she did, she rubbed her arms with her palms. I realized for the first time that she was dressed for the low desert—white cotton slacks, cable-knit cotton sweater, and velvet vest that made her eyes look more green.

I reached back into the rear seat and snagged my down vest. As Fiora took it, her hand brushed over mine. It was an accident, but we felt it just the same.

It had been a long time since we had touched each other.

"Thanks."

Fiora's voice sounded too husky, but her eyes were dry. I didn't like the look of defeat that lay just beneath her polite expression, though. Benny had been right. She was in deeper than she knew. Or had known. She knew now, and it wasn't helping her one bit.

I tried to drive 80 and adjust the climate control panel at the same time. Fiora noticed and leaned forward to help. She was still half asleep. Her fingertips slid over the back of my hand.

"Sorry," she said, snatching back her hand.

Then she laughed sadly at the irony of apologizing for touching the man who had been her husband for a short time and her lover for more years than either one of us liked to count.

"Maybe I should have it tattooed on my forehead," Fiora said. "Sorry, sorry, sorrysorry. . . ."

"Bradley's death isn't your fault."

"But you're in it just the same, up to your lips in shit, and that *is* my fault."

"I do my best work when I'm up to my lips in shit."

A ghostly, bittersweet smile crossed Fiora's mouth. "That's what Benny said. Damn him. Damn all men."

"And damn me in particular," I muttered.

She shook her head.

"I'm a man," I pointed out.

"You're different. You're the man I fell in love with before I knew how hard love was to live with.

So tell me, Fiddler," she whispered, "what's the secret to falling out of love?"

"How the hell would I know?"

"Because you've done it."

I turned and stared at Fiora in disbelief. Her eyes were closed, and tears were glittering again in her thick lashes.

"Fiora . . ."

"Please don't," she said huskily. "Just drive. It's one of the many things you do well."

I could talk to myself, but I couldn't talk to Fiora because she had closed me out. So I shut up and drove hard, lifting my foot only when we dropped down into the cleft of the Colorado River. The gorge was in twilight. The barren rise of desert hills still held color. Off in the distance there were glittering patches of white against the dark lowlands, flocks of waterfowl that dotted the sloughs of the Havasu Wildlife Refuge. We rumbled across the bridge into Arizona and began to climb out of the gorge and up the other side into the last of the light.

Once we cleared the roadside clutter of gas stations and homestead shacks at Topock, I put my foot down again. The 750's engine took on a deeper sound as I ran up to 90 and then leaned on the pedal a little more.

The BMW liked the new speed. The big car sort of flattened down onto the road's surface, getting every bit of traction out of the fat tires. The needle was touching 100 when Fiora glanced casually at the speedometer, then looked again in a classic double-take.

I waited for a complaint. It didn't come. She simply tipped her chair back and made herself more comfortable. Her air of relaxation wasn't a pose. Her body was utterly calm, right down to the slow beating of the pulse in her neck.

Fiora's silent, unconscious declaration of trust in me made a shambles of all the defenses I had spent months building. I kept thinking of the difference between something that was good and something that was perfect, and how I had once thrown away the violin when I was too young to know that good was attainable and perfect was not.

On the long ascent out of the Colorado Valley onto the shoulder of the Great Plateau, the BMW rushed to meet the night. Local traffic had been weeded out by now. What was left was a mix of cross-country eighteen-wheelers, pickup trucks pulling rented trailers, and a scattering of retirees in their motor homes. Everybody seemed to understand the rules: we were all Nowhere, headed for Somewhere Else, and speed limits never made sense out here anyway.

Because I was the fastest car on the road, I ran with headlights on high beam. That raised my visibility to traffic cops as well as to other drivers, but at the speed I was going I wouldn't sneak by a beat cop unnoticed anyway.

"Gum?" asked Fiora after a time.

I nodded.

She unwrapped two sticks of gum and popped them into my mouth with the ease and casual intimacy that only comes after years of being together. I had been expecting her favorite flavor—spearmint—but she surprised me. The taste of peppermint spread through my mouth. Instantly my stomach started to nosh on itself, as though anticipating food. I realized I hadn't eaten all day.

"When did you start carrying peppermint gum?" I asked.

"When I started missing the taste of you."

Fiora's words had come without thought, surprising her almost as much as me. She turned on the radio, as though trying to make conversation difficult. There was a country-western station in Needles. She killed that station as soon as she found it, but could find nothing else. The attenuated signals from Phoenix and LA were too scratchy to enjoy. She punched off the radio and jabbed another button on the other side of the console.

Suddenly the interior of the car was suffused with an outpouring of soft, gentle strings. Two measures is all it takes to recognize Vivaldi, even in the middle of a movement. The sound reproduction was stunning, vivid, clean, filling the car as though it were a small concert hall. I floated for a moment, caught in the maddening complexity of the notes, transfixed by the skill of the violinist.

Fiora made a startled noise and stopped the music in midphrase.

"Sorry," she said. "I didn't mean to . . . I was just listening to that on the way down to Palm Springs and . . ." Her voice died.

"Let it play."

"But it's Perlman."

"I know."

"I thought you didn't like to hear . . ."

Fiora's words trailed off again, telling me how close she was to the ragged edge of her self-control.

"I finally forgave him for being what he is and myself for not being what he is," I said. "Turn it on again. Please."

She started the music again. Concerto No. 2 in G Minor, first movement, *allegro non molto*. Summer. The string section picked up in the same place, undisturbed by the abrupt stop. Beauty filled the car, stringed instruments singing quietly to one another on a slow, sultry afternoon. The sound system was so clean I could hear the tonal idiosyncracies of individual instruments.

Then the round-cheeked little kid who broke my heart long ago broke it again with a beautifully controlled *glissando*, Vivaldi's description of a sudden wind and a stroke of lightning from a summer storm. Each descending note was distinct, vibrant, alive, so close to perfect that it made me physically ache; and the sound system did justice to every note.

"What the hell kind of player is this?" I asked finally.

Fiora touched a button and the music stopped. There was a gentle whir. A thin silver disc emerged from an almost invisible slot in the stereo console.

"Vivaldi, *The Four Seasons*, London Philharmonic Orchestra, Itzhak Perlman, conductor and soloist," Fiora read.

"I know that, but what's making the sound?"

"There's a compact disc player in the dash, eight speakers all around, and a pair of ten-inch subwoofers in the trunk. If you don't like the mix, there's an equalizer low on the dash to your left. If you punch the orange button, the sub-woofers are cut out of the circuit."

"Why would I want to do a damn fool thing like that? Run up the volume a bit."

She gave me an odd, disconcerted look and then her fingers moved gracefully, feeding the disc back in and adjusting the volume. The music picked up from the beginning, "Spring" in E minor. We sailed on toward the dark eastern horizon at 100 miles an hour, sung to by art that had survived for 250 years. The music was like a whiff of pure oxygen at high altitude, clearing the senses and deepening the ability to concentrate.

I needed that fine edge of focus as I accelerated more, letting the big car stretch out. Serious speeding requires serious attention to the road. It's not just a matter of avoiding the law. Like civilization, law is just a veneer over reality, and the veneer is thick only where people are thick. There aren't many folks out on the Great Plateau. At that particular moment, there were probably only a dozen traffic cops in all of western Arizona, and they were concentrated where traffic was heaviest, around the fringes of the cities and towns. Ten miles on either side of Kingman or Ash Fork or Williams, the chances of encountering a speed cop are only slightly better than the chances of encountering a kayaker in one of the sandy washes.

The real work of fast driving isn't dodging cops. The real work is keeping track of the other guys on the road and anticipating their reaction to the sudden appearance in the rearview mirrors of four blaz-

ing headlamps being pushed along at speeds just
short of Mach 1. The motor homes are the worst.
They're usually driven by someone who's accustomed to handling a passenger car, the kind of
driver who changes lanes before he looks over his
shoulder. But even the professionals, the long-haul
truckers whose kidneys and marriages gave out
years ago, aren't used to being overtaken by a silver
streak traveling 50 miles an hour faster than they
are.

Out on the long incline toward the San Francisco
Peaks and Flagstaff, there's another little wrinkle to
driving fast. Or rather a whole lot of wrinkles. The
old gray interstate ain't what it used to be. In the
last twenty or thirty years, a few hundred million
heavy trucks have broken down the right-hand,
slow lane. Now everybody has gravitated over to the
relative smoothness of the left lane. That means you
drive slow in the left lane and pass fast in the right,
as if you were in Europe. It seems simple enough,
except that in America, everyone's reflexes are
tuned to the opposite way of driving.

Fortunately there were long stretches where the
traffic was so thin that I could treat the interstate
like the Autobahn. The 750's glowing orange speedo
touched 140 for a few bars the second time
"Spring" came around on the disc, somewhere east
of Seligman. The pedal still had some bottom left
but the roadway was too rough, so I backed off to
120 and held it there for miles on end.

It had been full dark for an hour when we hit
Flagstaff. Coming off the freeway at the downtown
exit, I touched the brake for the first time since we

bought gas in Desert Center. A cold, hard wind buffeted the car as we turned left down the main drag toward the Flagstaff Mall. I pulled into the parking lot closest to the entrance and pointed.

"You need warmer clothes," I said. "Try REI or Eddie Bauer, if there is one, otherwise a sporting goods store or western wear should get the job done. Get boots, walking-style. If you see a good winter parka—lined Gore-Tex would be nice—get it for me. I'll be back to pick you up in fifteen minutes."

"And if I'm not here?"

"I'll wait and you know it."

"No, I don't know it."

"Fiora, that's ridicu—"

The door shut quietly behind her. She ran through the cold wind to the shopping center and disappeared inside. Too late I realized that she had left my down vest on the seat. If she had been angry and left the vest behind I would have understood the message—she'd rather freeze than wear something I had worn. But she hadn't been angry, so why had she left it?

It was cold enough that I pulled on the vest myself. The cloth smelled like Fiora's perfume. Abruptly I was flooded with the kind of bruising memories I had been trying to bury for eight weeks, and then I knew that Fiora had left the vest behind for the same reason.

Too damn many memories of me, of her, of us.

tWENTY-FOUR

The Chevron guy pumped gas while I stretched for the first time in three hundred miles.

"Check under the hood, mister?" he asked hopefully when the tank was full.

He had been politely salivating over the BMW the whole time he had been filling the tank. His hands were clean, so I let him look over my shoulder while I checked the car myself.

Cracking the 750iL's hood was like entering a church. The pump jockey stood at my elbow in hushed respect. The V-12 looked as though it had just rolled out of the factory, high-tech black and cool cast aluminum. The oil on the dipstick was clean, and the coolant overflow tank was full. I resisted the temptation to fiddle. The engine had run fine for four hours without my advice and counsel. There was another five hours of work ahead. Well, not quite work. When you're doing what you were created to do, it isn't work.

And if it ain't broke, don't fix it.

I left the attendant to clean the windshield and jogged across the street to a Safeway. Cheese, dry salami, fruit, crackers, all six kinds of Coca-Cola. They even had a Coleman chest and ice to fill it. I was through the checkout line in seven minutes flat.

Sixteen minutes by the clock after I dropped Fiora, I drove by the entrance and sat in the loading zone with the motor idling. We had been out of cellular range for a while but I got a Rocky Mountain Bell connection immediately. Benny answered in Newport on the third ring. I kept the conversation oblique.

"Any really special reason I should avoid contact with law enforcement at the moment?"

"No, but what you did to that car was criminal."

"I didn't do it, remember?"

Benny sighed. "What the hell did you say to make her do that?" Then, quickly, "Forget I asked, mate. I promised myself I'd stay out of it, whatever it might be."

"No sign of cops around my car?" I asked, ignoring the rest of Benny's noise.

"Not a one. How do you like her Autobahn Express?"

His voice was too casual. I had suspected that Fiora had had advice before purchasing her new car, but I had assumed that Valenti had provided it. Wrong again.

"The seats are a hell of a lot more comfortable

than the Cobra's," I said. "Adjustable lumbar support, built-in heater, more positions than the Kama Sutra."

Benny laughed. "It's nice at a hundred and ten, isn't it?"

"It's even better at a hundred and forty."

"Bloody hell," he said, delighted. "She wouldn't let me drive it that fast."

Before I could reply, Fiora opened the back door on the passenger side and dumped in a load of parcels.

"We're on the road again," I said to Benny. I hung up and said to Fiora, "Keep your ears open for anything on the news about the picture or about anybody involved with it."

"All right. I'll drive while you rest."

Fiora dumped a Gore-Tex jacket in my lap. She wore a tailored wool shirt—it looked dark green in the mercury-vapor lamps—over a white turtleneck and blue jeans that had been cut to her size and then shrunk. The jeans were tucked into a new pair of leather storm boots with fleece lining. She was barely two minutes late and God only knew what else she had in the two bags she had thrown in back.

"I'll drive," I said. "I'm in a hurry."

"This is an equal opportunity car. It goes fast without checking the driver's crotch for racing equipment."

I smiled in spite of myself and began sliding out of the driver's seat. "What did Benny use for foot controls?"

"He had a cane with a rubber tip. We drove to Nevada, where they don't care how fast you go."

A few minutes later we were out of town and flying. I wasn't worried. Fiora has good reflexes and steady hands. She kept the needle just below 100.

Dinner was the luck of the draw. We ate whatever my hand encountered in the ice chest. My pocketknife pared off the Tillamook Sharp Cheddar and Gallo Dry Salami a piece at a time. I fed myself and cut hors d'oeuvres that I fed to Fiora. The crackers crumbled all over the thick wool carpet and I smeared a little Gulden's mustard on the hand-sewn leather seats when the roadbed got kinky, but Fiora didn't complain. We were both hungry. I wondered if she knew there was a spot of mustard in the corner of her mouth . . . and if she would mind if I licked it off.

The knife slipped, nicking my finger. I swore and licked blood for a few minutes and told myself to keep my mind on what I was doing instead of on what I wanted to be doing.

Just east of Winona, the moon broke through low clouds to the east, spreading a tranquil silver light over the land. Without the wheel in my hands to stimulate and concentrate my senses, I started to sag and fold up around the meal.

"There's a blanket in one of the bags," Fiora said. "Why don't you sleep?"

Sometimes the woman reads minds. Sometimes I resent it, too, but not at that moment. I reached over, rummaged until I found the correct bag, and shook out a Pendleton lap robe. My new Gore-Tex jacket made a passable pillow. I dozed off and on, then slept. I awoke with a start when the tires hit a wide seam between two slabs of concrete. I looked over at the speedo. It dropped from 100 to 80 as I watched. The road was a rough bastard.

The landscape wasn't any softer. Black rocks and hammered silver moonlight and nothing in sight but road and more road. I turned and looked at Fiora. She was alert, but there were frown lines around her eyes and her shoulders were hunched, as though she had been sitting too long in the cold, squinting too long into the darkness. I dialed in a little more heat for her side of the cabin.

While she concentrated on passing a double-trailer rig with orange and blue running lights on its fairing, I felt around in the back seat until I came up with a one-pound bar of Hershey's bittersweet. I broke off a row of four squares and handed it to Fiora. She held the chocolate to her nose and inhaled the aroma as though it were a good red wine. She ate the entire portion in two minutes.

"More?" I asked.

"Please."

I fed her chocolate and tried not to remember all the times she had licked sweet crumbs from my fingers and we had both laughed. I wondered if she was remembering too, but I didn't ask.

At Gallup I pumped gas because I didn't know when we would have another chance. Fiora walked around on the frosty ground beside the pump island, scuffing the soles of her new boots and watching the burning white moonlight give definition to the stone mesas that lay along the road. The new down jacket she wore looked like a giant quilted potholder.

I got back in the driver's seat. Fiora didn't object. When I pulled onto the ramp leading to eastbound I-40, she ran the back of her seat down and spread the wool blanket across her lap. She closed her eyes and turned her face to the door before I could ask her a question. Not that I knew what question I was going to ask her.

Like hell I didn't know.

The realization of how much I wanted Fiora galled me. I moved the radio dial around until I found a Gallup station playing an hour-long tribute to Charley Pride. Fiora doesn't care much for Charley Pride. She thinks he's a bigot. In addition, she thinks almost all country-western singers are idiots who blow it through their noses and points farther south.

But she was asleep, right?

Besides, this Charley Pride festival was unique. It had educational value. Gallup is Indian territory, the only place in the world where you can hear a black man singing cowboy songs paid for by used car sales pitches rendered in the most dissonant and atonal language ever invented—Navajo.

If Fiora wanted to pretend she was asleep rather than talk to me, she could pretend not to hear country music while she pretended to sleep.

Her nerves were better than mine. She lay there patiently feigning sleep until Charley's Greatest Hits wound down to "Is Anybody Goin' to San Antone?'' That was one more than the limit, even for me. I reached over and punched a button at random and hit KOA, Denver. It was clear, so I left the tuner alone.

"Why give up just when ol' Charley was hitting his nadir?'' Fiora asked in a voice as astringent as the pickleweed that lined the roadside ditches.

"You're welcome. All you had to do was ask and I would have put you out of your misery sooner.''

"But you thought I was asleep, right?''

The sardonic yet somehow amused tone of Fiora's voice made me laugh against my will. I caught myself just before I reached out to touch her knee in a gesture of affection I'd used so often with her that it had become a reflex.

"This is the voice of the Rocky Mountain West, where the time is eleven p.m. Here's the latest news from the wires of the Associated Press. Authorities in Southern California have launched a nationwide search for the thieves who stole a Georgia O'Keeffe painting worth nearly four million dollars.''

Fiora straightened and turned up the volume.

"The painting, a newly discovered canvas known as Private Skull, *apparently was stolen in transit from Santa Fe, New Mexico, to Newport Beach, California, where it was to become part of a museum collection of southwestern art. Lieutenant Bob Keene is with the Newport Beach police department—''*

The report switched to a sound bite from what probably had been a press conference. Newport Beach is very publicity conscious. Their public affairs spokesman sounded more professional than most anchormen.

"We have a number of people to interview, both here and in New Mexico. We certainly can't rule out the possibility that it was an inside job."

The report cut back to the KOA newsman.

"The painting had been purchased this week by a Newport Beach businessman for four million dollars. And now, in local news, two men were killed following an accident in which—"

I turned the radio off. Lillian Bradley's body hadn't been found, or else her death hadn't been connected to the O'Keeffe. Either way, we were still ahead of the cops.

"Who's going to stand the loss on the painting?" I asked. "Nickelaw or Valenti?"

"Neither. It was insured." Without missing a beat Fiora asked, "Do you know where Maggie Tenorio is?"

"I know where to start looking for her, but I wish the theft story hadn't gone national so fast. Now that the word is out, she's going to be harder to find."

"Particularly if she stole the thing herself."

"What about Nickelaw and Valenti?" I asked, ignoring Fiora's remark about Maggie. I was after information, not opinions.

"Last I heard they both were sitting tight, waiting for the phone to ring."

"Ransom?"

Fiora nodded. "That's logical in a theft like this. A unique piece of art can't be peddled at your friendly neighborhood swap meet."

I made a skeptical sound.

"Where else could a thief get anything like the painting's true value?" Fiora demanded.

I shot her the kind of look she hates and said, "Harvey had the right idea when he asked you to shake down your client list for potential buyers of hot art."

"Are you suggesting that any of my clients would buy a painting if they knew it was stolen?"

"Yes."

Fiora drummed her fingers irritably on the cellular phone console between us.

"Dammit, Fiddler, where are your much-vaunted powers of detection? Are you so blinded by a sloe-eyed exotic that you can't see that Maggie Tenorio is the only one who had a reason, as well as the opportunity and the means, to steal the O'Keeffe? Why would Roger steal the painting? Or that odious schlep Nickelaw, for that matter. He can only sell the painting once."

I didn't have an answer for Fiora, because she was probably right. I'd been looking at the same facts myself. Given what we knew, Maggie probably had stolen the painting herself, and in doing so had triggered her lover's suicide. Or murder. There was always that, as ugly as the pattern made by a high-caliber bullet going through the palate into the brain and then out again, taking everything with it, memories and pain and life itself.

The next two hours were both too long and too short, but they passed just like time always does. As I pulled into the outskirts of Santa Fe I checked my watch. The trip had taken just over eleven hours.

All that was left was to see if Maggie was at home and, if so, how long she had been there.

I hoped that Maggie's arrival matched the airline ticket schedule in the dead professor's date book, because then Bradley could not have died at Maggie's hand.

tWENTY-FIVE

Maggie's neighborhood in Santa Fe was deserted. There was a faint area of illumination in the house next door, probably a night-light, but Maggie's place was dark and looked as though it was locked up tight. She could have been home in bed or she could have been a thousand miles away. Considering the arsenal she kept on hand, I wasn't looking forward to sneaking in and finding out which.

I pointed out the house for Fiora, then pulled back out of the little neighborhood onto Cerrillos Road. The Quality Inn down the street does lots of weekend ski business, but the VACANCY sign was lit as we turned into the parking lot. The air was cold and still, like an unsheathed knife against your throat. Except for the bright white lights on the self-serve islands of the Mobil minimarket across the street, Santa Fe was an empty stage set waiting for the cast to arrive. A city patrol car cruised past slowly. It paid us no attention.

Fiora got out of the car with me and stretched sleepily. She had been awake but silent since we heard the news on the radio. She drew a deep breath of the cold air and shivered as I opened the door of the lobby.

There were two desk clerks behind the counter. One was a Latina, slender and fashionably dressed in a wool sweater and slacks. She stood behind the registration counter, logging some kind of daily statistics on a clipboard. The other clerk was a young Anglo with dark circles who sat at the desk pondering an organic chemistry text.

"May I help you, sir?" asked the Latina with a smile far too bright for the middle of the night.

"I need a room, third or fourth floor, south side of the building toward the back."

The clerk checked the floor plan. "The only thing we have in that location is a single room, one king-size bed."

"Sold." I started filling out the registration card.

Fiora gave me a sideways look, but she didn't say anything as she turned and walked back toward the lobby entrance. By the time the clerk had taken an imprint of my credit card, Fiora had the car idling. I got into the passenger side and pointed in the direction of our room.

"You want me to take the first watch?" she asked.

Her voice was calm, almost casual. Maybe some of the implications of sharing a bedroom with me simply hadn't occurred to Fiora. I wish to hell they hadn't occurred to me.

Fiora parked the car head in. We took what we needed and rode the outside elevator to the third floor. Room 324 was halfway down the hall on the street side. The light switch was just inside the door. When Fiora reached to turn on the light, I put my hand over hers. Her fingers were cold.

"No light," I said. "I don't want anyone out there to know we're here."

Using the hall light for illumination, I crossed the room to pull open the curtains and the heavy blackout drapes. The moon and the city lights flooded in, strong enough to throw shadows but too dim to define colors. As I handed Fiora the field glasses, I pointed out the lights of Maggie's street two blocks away. Fiora located the house without difficulty. I went to the room's climate-control unit and punched buttons until the fan began drawing outside air into the room.

"Cold air will keep you awake," I said. "I'm walking. Unless I'm sloppy, you won't see me. But if a squad car shows up looking like he's on a burglary call, give me a jingle."

Fiora had plenty of time to object while I wrote Maggie's number on the motel note pad beside the phone. There were no objections made, no questions asked, nothing but Fiora watching me with her eyes wide and much too dark against the pallor of her face. As I closed the door behind my back, I wondered what her dreams had been like lately, if they had included me, and if they had made her twist and cry out in her sleep.

Not the most comforting kind of thoughts to have while sneaking through cold streets in the dark to-

ward a house with Mace on the bedside table, a
loaded shotgun underneath the bed, and probably a
hunting knife under the pillow for good measure.

I hopped the wall behind Maggie's house and listened at the back door for a full minute. The interior
sounded dead. The windowpanes in the bedroom
were icy to the touch, as though the furnace had
been off all night or longer. I slid the blade of the
screwdriver from the 750iL's tool kit between the
jamb and the back door. The wood was dry and well
seasoned. When I leaned on the blade, the wood
gave a short sharp yap, like a small dog that had
been stepped on. The latch dropped onto the floor
inside. The door swung open. No sounds came from
the house.

I stood in the doorway, listening again to make
sure I was alone. As I stepped into the kitchen, my
foot tapped the remnants of the broken latch. Its
presence bothered me but I didn't know why. In the
next moment it came to me. The back door had
been locked securely the night Maggie's place was
trashed. I knew because I had checked it. The front
door had been intact, too. Same for all the windows
—which meant that whoever had done the trashing
had either picked locks or had access to a key. If it
were the latter, Maggie probably knew who had
been painting on her easel.

I made a mental note to ask her just as soon as I
got my hands on her graceful throat.

The air in the kitchen was cold and stale, as
though the place had been closed up for some time.
There was the faint, sharp odor of an art studio and

a vague smell of garbage, but that was all. No smokeless powder, no death.

I flashed a shielded light around the kitchen. The mess from the previous intruder hadn't been touched. The soup that had been splattered about was frozen in odd places. I passed down a short hallway into the sleeping area. Still trashed. It was the same in the living room studio. No one had come by to clean up the debris. The broken oil-encrusted palette flashed a rainbow of impossible color combinations back at the light. The canvas lay where it had fallen, its message still intact. Furniture was still overturned. The slashed couch cushions still lay where they had been thrown.

If Maggie had been here since I took her to Palm Springs, she had left no more sign of that visit than I was going to leave now.

I shut off the flashlight and let myself out the back door. I didn't see anyone until I stopped at the Mobil minimarket across from the hotel. Five minutes after that, I knocked quietly on the door of Room 324 with two big paper sacks in my hands. Fiora let me into the darkened room and closed the door behind me.

"Room service," I said, moving the binoculars aside so that I could set the sacks on the table in front of the window. One of the two Naugahyde easy chairs had been turned around to face the view. The room was nearly as cold as Maggie's house had been.

"Anything?" Fiora asked as she turned the other chair around and sat down.

She looked cold even though she still was wearing her down jacket.

"I don't think Maggie has been to the house. But I have a hunch she's nearby. Nickelaw and Harvey are both in Southern California, beating the bushes for her. She's running scared, and this is the land she knows best. She'll go to ground here."

"You sound like you know her . . . well."

I shrugged. "You want hamburgers or hot dogs?"

Fiora didn't want either but she drank her coffee with three sugars. I ate from the paper bags I'd bought at the minimarket. After a few tries I prodded Fiora into taking some more chocolate. I was worried about her energy level in the cold. Small things lose heat more quickly, and she was a hell of a lot smaller than I was—and I was cold.

We sat back from the window, watching the night outside like a big-screen Sony. After fifteen minutes Fiora yawned. Ten minutes later she yawned again.

"Go to bed," I suggested. "I'll let you know if anything happens."

She shook her head and rubbed her hands together to warm them. A minute later she yawned again.

"Dammit, go to bed. You keep yawning like that and you'll start me doing it."

Without a word Fiora got up. A few moments later the bathroom fan revved up, adding its noise to the sound of the wall fan. I couldn't imagine why she wanted both of them on, but I didn't say anything.

I watched Maggie's dark house through the binoculars. Despite the fans, I thought I heard the soft,

intimate, familiar sound of Fiora stripping the cover-
let back and crawling under the blankets. It made
me wonder if she was still wearing her clothes or if
she had picked up a nightgown during her lightning
raid on the shopping mall.

For a while I tolerated the noise of both fans, then
decided that the room was cold enough and turned
the wall unit off. Beneath the mindless hum of the
bathroom fan, I heard what sounded like a frag-
mented sigh, followed by a strained noise, as though
Fiora were trying to cover the sounds of her shivering. It wouldn't have surprised me. She always got
chilled 15 degrees before I did. Not only that, she
was trying to warm up a huge icy bed.

The glasses made a small thump as I set them on
the table. I went to the unoccupied half of the king-
size bed, picked up the surplus of coverings, and
folded them back over Fiora. Then I reached for the
heat switch on the wall unit.

"Don't," Fiora said in a strained voice. "You'll fall
asleep if it's warm."

From the sound of it, she was gritting her teeth to
keep them from chattering. When I bent over her
side of the bed I sensed that she was shivering un-
controllably.

"I'll be okay—in a minute," Fiora said.

"In a minute you'll be a Scots popsicle," I muttered, reaching for the climate-control unit again.

Her hand came out quickly from beneath the covers and caught my wrist. Her fingers were cold. Despite that, they felt familiar, wonderful, electric.

"It's all right," she said. "It just took a few minutes for the sheets to thaw out. I'll be fine now."

But Fiora didn't loosen her grip on my wrist. I put my hand over her fingers, rubbing gently, warming her skin.

The silence became a living, prowling thing.

"When did you start listening to the violin again?" Fiora asked quickly, as though she too sensed danger in the restless silence.

"A while back."

My answer was absent, for I was absorbed in rubbing the sensitive center of my palm over the back of her hand, her forearm, her upper arm. Her skin was cool and smooth, drawn taut by health and life. The feel of her fascinated me. I ran my fingertips from the rapid pulse in her wrist to the sensitive crease of her inner arm. When I smoothed my palm over her arm again, the skin was roughened by gooseflesh.

It wasn't cold that had drawn that primitive reflex from Fiora; it was the same passion that made my body grow heavier with each breath, giving me the feeling that gravity had just doubled. I couldn't have moved if I had wanted to—and I didn't want to.

"Maggie reminds me of myself, when I both loved and hated the violin," I said, pursuing both the subject Fiora had introduced and the living warmth of her arm. "As Nickelaw put it, she's a good artist in a world where good is another word for second-rate."

"Maggie paints?" Fiora asked with an odd catch in her voice.

"Yes. She loves it. She's a good painter, but not perfect. Not even great. She knows it. It sits in her gut like acid."

Fiora breathed a ragged sigh whose dying warmth

flowed over my hand. "It's . . . destructive . . . to fight something you love simply because you can't do it perfectly. Nothing human is perfect. Not even love."

"I know. I just don't know what the hell to do about it."

For a time the room was so still that I could hear the soft, fluttering sound of my quartz watch and the intimate whisper of skin over skin as I stroked my palm over Fiora's arm.

"Is that why you don't want to believe Maggie is a crook?" Fiora asked softly. "Because she reminds you of yourself?"

"I suppose."

I picked up the hand I'd been warming and tasted the center of the palm. Fiora shivered. The tremor passed from her body through her hand to me.

"Maggie likes women better than men, but even before I knew that, I knew I wouldn't end up in her bed." I brushed my beard over Fiora's palm for a few moments before I continued. "No matter how angry I am with you, every time I look at a woman, I'm looking for you. It's been like that before when we've been apart, but it always passed after four or five weeks. Not this time. It just got worse. None of the women were you."

I closed my eyes, knowing I was holding Fiora's hand too hard and unable to do a damn thing about it. Running from the truth hadn't helped. Maybe honesty would. "So when you find a way to fall out of love, let me know. It's a secret I'd kill for."

Fiora whispered my name and then her arms were around me, holding me with the fierce strength that always surprises me in a person half my weight. I held her in return and began to understand how much of myself I'd been living without. The realization would have been frightening if I were still alone, but I wasn't.

After a long time Fiora stirred, put her hands on either side of my face, and looked at me. Just looked at me.

"As long as you don't have the secret of falling out of love," she said, "I don't want it."

Her hair felt like cool satin against my hand. She was wearing a flannel shirt that went the length of her elegant back and vanished into the waistband of her jeans. Her face was pale, her hair bright, her eyes half closed in pleasure as I ran my fingertips from her earlobes and along her jawline and then down her throat to the barrier of the shirt's first button. I stopped there and looked back at her eyes.

"I thought you'd never ask," she whispered.

A shrug of her shoulders helped me slip the unbuttoned shirt over her head, but before the sleeves reached her elbows, she was kissing my cheek above the beard. Her lips were full and soft and resilient. Her breath was warm on the patch of skin behind my ear. She tried to put her arms around my neck, only to find that she was imprisoned by the half-removed shirt. I could have helped her, but I had found other flesh that was full and soft and resilient, and it felt too good for me to stop. The hard rise of her nipples against my hands told me she didn't want me to stop either.

Finally Fiora managed to unbutton the cuffs and throw aside the shirt. Her breath caught when my hands slid inside her unfastened jeans. Long fingers are a distinct advantage at times. I used every bit of that advantage, teasing both of us in the process. When I could take no more, I peeled away our clothes and slid between the sheets. They must have been cold, but I didn't notice. Fiora tasted of coffee and bittersweet chocolate, and she fit me even better than my memories.

When we couldn't get any closer, I forced myself to stop. I wanted one answer from Fiora, and I wanted it from the elemental, fey level of her mind, not from the businesslike top.

"Fiddler?" she asked, moving against me until I pinned her in place with my greater weight.

"Not yet, love. Why did you plant the lemon tree?"

"To remind you of me," Fiora said without hesitation, locking her legs around my hips. "Of us. Of this."

I looked at the radiant tumble of her hair against the pillow and the dark mystery of her eyes. She had never been more beautiful to me. I tried to say something but it was too late; it had been too long; control was slipping away from me.

It had been just as long for her. She twisted and reached up for me even as I came to her. My last coherent thought was that her mouth tasted not of chocolate but of lemonade, tart and sweet, focusing me in the wild instant when there was one of us, not two.

tWENTY-SIX

"**I** told you we needed two beds," Fiora said.

She was sitting next to me in front of the window, curled up in the cocoon of a king-size blanket and nothing else. I had on my down vest and jeans, period.

"The other side of the bed is still dry," I said, putting down the glasses and glancing at her.

She smiled an intimate, remembering kind of smile that made gravity slide down to the heavy end of the scale.

"I'll stay up for a while anyway," she said, stretching, then shivering and pulling her bare arms out of sight once more. She looked at me and smiled. "I like the view."

"Yeah, cities are pretty at night, aren't they?"

Fiora shifted the blanket and aimed a lazy overhand right at my head, giving me plenty of time to catch her fist and hold it against my thigh while I used the binoculars on the view. Her fingers flexed and burrowed closer to my body.

"How do you stay so warm?" she asked.

I lowered the glasses and gave her a sideways look of disbelief. She laughed at me and flexed her fingers again.

"I was distracted from my post in a moment of weakness," I said, lacing my fingers through hers. "It won't happen again."

"What a pity." She sighed and added, "You didn't seem weak to me. Not until the third time, anyway."

"You complaining?"

Fiora smiled and shook her head emphatically. "Only a fool would complain about something that feels that good and goes on for twenty minutes."

I laughed silently and hugged her close, knowing that the moment couldn't last. Nothing had been settled, not really, which meant that the war wasn't over; and that made the feeling of peace right now all the more intense. Holding your breath in the middle of a relationship can be maddening, but that kind of sweet tension has its reward—a love affair that's new enough to be compelling and old enough to be perfectly choreographed.

"I wonder if Perlman ever gets tired of playing Beethoven's violin concerto," I said. "Does familiarity make him lose concentration?"

"Asks the bloodhound who's never been distracted from the scent," Fiora muttered. "Well, almost never."

I lifted her hand and kissed the knuckles, then

tucked the cool fingers inside my vest. "I'm serious."

Fiora said something that was lost against my neck. Her free hand was inside my vest now, fingertips finding every different texture and enjoying it.

"I love to see that kind of concentration," I continued, even though she seemed to be French-braiding hairs in a line to my navel. "It's the hallmark of true intelligence. It's the thing I admire most in you." My breath sucked in hard. "Besides your body, of course."

"I always wondered which you liked better."

"That's the beauty of it. With you I'll never have to choose."

"Yes," Fiora whispered against me. "That's why we both keep coming back for more. When we're together it's the best we've ever had and we're the best we'll ever be."

"And if you keep that up, we're going to get real close, real soon."

Even as I turned to kiss Fiora, I caught a flash of movement on Maggie's street. Fiora must have seen it too. When I reached for the glasses she was already handing them to me. The white, sharky nose and the whale tail of the Dage Porsche was unmistakable, even in moonlight.

"What kept you so long?" I muttered as the car slid to a stop at the curb in front of Maggie's little adobe house.

"Is it Maggie?" whispered Fiora.

"I can't tell."

The driver killed the lights, opened the car door, and stepped out into the night. I twisted the fine focus on the eyepiece, trying to clarify the view, but the driver was already gone. It could have been Maggie.

In winter clothing, it also could have been a hitchhiker from Mars.

The figure crossed the sidewalk and was swallowed up by the shadows of the porch. A moment later light flared behind the blinds in the living room. Either it was Maggie, or the same intruder who had trashed the place, or Maggie had loaned out a great many keys.

Fiora threw me my shirt and started pulling on her own clothes. By the time she stamped into her boots I was already fully dressed and grabbing what little gear we had. A minute later I was throwing stuff in the car. I went around to the trunk and popped the latch. The Germans are such relentlessly logical designers; it took me less than ten seconds to find and disconnect the wiring harness on the taillights. The engine fired up instantly. With a motion that had become almost habitual, I locked the transmission in SPORT.

The front passenger door opened and shut quickly as Fiora threw herself into the car and rammed home the seatbelt latch.

"The lights in the house went off about twenty seconds ago," she said.

I pulled the shifter into drive and rolled across the frosty parking lot without lights. I nosed past a concrete wall until I could see Maggie's street. Engine idling, we waited. Ten seconds later the long, swoopy nose of the Porsche appeared, sporting bright white headlamps and fog lights and orange fender lights. The car turned north, away from us.

After a few moments I turned on my own headlights and rolled out onto Cerrillos Road. The Porsche was five blocks ahead. On deserted streets in the middle of the night, that was as close as we needed to be. As I followed the Dage, I whistled a few bars of Vivaldi's "Summer" over and over.

"You want real music?" Fiora asked.

"That was real music."

The red eyestalk light on the whale tail was a perfect tracking mark. Combined with the wraparound strip of Porsche taillights, there wasn't another light profile like it in New Mexico. The driver bore left on St. Francis and pushed on through town, across the river and up onto the highway toward Taos.

Out on the four-lane highway I laid back two miles, letting the rolling landscape cover us. The Dage moved erratically, pushing ahead, then falling back, then picking up again. But the variations in speed were those of a tired driver, not of someone trying to expose a surveillance. I held the 750 to a steady 80 and waited. There was very little traffic around, but I hid in it when I could. From time to time I changed my profile—low beams, high beams, right lane and left, just to vary the look in the Porsche's rearview mirror. Fiora sat quietly with the glasses on her lap, watching the night.

Pojoaque flashed by, dark except for the Coors and Bud logos behind the wrought-iron window grills of the liquor store and taverns. I wasn't worried about speed traps: the Porsche was going to trigger any state-trooper land mines long before I would. A few miles south of Española, I pushed up a little closer, cutting the interval to a half mile.

"I can read the license plate," Fiora warned, staring through the glasses.

"No help for it. We're coming up on a choice. Left for the Chama River Valley, straight ahead for the Upper Rio Grande Valley, hard right for the High Road to Taos."

"Any guesses?"

"I'm not guessing any more. I've been wrong about too many things."

The leafless cottonwoods at the river junction shone like polished sterling in the moonlight. A Conoco station on the left was open, and three cross-country livestock rigs were parked in front of a coffee shop on the right. A plastic steer surveyed the roadway from atop the flat roof of a feed store.

Halfway through the long strip development that passed for a town, the Porsche turned right onto New Mexico 76 and disappeared into the night. I slowed and let it go. Then I killed the headlights and made the same right turn onto the two-lane road. The sensation was wonderful, like becoming invisible between one breath and the next. The BMW flowed along the deserted blacktop like a drop of mercury going downhill, silvery and silent in the moonlit night.

Fiora didn't say a word, even though we were suddenly without headlights, rocketing down a frosty, twisting, unlighted two-lane country road at 80 miles an hour in her new $70,000 car. Three quarters of a mile ahead, the Porsche bored on into the night. The car was the only spot of light on the whole landscape.

"You watch the road," Fiora said. "I'll watch the Porsche."

"Tell me if I get too close."

I pulled the shifter down to slow the BMW, third, second, then up to third again, like the Cobra without the clutch. The transmission was smooth, fast, solid, responsive. It was like somebody had reinvented driving.

"How close is too close?" Fiora asked.

"Half a mile," I said, braking hard for a sudden sharp right-hand bend, where the road dropped down into a dry ravine and popped up the other bank. "The silver finish on this car doesn't stand out, even in moonlight. But we're going up the hill. I don't want to be spotted on the switchbacks."

Fiora knows when to be quiet. Nothing else competed for my attention when the BMW started the climb up from Santa Cruz. The V-12 gave a low, contented growl when I punched the accelerator on the hundred-yard straightaways, and the brakes bit securely when I overreached myself at the end. The cottonwoods along the little creeks threw deep shadows. The High Road hasn't been reengineered since the sixteenth century, but the Germans had pushed traction control into the twenty-first century. I drove the car harder than I should have, but it seemed impossible to spin the fat Michelins on acceleration or to lock them up on heavy braking.

When the chips are down, Fiora doesn't whimper. It's one of the things I love best about her. She sat in the passenger seat, acting as though we were travel-

ing the Harbor Freeway on a Saturday morning.
Trees whipped past in a blur. She said nothing. She
didn't even move her feet on the floor mat when
she thought I ought to brake. She didn't flinch
when I snapped the shifter up and down the scale
and the needle teleported to the red line. She just
sat in the big leather chair and watched the moving
pool of light that was the Porsche.

The road abandoned the river valley and began to
climb up the shoulder of the Sangre de Cristos,
heading back toward the place where I had run over
the broken wine bottle and been drawn into Nickel-
law's gallery by a black stone bear. Life curves and
recurves, a tight spiral going up and up while twisting back on itself, skimming over all the old ground
yet never touching down in exactly the same place
twice. Turn and turn and turn, each vista new and
déjà vu at the same instant.

As we went deeper into the mountains, the modern world became little more than a rumor. The
half-acre private graveyards beside the road were inhabited by arcane, idiosyncratic crosses and handmade flowers glistening in the cold moonlight.
There were very small, pitched-roof adobe houses
set back only a few feet from the pavement, relics of
the days when wagon traffic was the rule. There
were tiny settlements, each with its own small,
thick-walled adobe church, the doors and gates
locked against the inexorable forces of the modern
world.

We flashed into Truchas and made a hard left just
past a little general store. The moonlight caught a
hand-painted sign in front: INDIAN JOYERIA, MILAGROS,

BACK-HOE WORK. WE ACCEPT FOOD STAMPS. The BMW flew past and on up the hill. I gave myself to the rhythms of the road and the chase—second, third, second, and brake, around the curve and on up the hill, second, third, second, and brake for another curve, climbing, climbing, climbing into the night.

There must have been a seep hidden on the uphill side of the highway. I had a second's warning when I saw the glitter of fresh water at the edge of the pavement. The temperature was so cold that the flowing water turned to black ice a few yards beyond the seep. One instant the 750 was rocketing down a short straightaway, setting up for a right-hand uphill bend; the next instant we were skating on a sheet of ice two hundred feet long and the car's tail end was starting to snake around to the left because I had already set up for the curve.

The slide registered in the seat of my pants before my hands picked it up in the steering wheel, but it was already too late. When I steered a few degrees right, the back end came around a little farther, inching toward disaster. All of the big car's computer-brain sophistication and V-12 power were useless because there was nothing for the tires to grab.

I could see that the ice slick ended with the straightaway. Until the tires hit dry pavement, there was nothing to do but hang tough and hope the car still had a semblance of a line for the curve at the other end. I kept a little power going to the back tires. From the corner of my eye I watched the outside radius of the curve come at me like the background on a video game, everything whipping by too fast. When the slick ended, I tapped the throttle.

The tail was already too far around. The tires bit but didn't immediately hold. It was too late for brakes. I cranked more wheel against the skid and fed gas and prayed. The Michelins thought about spinning; then the electronic brain cut the power until it matched the traction. I was already correcting the other way. We shot through the curve like we were on tracks.

"You bought a nice car."

"Benny thought you would like it."

We wailed up the road, chasing a speeding white ghost. The next corner was rough, potholes in the pavement, but the 750 took it, flattened it out, and sped on.

"Scared?" I asked.

"Should I be?"

"I was, on that ice."

"Yeah. That's why you were smiling."

"The light's bad. That was a grimace of fear."

Fiora laughed.

The Porsche had the advantage of lights, and perhaps the advantage of knowing the road. Even so, the driver was playing over his—or her—head, speeding in the wrong places and jamming on brakes well into a curve. I had to be careful not to get too close. Off toward the east, the night had just begun to fade toward dawn. In half an hour we'd be visible even without headlights or brake lights.

We raced through another little village, made a hard left, then a hard right a few miles later. Scattered lights burned in barns and outbuildings. Other than that, the only sign of life was a big dark dog that got up from his bed on the doorstep of a mobile home to watch us go past. Highway 76 made a tight left at Penasco. I looked ahead, trying to find the lights of the Porsche.

"It made a turn about a half mile farther on," Fiora said.

We were on a flat bench of farmland and pasture. Finally there was a straight piece of road ahead. I nailed the accelerator and the V-12 growled with pleasure. The speedometer console was dark, but as we passed under an overhead light at the edge of the village I could see the needle touching 110. There was a lot of accelerator left but no sane reason to use it.

Ahead of us the Porsche's headlights popped up on the far side of an arroyo. We were much too close. I braked just as the road pitched over the edge of the bench and started downhill. Immediately I saw why the Porsche had lost speed. A half dozen range cows were milling around in the middle of the road, their eyes glowing with moonlight.

The BMW was among the cows before they could react, which was fine, because range animals have a tendency to do exactly the wrong thing at the worst possible moment. I whipped the big car over to the left lane of the road and then some, keeping only the right-hand wheels on the pavement. I didn't see the paddle marker on the left shoulder until too late, but even if I had seen it, I'd have taken the same line. A small piece of sheet metal is preferable to a thousand pounds of beef.

There was a crack and thump and glass breaking

as the paddle marker disappeared; then we were through the cows and back on our own side of the road. None of the idiot lights on the dash came on, so I nailed the accelerator and kept going.

"Sorry," I said.

"I'd forgotten how big cows are," was all Fiora said.

The road shot up the other side of the arroyo and climbed into the trees—pines, not cottonwoods, and the snow was deeper beside the road, clean and blue-white in the moonlight, chalk-white in the shadows. I caught a flicker of movement in a road cut as a shadow leaped up the bank and disappeared, a cat of some kind, bobcat or cougar.

I remembered this stretch of road. There was a long straight run for a mile, then the highway pitched over the divide and down into the next valley. The surface was icy in spots. I held the shifter in third and tiptoed as fast as I could. As long as the road was straight, I was okay, but I could see only a hundred yards ahead. You can live at the edge of your vision like that for a long time, but the monochrome of moonlight deprives you of the color cues that give you depth perception. It's dangerous and exhilarating as hell.

"You really like this," Fiora said.

There was no point in denying it. I had learned long ago that adrenaline was my drug of choice.

"What about you?" I asked.

There was silence, then a long sigh.

"Oh, I can see the attraction," she admitted as the night divided around us and whipped past in black and silver array. "But I can get the same high from picking up the pattern in a stock-market scam, and I don't run the risk of ending up DOA with a herd of cows. Most people would think you were crazy to be doing this and I was crazy to be with you."

"I don't give a damn what most people think. Just a few."

"I don't think you're crazy," Fiora said. Her fingertip went lightly over the back of my hand, and she smiled. "Maddening, sexy, sometimes unnerving . . . but not crazy."

The straightaway ended before I could answer. I lifted my foot and shifted down twice in rapid succession. The V-12 made a sound like a happy cougar, gripped the road with tangible strength, and whipped through the black curve.

tWENTY-SEVEN

Though the sky still held the full darkness before the dawn, lights shone in several of the houses, reminding me of my childhood in a place not unlike this, where farmers got up well before sunrise to do stock chores and their wives pulled on overshoes and heavy coats and drove down the hill for the early shift in small cafés along the interstate.

"Traffic will start picking up now," I said, thinking aloud. "Hope to hell that Porsche roosts pretty soon. I don't want to tangle with a lot of sleepy civilians."

The road twisted down from the heights before it crossed a small valley and started back up the other side. Along the length of the valley, farmhouses were laid out randomly beside small flat meadows. Fields of weathered cornstalks poked up through the snow. We flashed past a stand of a dozen mailboxes at an intersection and then, a half mile farther, another cluster of a dozen more.

Fiora lifted the glasses to her eyes and studied the taillights ahead of us on the road across the little valley.

"Fiddler."

My foot was coming off the accelerator even before before Fiora spoke. The pattern of the taillights ahead was wrong.

"That's not the Porsche," she said. "It's a pickup with a light on the tailgate."

I was already braking.

"I'm sorry," she said. "I shouldn't have taken my eyes off the lights."

"Forget it. I lost him too. When was the last time you were sure of the Porsche?"

"Just after you missed the cows. The Porsche was climbing the hill opposite us. The pattern of the taillights was very clear."

"Then he has to be in somewhere in this valley." I braked to a stop in the middle of the highway. "There aren't that many roads."

I ran my side window down and shut off the engine. The pickup truck rattled up the rise ahead of us and vanished, taking the noise and leaving silence behind. There was no ripping-canvas turbo sound, no rumbling Porsche exhaust, nothing but moonlight, darkness, and cold. The Porsche had gone to ground.

I thought of the houses scattered behind me. Button, button, who's got the button?

A few seconds later we were headed back up the hill. I found a place that looked out over the entire valley. There were at least fifty houses scattered in clumps along the meandering river course. I got out and used the glasses on each patch of light. Dawn was coming on from the east, giving a bit of definition to the working ranches and new weekend homes along the river. The cottages had a gentrified look about them. I concentrated my search there, seeking the shape of a Dage Porsche.

As I skimmed over the landscape with the binoculars, there was a ghostly stirring beneath my conscious mind, a sense of having missed something. I put down the glasses and let my eyes not quite focus on the scene in front of me. Abruptly I realized that I had seen this landscape on television just before some clever technician had made the picture dissolve into O'Keeffe's *Private Skull*.

Fiora came out and stood next to me, shivering in the cold air. "Do you know where we are?"

"Close to Las Trampas. Come on."

I hurried her into the car. A few moments later we had turned around and were racing back down the hill.

"What are we looking for?" Fiora asked.

"A country house. It's a renovated adobe with a flat roof and a low wall around the front courtyard. There's a dry fountain with blue and white tiles in it."

"When were you there?"

"I wasn't. I saw it on television. Look for the name Quinones on the mailbox, or Tenorio. Hell, even Nickelaw."

I slowed for the line of mailboxes on a fence where the main road passed a side road. Without turning on the headlights I couldn't read the names. I stopped and got out. The glove-box flashlight picked out the word "Quinones" on the second mailbox from the end of the row.

The renovated adobe was a mile off the main road, isolated at the end of a little loop. I let the car idle along almost silently until we rounded a curve and saw the white Porsche tucked out of the way behind a big rock. I parked behind it.

"Do you have the Beretta?" I asked.

"Yes."

"If anyone comes out of that house but me, get the hell out of here."

The air was as still and dry as crystal. Frozen gravel crunched softly beneath my boots, but I wasn't worried about giving away my presence with such small sounds. From the house came the mournful cry of a Spanish ballad, the same notes over and over, a phonograph needle caught in a deep groove and left to repeat the same meaningless loop of music.

When I was twenty feet from the house I pulled out the D-Mag, noticing again the unexpected heaviness of the big gun. The courtyard wall was an easy one-handed vault. The dry fountain was right where I had expected it, in the center of shining tiles. I kept the thick fountain between myself and the front door. There was no sound but that of the trapped needle mindlessly gouging notes out of plastic.

At the corner of the house was a window with the curtains only partly drawn. I walked to one side of the bar of yellow light, then grabbed a fast look. The interior room was a cross between a stylish gallery and an artist's studio. Large, paint-stained, open, the room had no places for concealment. In the far corner, two easels stood with their backs to the room beneath a hard spotlight. On a rolling table between them were oil paints, brushes, and cleaning materials.

The walls were hung with Maggie's landscapes. The paintings reminded me of her—strong, ambitious, oddly compelling in their imperfections. The paintings were separated and accentuated by Navajo weavings and chile *ristras*. A huge bleached horse skull dominated the wall above the fireplace. The rest of the place was done in Santa Fe style, but it was comfortable rather than artful. In the fireplace piñon logs had burned down to silver-orange embers and almost invisibly fine gray ash.

Maggie Tenorio stood in front of the fire, her hands shoved deep into the slash pockets of a long wool skirt. I wondered if one of those fists was closed around a knife. It wouldn't have surprised me. She was arguing fiercely with someone I couldn't see.

I slid away from the window and moved to the big iron-bound front door. The latch was well oiled, making no sound when I lifted it and slowly pushed the heavy door open. The house was warm. The air smelled faintly of wood smoke. The tile floor of the entryway was covered with Navajo wool rugs. I moved toward the sounds of the two voices.

"What is it? You want more money?"

It took me a moment to recognize the breathy voice because I had heard Nickelaw's blond girlfriend speak only once before.

"No, I don't want more money," Maggie replied.

Her voice was tense, angry. "There was a time when I did. God knows I've gotten sick of watching Olin make himself rich off artists he bought for a penny on the dollar. But I'm past that point. Now I just want out."

"Don't want to play any more, huh? You always did quit just when it started getting fun. Didn't the reservation teach you anything? It always hurts the first time, but after that it feels pretty good. At least it quits hurting, and it gives you a lot of power. But then, you wouldn't know about that kind of power, unless your dyke lover is more of a man than I think."

It wasn't Vikki's words so much as her tone—flat and husky at the same time—that made the hair on the back of my arms prickle uneasily. There was a something just beneath the surface of her words, something ugly that cut through civilized consciousness and screamed danger to the reptilian brain beneath.

"Lillian is a good person," Maggie said, her voice resonant with anger. "She's shown me more kindness than anybody else in this shitty world. That's why I took the painting. I didn't want to see her hurt. She deserves better than that."

"Too bad," Vikki said carelessly. "She found out anyway. Know something else? Being set up by you hurt her even more than you thought it would."

The pleasure in Vikki's voice was almost sexual. I remembered her empty eyes and slick smile when she had handled the D-Mag. She liked guns, but she liked pain even better. Other people's pain.

Pressing against the wall beside the doorway into

the studio, I slipped forward another few inches. I could see Maggie's indistinct reflection in the window and, beside her, the flickering image of the fire. I eased forward another inch. Now I could see the edge of Vikki's white coat. No opening, just seamless white, which told me that she was facing in the other direction, toward Maggie. I slid forward a bit more.

Vikki didn't quite have her back to me. She was partially turned in a way which let me see the blue-steel shine of the revolver in her hand. It was pointed at Maggie's stomach.

"What are you saying?" Maggie demanded. "Did you tell Lillian about the painting?"

"Yeah."

"You fool! Lillian's not like us. She'll never be able to keep a secret like that! Why did you tell her?"

"She wouldn't tell me where you were. But after I told her what you'd done . . ." Vikki laughed, then said savagely, "Don't move. Your brains won't look any better than hers when they're splattered all over the wall."

"What?"

"She told me where you were. Then she shot herself. Don't worry about our secret. Dead dykes don't talk."

I slid forward until I could see Maggie instead of her reflection. Her hands were still thrust deeply into the pockets of her skirt as she stared in growing hatred at the blond woman in the white coat. It was the first time I had ever seen the two of them standing together. Suddenly I realized who Vikki reminded me of—Maggie. It wasn't coloring. It was the angle of cheekbones and eyes and how each woman held herself. And their hands. Most of all it was their hands. Slim, elegant, perfectly proportioned, capable of artistry or death.

Abruptly I understood how Nickelaw had come into possession of *Private Skull*.

"You never should have stopped seeing that shrink," Maggie said, her voice low and cold. "You're crazy, Victoria. Stone cold crazy."

Vikki laughed. "It's not that easy. I'm the same as you. I know what I want and I know how to get it. I want that painting."

Maggie didn't move. I took aim at Vikki but held off on the trigger. She might have been crazy but she wasn't stupid or out of control. She wasn't going to shoot until she had what she wanted—*Private Skull*.

But just in case Vikki changed her mind, I held the D-Mag steady and watched her head over the barrel, wondering whether she was wearing a blond wig now or if she had worn a dark wig for the TV crew. I could wait for the answer. Listening to this family quarrel was the closest I had come to the truth since I'd laid eyes on the black bear in a Santa Fe snowstorm.

"Come on, Maggie. You'll get your share even if Olin won't. Get the painting for me."

"No." Maggie's voice shook with the same barely controlled rage that made her dark eyes shine like black ice. "You went too far this time. You and Olin will both be in hell before I give you that canvas."

"Olin's history. He doesn't want the painting

back. All he wants is the insurance money, and he won't share it with either of us. He told me so." Vikki's body jerked slightly. "I'll bet you hid it above the *lateens*, didn't you? That's where you used to hide things you didn't want me to have. I always got them anyway."

"Get out of here, Victoria. Don't ever let me see you again. If I do, I'll break your back like I would any snake's."

Vikki's hand twitched suddenly. I wondered if she had used amphetamines to stay awake on the long drive from Palm Springs. Not a comforting thought. Crystal meth does bad things to minds. I eased forward a few inches more, making dead sure of my aim. Keeping the edge of the adobe doorframe between me and Vikki, I cocked the hammer on the D-Mag.

"Put the gun down."

Vikki spun toward me. She wasn't accustomed to targets that were also armed. She fired the first shot too fast. The bullet zipped past two feet to my right. I had plenty of cover so I held my fire.

"Drop it or die," I shouted over the report of the .38.

She heard me but she wasn't buying it. This time the shot gouged the adobe close enough to spray me with dust. Before I could flinch, other pistol shots rang out. The sounds were sharper than the .38 had made, which meant the second gun was smaller.

At least one of the four bullets hit Vikki in the back of her head, knocking her hair askew. A wig. She jerked as other bullets penetrated, but she was already falling. Out of the corner of my eye I saw her hit the tile floor in a distinctive, boneless sprawl that was a travesty of normal human grace.

I was face-to-face with Maggie. She was holding a small-caliber handgun at arm's length. She recognized me but her gun was still aimed in my direction.

And my D-Mag was aimed at her.

"Put it down, Maggie."

She stared at me another three seconds over the barrel of the little gun. "It's not what it looks like."

"It never is. The gun, Maggie. Put it down. Don't make me shoot you before you have a chance to tell me how I've got it all wrong."

Slowly she lowered her hand. When her fingers touched the folds of her skirt, she let go of the little gun. It clattered coldly on the tile.

"Fiora?" I called, knowing that the sound of shots would have brought her out of the car. "You can come in if you don't mind a corpse. Otherwise, stay put."

"I'm coming in." Her voice was tight.

I walked across the room to Maggie, bent down, and picked up her gun. The safety was still off. I set it before I dropped the piece into the pocket of my vest and turned to Maggie.

"Go stand by the fire."

Maggie reached the fireplace just as Fiora came through the front door. Her hands were rammed in the pockets of her down jacket. I had no doubt that the Beretta I had given her was in her right hand— and that this time she would remember Volker's advice: If you really want to kill someone, don't waste time pulling the gun out of your pocket.

Fiora looked at me urgently, checking for wounds. When she realized I was all right, color slowly began to return to her face. She gave Vikki a quick glance, grimaced, and looked away.

I went and sat on my heels near Vikki's head. Her beautiful face was intact, her eyes open. One was brown and one was green. The green was slightly off-center, revealing a crescent of brown iris. The other green contact lens must have been knocked loose when the bullet hit. I looked at her face more closely, seeing other faces she had worn.

"Amazing," I muttered.

She had a real flair for makeup. She must have deliberately blurred the flawless lines of her face for her television appearance as the proud Indian niece of the woman who had pulled a Georgia O'Keeffe out of a barnyard manure pile. Victoria Quinones was a second, darker incarnation of Vikki, the drop-dead blonde.

Not that it mattered any more. Brunettes died just as dead as blondes.

More out of ritual than hope, I probed the cooling skin of Vikki's neck, seeking a pulse. There wasn't any. I stood up.

"Your sister or cousin or whatever is dead."

"Half sister," Maggie said, staring into the flames, her eyes concealed by shadows.

I heard Fiora's sharp intake of breath.

"The painting," I said to Maggie. "Get it."

Maggie looked up from the fire. Without a word she walked across the room to the easels. Slowly she turned one easel so that we could see the canvas. The malevolent eyes of *Private Skull* stared out at us.

Then Maggie rotated the second easel. A second skull stared out at the room. The poppy in this one was only half complete. The second painting was signed MT. Other than those two details and the still-wet oil on the second, the paintings were identical.

I looked at Maggie. She gave me a small enigmatic smile, Mona Lisa with teeth.

"Yes. They're mine. Both of them." There was a savage kind of pride in Maggie's voice. "I stole the first one out of the shipping crate the night of the unveiling. I painted the other one today."

"Was Bradley in on it?"

"Lillian . . ." Maggie's voice cracked. She swallowed and tried again. "Lillian loved this painting. She saw the agony in the poppy and she believed in it. She saw . . . greatness."

Somewhere in the back of my mind I heard Perlman's Vivaldi. I could understand the savage love that had driven Maggie to paint *Private Skull*. I could also understand the savage hate that had driven her to paint a second skull and sign her own name to it.

"Why did you steal *Private Skull*?" I asked.

"Lillian had cancer. Inoperable. A few months, a year. No more. I was afraid she would spend all her time fighting off snipers."

"And maybe, just maybe, you were afraid that cancer wouldn't kill her soon enough," I said softly. "Maybe you were afraid that one day she would look at the painting and see you instead of Georgia O'Keeffe."

Maggie flinched. She took her hands out of her pockets, spread her fingers wide, and looked at the perfection she had never been able to transfer to canvas.

"In art, appearance is the only reality that matters," she said finally. "Lillian never believed that. But it's true."

Maggie balled her fingers, shoved her fists into her skirt pockets once more, and watched her half sister with unforgiving eyes.

tWENTY-EIGHT

I wrapped both canvases in a red and black wool blanket and put them in the trunk of the BMW. Then I put the taillights back into working order. Behind me the sun was outlining La Cueva Peak in molten gold, and the sky overhead had begun the transition from black to blue to lemon. The air was thin, cold, and still. Fiora came out of the house with Maggie, who had changed into a pair of jeans.

"Last chance, Maggie," I said. "You might have an easier time with the local sheriff if you stayed here."

She gave me a bleak sideways glance. "I'm an Indian and this is New Mexico. I'll take my chances with city cops in some other state."

I didn't push it. I had a lot more questions, not much time, and Maggie was a woman on the edge. It showed in her body language, the tiny hesitations as she chose her words, the tense flinching of her eyelids. Beneath her composure something wild was prowling, looking for a way to be free. It could have been anger, guilt, grief, or a volatile mix of all three.

Without discussion Fiora got behind the wheel and drove, proving once again that she can read me like large print. I got in back with Maggie, where I could keep an eye on her.

"Whose idea was *Private Skull*, yours or Nickelaw's?" I asked as we left Las Trampas behind.

For a few moments Maggie didn't answer. Finally she made a hesitant, futile gesture with her beautiful hands.

"It started as a game," she said in her low voice. "I wanted to show the fine arts world how clever I was and how esthetically blind they were."

Fiora glanced at me in the rearview mirror. Her expression was skeptical. Not unkind, just skeptical. But I thought I knew what Maggie was trying to say.

"Yeah, I know how you feel," I said matter-of-factly. "Nobody has ever been able to explain—really *explain*—why one artist's work is worth two million bucks and another's is worth two hundred. Nobody has ever been able to explain why the critics go ballistic over one artist's painting and dismiss another's as 'derivative and second-rate.' But nothing, and I mean nothing, is as killing as the critic who lives within every artist, the critic who whispers that they will never be great, much less perfect."

Maggie looked up from her hands and for an instant the bleak fury in her was almost tangible. "You said you weren't an artist."

"I'm not, but if I thought I could fake a violin solo as well as you faked that O'Keeffe, I'd be tempted as all hell to hang it out for the world to see."

"I didn't start out to sell forgeries. I did the first one to get even with Lillian. We were fighting and . . ." Maggie shrugged. "What we were fighting about wouldn't make sense to anyone else. It doesn't even make sense now to me."

Fiora's eyes met mine in the mirror, but neither of us said anything. Her expression was a little softer now, as though she were beginning to understand Maggie. One thing was certain: Fiora understood two people who loved each other fighting about things that wouldn't make sense to anyone else.

"So I did a little sketch," Maggie continued, "and I made it look like a study O'Keeffe had done for one of the river paintings. I hung the sketch in a side gallery at Olin's place and waited to see what happened." She closed her eyes. When they opened again, they were empty. "Lillian saw the sketch and went crazy. She was so happy. She went on and on and on about the purity of line and the intense, controlled emotion and the elegant balance of shape and color."

Maggie's hands lifted, turned, found nothing to hold onto, and settled back into her lap. "I had proven that there was no esthetic difference between a real O'Keeffe and a well-executed fake. I had won. Yet when I tried to tell Lillian, the words just wouldn't come. I understood too late that, if I told her, something would be lost that I didn't want to lose."

"Lillian?" asked Fiora.

Maggie's hands lifted and fell once more. "Lillian believed in art the way most people believe in God. Art was her soul. I was . . ." Maggie's voice died and then began again, so soft that I had to lean forward to hear. "Jealous, I guess. But I couldn't do it. I couldn't take Lillian's faith in herself, in art, and give her humiliation and bitterness in return. I didn't want her to be like . . . me."

I waited. Fiora asked no more questions. Maggie offered no more answers. She simply sat and stared at the dry horizon, her face a mask.

"What happened to the sketch?" I asked.

Maggie blinked. She hesitated, then sighed. "Victoria told Olin about it. He wanted to sell it. I didn't. Victoria threatened to tell Lillian if I didn't go along with the sale. Some Texas brain surgeon paid fifteen thousand dollars for it. Olin gave me three thousand and told me to do more or he'd tell Lillian." Maggie shrugged. "After that, one thing just led to another."

Victoria. Vikki. The ever-changeable, ever-savage beauty.

"Victoria was getting even with me," Maggie said. "My father was an Apache drunk. Hers was a Mexican drunk from Guanajuato. She made up lies about an exiled Russian aristocrat being her real father. She said she was from royal blood and I was just a peon. I called her Victoria to remind her of where she came from, where we were both from. Victoria hated that, and me. That's why she told Lillian."

Tears gleamed in Maggie's eyes until she blinked rapidly, banishing them. "Victoria hated being part Mexican, part Indian, and all nothing. Her hair was lighter than mine, but she made it even lighter. She bobbed her nose and stayed out of the sun and taught herself to speak without an accent. And she hated me because I was dark and her own blood. She looked at me and saw a part of herself that no makeup could change.''

The car was silent except for the faint sound of the engine and the dry hum of tires on smooth pavement. I wondered if Fiora was thinking about her dead twin brother, who had hated her even more than he had loved her.

''Whose idea was *Private Skull*?'' I asked.

''It just happened,'' Maggie said tiredly.

''That's not good enough.''

Her hands lifted and fell once more. ''You've got to understand. Lillian taught the first art history class I ever took in the East. She used to talk about how much O'Keeffe must have resented Stieglitz. Lillian just *knew* there had to be paintings that grew out of O'Keeffe's resentment.'' Maggie hesitated, thinking, remembering. ''Then I found out Lillian was dying. *Private Skull* vindicated Lillian's whole life. I would have painted it for nothing.''

''But you didn't.''

Maggie smiled bitterly. ''Don't bet on it, white man. All Olin did was get me the right materials. I had painted that first forgery on plain paper. It wouldn't have passed any scientific examinations. *Private Skull* would have to. Olin got me some blank 1930s canvases from one of the forgers he knows in New York. He got the oils from the same source. Everything was historically correct. I made three tries before I was satisfied. We burned two. Olin treated the third with a wash and then heat to dull the paints, make them look as though they're aged. He took care of all the technical details himself."

"Sounds easy. Too easy. Why isn't there more of it done?"

Maggie's bitter smile flashed again. "Maybe there is. Maybe we just don't know it. Art is like religion. If people want to believe, they will. Art experts are no different. If you tell them what they want to hear, they're not nearly so critical of a canvas as when you give them bad news. If my painting had been a happy monument to O'Keeffe's and Stieglitz's love, Lillian would have treated the painting a lot differently. But it wasn't and she didn't and now she's dead and what the hell difference does make anyway?"

The hum of tires over the cold road was Maggie's only answer.

After a long silence Fiora asked, "Did Roger Valenti know the O'Keeffe was a fake?"

Maggie's laugh was even more bitter than her brief smiles had been. "No way. I don't know about Olin's other paintings, but I know what he actually got paid on this one down to the last bright penny. Olin offered Valenti the painting for a million dollars, cash, but the sales contracts were going to make it look like he had paid three point six."

"I see," Fiora said. "In effect, Nickelaw makes a million, Roger saves more than a million in tax write-offs, and the world has a new O'Keeffe. That's what the media hype was for—to make the purchase price seem reasonable to an IRS accountant."

"Yeah. That was Valenti's idea. He's real shrewd.

Even taught Olin a few tricks.'' Maggie glanced at Fiora, then away. "Don't count on cashing Valenti's checks much longer. He was pissed that you kept questioning the value of his precious fake.''

Fiora shrugged. "I said it was overpriced. It was.''

"You were making Olin nervous too. Everybody was getting nervous but Victoria, and she's as cold-blooded as they come.'' Maggie shrugged, but her shoulders were too tight to make the gesture work. "Now they're all safe. Olin gets the insurance money, Valenti gets to fire you, and nobody has to worry about fakes or forgeries. Just one big happy family.''

"Not quite,'' I said. "Some of us are dead.''

Maggie's black eyes focused down the slope toward the Cañon del Rio Grande and the flat plateau beyond. The morning haze was beginning to rise from the land, but the details of the small peaks and long black mesas still stood out sharply. So did the expression on Maggie's face. It said that men and women had been living and dying in this dry country for a long, long time, and they would go on living and dying.

The thought comforted Maggie, if her bleak smile was any sign. She leaned against the headrest of the back seat and closed her eyes.

There were other questions I could have asked, but the answers wouldn't help me decide the best way to nail Nickelaw's ass to the wall, and Valenti's right alongside him. So I shut out the recent past and the dead half sister and the surviving half sister's haunting, haunted smile.

I caught Fiora's eyes in the rearview mirror and

silently asked if she wanted me to drive. She shook her head. I settled back in my seat and started to draw up scenarios in my mind.

We were somewhere in western New Mexico before I came up with a scenario I liked. It wasn't perfect because it relied too much on a man I didn't entirely trust. But California was only ten hours away. Sooner or later, Maggie and Fiora and I were all going to have to start explaining the dead bodies and forged paintings that were littering the landscape. I'd rather do a show-and-tell in public than in the back room at some police station.

Besides, Nickelaw and Valenti had wanted a media event, hadn't they?

I got a scratchy cellular phone connection and gave Benny a shopping list. Then I hung up, dialed information, and got the number for Channel Four News in LA. Channel Four News was only too glad to connect me to the blond fence rail who had sat next to me at the press conference the day Bradley died. I was switched to her extension. She hit the phone on the first ring.

"Maura May."

Her voice was clipped and rushed, showing the effects of the full flush of a deadline adrenaline jag.

"You've been chasing the story about that O'Keeffe painting," I said.

There was a two-beat pause. "That's right. I broke the story about the theft."

"Then you'll want to drop by Valenti's museum tomorrow morning around nine. With a camera crew."

"What's happening? Another press conference?"

"Better than a press conference. An exclusive."

"About what?" she demanded.

"You'll find out tomorrow."

"I don't have time to chase speculative stories."

"Fine. I'll give it to Channel Two."

"Wait! Is it the O'Keeffe?"

Hook, line, and sinker.

"It's the O'Keeffe, but if you call the museum or anyone else and start asking questions, there won't be a story. They'll plug the leak and you'll be left wishing you'd kept your mouth shut. Understand?"

"Yes."

I started to hang up.

"Wait, how do I get back to you?" she asked quickly.

"You don't."

I hung up and dialed the federal building in LA. Like all cops who rely on snitches for their daily bread, Harvey Durham could always be reached by phone. It took a little waiting and a lot of patching through, but I finally heard his low, hoarse voice.

"CID, Durham."

"You still looking to make your case on Olin Nickelaw?" I asked.

There was the silence of pent breath and sudden adrenaline, telling me Harvey still had hope of cutting off Nickelaw's balls and taking early retirement in a haze of governmental congratulations.

"There's going to be a little art show first thing tomorrow morning at Valenti's museum," I said. "Be there and you'll make your case. Be late and I'll give everything I have to the first cop who walks through the door."

"Why should you do me any favors?"

"Because we finally have a common goal. We both want to see Olin Nickelaw in federal prison. Hell, I'll even give you Roger Valenti, if you think he's worth the trouble. Are you in, or do I call the FBI and start talking about wire fraud, possible money laundering, and stolen property crossing state lines?"

"You've got to give me more to work on. I can't go charging off on your say-so. I've got a supervisor to convince."

"Bring him along. Just be there tomorrow morning when the museum opens. Don't be late. The show opens first thing."

I hung up before Harvey could say anything more. Unfortunately, I couldn't hang up on Fiora.

"Why did you call that scum bag?" she asked.

"Don't take Harvey personally," I told Fiora. "Just use him and throw him away."

"I'd rather use toilet paper."

I reached over and touched Fiora's shoulder. Beneath the flannel shirt I could feel flat muscles between her neck and shoulder. They were hard, tense. I rubbed gently.

"Harvey's a cop," I said, "but he's also a bureaucrat. He needs to justify his time by making cases, so I'm handing him one that's ready-made. Even he couldn't screw this one up."

"And what do we get for our generosity?"

Always the pragmatist.

"In case it has escaped your notice," I said, "we're

up to our lips in shit. Harvey is a cop and a bureaucrat who's used to intricate scams. We'll let him do the explaining to all the cops who aren't used to anything trickier than busting hypes and hookers. Cops like the homicide detail at the Riverside County Sheriff's substation in Palm Springs and the Taos County Sheriff's Department in New Mexico."

She looked unconvinced.

"Fiora, take my word for it. It will be easier this way. Cops are really narrow. Five civilians tell them a story, and they'll check it out to the last detail and still not believe it. But let another cop tell them the same story, and they'll all line up and swear it's gospel. Harvey's going to save us a hell of a lot of explaining."

"I'd rather make a deal with the devil."

"You can cut your own deal with whoever you want," I said impatiently, "but Maggie's got some very delicate problems. Lay aside the two murders, and she's still got the canvases to explain away. Forgery, conspiracy, the tax-evasion scheme, fraud by wire, transportation of stolen property across state lines, flight to avoid lawful prosecution: every one of them is a federal crime, and every one of them could land Maggie in Pleasanton."

"What makes you think Harvey won't put her there?"

"Because he knows how the game is played. He'll trade Maggie's testimony for Nickelaw's ass any day the deal is offered."

"But—"

"It's too late," I interrupted curtly, tired of Fiora's objections. "I know you don't trust me not to fuck it up. That's tough, pretty lady. You invited yourself along for the ride, remember? If you're really nervous, pick up the phone and call the FBI.''

The car became very silent. I closed my eyes, ignored the big D-Mag digging into the small of my back, and tried to sleep.

After a while I succeeded.

tWENTY-NINE

Benny's van was parked in Crystal Cove when the three of us drove up. I went right to the new koi pond. As I expected, Benny was there with a bag of fish chow, feeding the koi with one hand and Kwame with the other. To the dog, kibble is kibble.

"Did you look into the MOSA alarm system?" I asked as I watched Lord Toranaga rise to the food in a muscular swirl of power, making water dance in the spotlighted pool.

"Piece of cake. Took the Kid about ten minutes."

"The Kid?"

"That tow-truck driver who brought in the Cobra." Benny grinned. The reflected light from the pool made him look diabolical. "The Kid decided chop shops have a limited future, so he's learning to be my legs."

"God save us all from your prosthetic devices.

What did the sorcerer's apprentice find at the museum?"

"Pressure pads in the flooring, latch alarms for the wall art, secured mantrap entries, IR and sonic sensors in the hallways. Great stuff, really great. That museum's going to be tamper-proof . . . once they get it all hooked up again."

Benny's grin had a lot of teeth and no comfort at all. I grinned right back at him. Fiora and Maggie came up behind me. I ignored both of them.

"Will I get ten minutes without having the world come down around my ears?" I asked Benny.

"You can have ten hours, boyo. There were only two operational circuits, so I had the Kid cross-wire the one that runs under the street to the Newport Beach PD dispatch desk. The sender unit still goes off, but the impulse goes around the horn and comes right back into the museum and nobody's ever the wiser."

"What about the second circuit?"

"Internal alarm to summon the duty guard. The Kid took the bell box out with a can of Freon-driven quick-set Styrofoam."

"So I can just walk in?"

"There might still be a guard around somewhere. You didn't give me enough time to figure out if they ever vary the two-hour sentry rounds."

I shrugged. If the guard I had seen in the parking garage was any sample, I wouldn't have to worry about original thinkers. "Did you get the stuff?"

Benny pointed toward the grocery bag on the patio next to his chair. I pushed Kwame's drooling muzzle out of the way and looked. Inside the bag were several large, double-barreled hypodermic-style contraptions.

"Thermosetting synthetic resin—probably phenolfurfuraldehyde," Benny said. "Don't put it where you don't want it to stay or you'll know why they call it Super-Glue."

"I'll keep it in mind."

"Want me to go along?" he asked.

"No. I want you to stand guard over Maggie and Fiora."

Benny is the other person in the world who reads me too well.

"Love to, mate," he said. "How does Fiora feel about it?"

"She's not buying it," Fiora said from behind me.

Benny looked from one to the other of us, reached for his wheels, and rolled toward his van. "Thanks for the Indian ring, Fiddler. Give me a call when you two can agree on the time of day."

I turned around to confront Fiora, but I knew it was futile. The look on her face said she wasn't going to be budged on this one. I could leave her here and she would take a cab to the museum.

"You need someone on the outside," Fiora said reasonably.

"Benny could do it."

"Roger Valenti is my problem, not Benny's. I want to have a part in solving it."

If my plans at the museum had involved anything dangerous, I would have tied Fiora up and dumped her in Benny's lap right then. But I gave in because I figured that even if I got caught on the inside, she would be in the clear on the outside.

I should have remembered how many times I'd been wrong lately.

"Fine, pretty lady. You can go. Bring Maggie too, so I won't have to worry about Nickelaw cutting his losses and her throat at the same time. Just goddamn sure neither one of you gets out of the car. I'm going to assume that anyone moving is an enemy, because all my friends are staying put."

I waited for an objection. There wasn't any. I looked at my watch. "Come on. It's time to put the cat among the pigeons."

There were still shoppers in the Plaza de Bellas Artes when we drove up at a quarter of ten. Headlights off, I found my lookout spot across the gully from the museum and parked the BMW nose in. Neither Fiora nor Maggie said anything. Fiora had given up trying to talk me out of going into the museum, and Maggie had apparently given up trying to talk, period. She was so damned quiet I had to keep reminding myself that Fiora and I weren't alone.

I shucked the binoculars out of their case and focused on the museum. The eyepieces were cold and smooth against my skin. At high power, the lobby was visible through the curtain of water from the fountains in front of the museum. I braced my arms on the steering wheel, watched the building, and waited, ignoring the two people in the car with me.

Ten minutes passed. Nothing doing. Nobody home.

I waited some more.

By eleven P.M. the marine layer had nestled almost down to the ground, leaving only the last few feet of air clear. All that held the fog at bay was the residual warmth of the ground, and that was fading quickly. Wet, damp air haloed the streetlights and softened the distant lights of the high-rise office buildings in Newport Center.

The private security patrol slowly cruised up the horseshoe drive in front of the museum. He flashed a spotlight across the front of the building, then went down the driveway again and turned back onto Jamboree Boulevard. I checked the LED clock on the dashboard. Time to go.

"Can't you just take that roll of canvas to the cops?" Fiora asked.

I looked into the back seat, where one-and-a-half phony O'Keeffes lay rolled together into a single fat cylinder. I reached for it. Fiora's hand came out swiftly and wrapped around my wrist.

"Fiddler?"

Fiora's fingers were cold and trembling. Her voice hovered on break point. I looked up and saw the raw fear in her eyes. I could have explained all over again how simple and safe things were going to be, but she wouldn't believe me. She has the gift—or the curse—of a keen sense of the future that is just short of prescient and unnervingly far away from accident. She isn't infallible, but she has been right often enough to scare both of us.

"Nickelaw is a smooth son of a bitch," I said, "but he's going to have a hell of a time explaining away these ersatz O'Keeffes on their nicely aged canvas. Ditto for the boy billionaire explaining away a public price of three point six million dollars and a private price of one million cash. Now, unless you can think of a better way to get Maggie and you off the hook and Nickelaw and Valenti *on* it . . . ?''

Fiora closed her eyes, bit her lip, and shook her head. "I can't. I've tried and tried. But I don't like it, Fiddler. Do you understand? I don't like it!"

"Ten minutes' exposure, max."

She said nothing, simply released my wrist. I pulled the paintings into the front seat, started the car, and went down into the hollow in front of the Newporter Inn. The fog was heavier in the low spots. Traffic was sparse, a single car here and there.

We rolled past the front of the Museum of Southwest Art. The fountain and reflecting pool shimmered within cones of blue and white light. The museum's glass front glittered like a polished zircon. There were no cars parked nearby. The small security office beside the entrance of the parking structure was dark.

"What about the guards?" Fiora asked.

"There's only one. He won't be back for an hour and fifty-three minutes."

I pulled into the horseshoe driveway and stopped. The sound of the fountain cascades was loud as I opened the car door, got out, and walked across the little plaza to the front doors of the museum. The lock bolt had been shot through the polished aluminum casements of the two center doors. I took the handles in both hands and gave them a sharp jerk.

No flashing lights, no bells, no police dogs barking in the night, nothing but the clammy breath of the marine layer settling over the land. I walked to the corner of the museum and flashed the Mag light up into the shadows just below the roofline. The blade of light caught the clean, green paint on the alarm box. I tilted my head and listened carefully. By letting out my breath and holding it, I could just make out the buzzing of a small electric motor working its little ass off, trying to ring a bell with a clapper that was frozen in place by a Styrofoam buffer.

When I walked back to the car, Fiora had switched over to the driver's side. As soon as I got in she released the brake and accelerated sharply.

"Gently, gently into that good night," I muttered.

Instantly Fiora eased off the gas. We left the traffic circle at a sedate speed. I pointed Fiora back onto Jamboree and around the corner onto Back Bay. A few minutes later I gestured to a wide spot in the narrow road. She pulled over, switched off the lights, and reached for her purse.

"Take my Beretta," Fiora said abruptly, pulling out the pistol.

It wasn't a request. Rather than argue, I took the damned gun and put it into the half-assed holster that was part of my left boot.

"Go back up to the parking lot and watch," I said. "You've got the number of the museum switchboard. If you see anything, call and let it ring. Otherwise, I'll call you when I'm done."

She nodded tightly.

I picked up the backpack, stuffed in the fake O'Keeffes and reached for the door handle. A hand came over the seat back and gripped my shoulder. Maggie.

"Why are you doing this?" she asked.

Before I could speak, Fiora did.

"Because he likes it and he's good at it. It's as simple and as complex as that."

There was no possible answer to the seething mixture of emotions in Fiora's voice. I got out and closed the door quietly. The BMW grumbled gently away into the night, leaving me alone.

tHIRTY

Fog scattered the lights of civilization, giving the entire night sky a vague white glow. As I stood and waited for my eyes to adjust, I listened to the brackish water of Newport's upper bay lap at the rocks along the one-lane road. After a few minutes I could see well enough to find the steep, narrow trail that trespassers and birdwatchers had made from the back bay to the top of the crumbling mudstone bluff. I shrugged into the backpack and started climbing, cursing the Beretta in my boot with every step.

As I climbed up the steep path, loose bits of dirt skittered down the slope behind me, making sounds like a fleeing army of mice. Below the crest of the bluff the path turned and meandered a few dozen yards, as though unable to decide where the best place was to make the final assault. After doubling back a few times, the path settled on a brush-filled cleft.

I fought through the mist-wrapped chaparral, stumbling more than once on roots and loose dirt. Then, without warning, I found myself up and over the edge onto the flat surface on top of the bluff itself.

Just ahead of me the museum was outlined against the lights of Newport Center. From my position I could see all the way through the glass panels in the museum walls to the courtyard and fountain out front. There were no lights on in the museum offices, no industrious junior curators working late, no secretaries typing on a rush assignment.

On the distant road I glimpsed the silver BMW as it slid by, then turned and went up the hill to the parking lot. Moments later Fiora stopped and turned out the lights. In the fog-shimmering darkness, the night was full of promise and regret, replete with a future that was not yet born. I stood silently, letting my eyes complete their adjustment to the ghostly light.

The gardeners had been at work, trying to replace what the earthmovers had ripped out in their efforts to teach God how to make the perfect landscape. The wild grasslands on top of the bluff had been stripped off, revealing a soil of unyielding, unpromising clay.

The barren ground was dotted with piles of redwood compost and sand that were being worked into the adobe soil. A few trees had been planted already, the standard eucalyptus and mimosa standing thinly against the dull pewter sky. In one corner of the plot the distant lights outlined the scalped topknots of five forty-foot palms, the kind that grow for decades somewhere inland and then are uprooted and taken to Orange County to impart an aura of instant permanence to a newly remade land.

Roger Valenti believed in the kind of artistic tradition that could be imported en masse. William Randolph Hearst had believed in that too. Tourists still line up to see the result at San Simeon. I wondered what tourists would be thinking of the MOSA sixty years from now, or if tonight would write *finis* to Valenti's self-congratulatory civic dreams.

Nothing else moved through the darkness as I walked quickly from the cover of a newly planted tree to a compost pile and from there to a parked earthmover. Shielded by the big machine, I stopped and listened. The first thing I heard was the moist sigh of tires against fog-slicked pavement as cars passed by beyond the museum. In the distance a coyote yap-yowled from the brush along one of the fairways at Big Canyon Country Club, reminding me that some wild creatures have made their peace with suburban man. As long as man keeps cats and small dogs, coyotes will thrive.

I walked quietly away from the earthmover. Just as I started across a patch of open ground, there was a flicker of movement low and to the side, no more than twenty-five feet away. The skin on the back of my hands prickled from the jolt of adrenaline rushing into my blood. I froze in midstep and tried to identify the shadowy form.

The motion came again—a quick forward glide, then a sudden stop, then another quick soundless glide. It was a pale house cat hunting in the darkness. The cat seemed unaware of my presence. So did whatever it was stalking. The attack was as soundless as the stalk had been. The cat covered the last ten feet in a blur of motion. There was a tiny shriek as the predator pounced and the prey realized that escape was impossible.

The silence that followed was total. Then came the hard, throaty yowl of the cat announcing its success to the night. The cry made my scalp ripple. Heart beating too fast, I walked forward. The cat vanished.

The back entrance to the museum was two double doors made of heavy glass. The service door on the office wing of the museum was glass too, but that door was less exposed to casual view. Standing in the deepest pool of shadow I could find, I dug the diamond glass cutter out of my backpack and ran a semicircular cut on the door at the level of the handle inside. Then I laid a cross-hatching of masking tape over the glass and tapped out the cut piece with the butt of the D-Mag.

The tape held. Not so much as a shard of glass fell forward to shatter noisily on the glazed tile floor. I set aside the half-moon of glass, reached through the smooth-edged hole I'd cut, undid the deadbolt, and released the latch. The door swung open.

My nerves anticipated the shrilling of an alarm. My mind had faith in Benny's thoroughness. My mind was right. After a slow count of five, nothing had happened. Not one sound came back to give me away. Quietly I stepped inside and pulled the door closed behind me.

The diffuse glow of fog filtered in through sky-lights and mixed with the reflected light from the fountain display outside. Though unfinished, the interior of the museum had already taken its final shape. I walked soundlessly through several side galleries where paintings were already hung—contemporary wildlife works and a few older pieces that showed the influence of Remington and Russell, if not the vision. The vague light heightened the surrealism of a Fritz Scholder canvas, but it flattened out most of the artists. Like second-rate diamonds, second-rate art needs precision lighting to dazzle the patrons.

The sculpture gallery was nearly complete. A huge cowboy bronze—all flailing hooves and spinning lariats, either a Remington or a knockoff of one —was mounted on a heavy pedestal at the center of the room. Smaller, less imposing sculptures and painted clay pots were in various stages of unpacking and display. The unearthly glow of Utah alabaster graced some of the large stone carvings. The frozen aboriginal figures somehow seemed more supple in the faint light, more alive. They haunted the night.

I remembered Nickelaw's gallery in Santa Fe and the black bear humped in muscular magnificence over the center of the world.

Keeping well away from the glass walls of the lobby, I gave the room a fast check to make sure there were no janitors or after-hours decorators around. Nothing was there but empty chairs and a quiet phone.

I started scouting the museum for a prominent,

permanent, empty wall. The second characteristic was most important, for despite appearances, the interiors of modern museums are designed to be ephemeral. Traveling collections and new acquisitions dictate that walls roll on metal rails and be illuminated by track lighting that is also on metal rails. The shape and size of display areas can be changed overnight.

But I wanted a solid wall, a real wall, a structural wall that couldn't be picked up and moved out of public view before the press arrived in the morning.

Finally I found a good wall in the sculpture gallery just off the lobby. There was enough illumination seeping in from various sources that I didn't need to fuss with my flashlight. I pulled off the backpack, unrolled the canvases facedown on the cold tile floor, and assembled the glue gun.

Super-Glue is two ingredients, an adhesive and a catalyst. The trick is to keep them apart until you're ready to fly, because once you've mixed them, you've got about thirty seconds to apply the adhesive and join the two surfaces; after that, the glue hardens and won't stick to anything new. The applicator Benny had given me worked like a twin-barreled hypodermic with a single fat needle as an outlet. I broke the seals on the two tubes, pushed the plunger to test the flow, then squirted a Jackson Pollock pattern across the back of each canvas.

The stopwatch started running in the back of my mind. Twenty-nine, twenty-eight, twenty-seven, twenty-six . . . one canvas down and one to go. Twenty-five, twenty-four, twenty-three . . .

The plunger jammed. I swore silently, pushed and

then pushed some more, and finally wrenched the damned thing but good. Glue spurted all over the second canvas, making a puddle.

I picked up the first canvas, stood on tiptoe, and slapped that painting as high up on the bare wall as I could reach. The glue had begun to thicken already. The canvas hit the wall and didn't even quiver, much less slide. It was so dark in the museum that the O'Keeffe showed only as a ghostly shadow.

Nineteen seconds to go . . . Seventeen, sixteen . . . and *smack*, the second painting was high on the wall a few feet from the first. Catty-corner, but that was tough. That canvas wasn't going to move any more than the paint on the wall.

I heard a sound, crouched down, turned—and dawn exploded in front of my wide-open eyes.

By the time my brain figured out the source was a four-cell flashlight rather than the sun, it was too late, my night vision was gone; but the image of a blue-steel pistol was imprinted on my retinas. Like me, the man was left-handed.

"Don't move, Fiddler."

I closed my eyes and froze and recognized the voice all at once.

Nickelaw.

A small part of my mind wondered what the hell he was doing here, but most of me was vastly more concerned with what the hell he was going to do next, shoot or talk.

The overhead gallery lights flicked on. They were aimed at the display objects, the bronzes and the alabaster stone carvings and the pots. The tightly focused lights did little more than intensify the shadows everywhere else. The fake O'Keeffe skulls blended right into the pale wall, and the dim light turned the poppies to just one more dark blotch.

More sounds. Footsteps. Silhouettes in the doorway with the flashlight behind. The unmistakable curve of a woman's hips, two women, both walking into the room.

Fiora. Maggie.

And just behind them the fierce flare of the flashlight, the deadly shine of a pistol, and a man moving with the lethal grace of a predator.

"Stand up slowly."

As I stood up slowly, I dropped the glue gun on the floor, wanting my hands free for the Detonics. Nickelaw turned off the flashlight, pushed it inside his waistband, and shoved Maggie in my direction, all with his right hand.

"Get over next to him."

Maggie went forward a few slow steps.

"Move it, bitch," snarled Nickelaw. His right hand snaked out and nearly lifted Fiora out of her shoes. "You too. Now!"

The gun in his left hand was a small automatic, probably a Walther, but at this range size didn't matter.

Both women moved toward me. Maggie's feet dragged. As she crossed a sword of gallery light, I saw a bruise on her temple. This time Nickelaw had hit her with something harder than the flat of his hand. Fiora crossed the beam of light. Her face was unmarked. She was pale and steady, never taking her eyes off the gun in Nickelaw's hand. She would make a try for it if she saw even the slightest chance.

I wished I had forced Fiora to keep the damned Beretta. Unarmed, she was no match for Nickelaw's trained, deadly hands. Yet as much as I wanted to, I wasn't going to warn her off. Nickelaw wouldn't expect an attack from such a small, fragile-looking creature as Fiora. In that might lie our best chance of living.

But it was agony to watch her watch him so carefully, waiting for an opening, an opening that would leave her wide open to his return attack.

"Stay where you are," Nickelaw said harshly to me.

Only then did I realize that I had started for him.

"Do you have a gun?" he asked me.

That was one of the most foolish questions I had ever heard, but I didn't laugh. "No."

Nickelaw was bright enough not to believe me and wary enough not to want to get within reach of my big hands—or feet.

"Open your jacket."

I did, showing Nickelaw my belt on the right side, then left, and the same for my armpits. A cop would have checked the small of my back, would have found the big D-Mag wedged there, and probably would have found Fiora's Beretta in my boot as well. Neither gun was handy at the moment, but moments change, and with them so do circumstances. It wasn't much comfort, but I wasn't in a position to be choosy.

Nickelaw walked closer to me, gliding on his spring-loaded feet. His hands moved into the light.

They had a very fine tremor. Adrenaline. He was edgy as a cat in a thicket. His combat training had been in a gym, with floor mats and body padding and the knowledge that he could always cry uncle.

I wondered whether Nickelaw had ever been hurt and had had to keep on fighting anyway. Survival, not sport.

"I'm sorry," Fiora said to me, her voice husky with restraint. "I was watching the front of the museum. He came up from the side."

"My fault, not yours." I smiled at Fiora, wanting her to know I meant each word. Then I turned back to Nickelaw. "Did Maura May call you?"

Nickelaw looked blank. "Maura May? Who the hell—oh, the television reporter. Why would she call me?"

I eased a quarter turn away from him, keeping my left side in deep shadow, concealing the movement of my left hand up my leg toward the small of my back.

"Because I called her," I said. "She's going to be here with bells and whistles and cameras grinding away while she holds a viewer call-in to decide which skull is the real one."

"You're not that smart," Nickelaw said casually. "Even if you were, by the time anyone shows up there won't be a damn thing to see."

"Don't bet on it. I just hung Maggie's most famous works on the wall."

Nickelaw almost fell for it and turned to look, pulling the gun muzzle off-target. At the last instant he corrected. He kept the gun pointed in our direction while he threw a quick look over his shoulder. His breath hissed out as he saw the skulls.

"Get them down!"

"No can do, pal. They're a permanent part of Valenti's collection."

Nickelaw walked diagonally to the unlighted wall, still pointing the gun toward us. He tried to peel back one corner of the canvas with his right hand. His fingers couldn't get a grip.

"What in hell . . . ?"

Reflexively, he turned to shift his pistol from left hand to right, freeing his superior hand to worry the canvas. It was the movement I had been waiting for. I reached for the D-Mag.

Before my hand even grasped the pistol butt, the gallery exploded with the sound of a shot from a large-caliber pistol. The effect of the bullet was even more violent than the sound. The slug penetrated Nickelaw's skull and brain, and the crimson poppy of death exploded from his forehead.

"Move and you die, Fiddler."

I let my hand fall away from the D-Mag. I didn't have to turn around to have answers for the small questions that had been nagging at me all during the long ride from Santa Fe and the short minutes in the gallery. I now knew who had told Nickelaw to come hunting in the museum tonight.

I also knew we were in worse trouble than we had been when Nickelaw was alive.

tHIRTY-ONE

The force of the bullet flung Nickelaw against the gallery wall. Hydrostatic shock ruined his perfect face and the skull beneath in the same shattering instant. Lillian Bradley had been gentle and erudite, Olin Nickelaw had been cruel and clever; and the contents of their skulls looked no different when splashed across a wall.

I turned toward the man holding the gun—Harvey Durham. I wasn't surprised to see him, but the gun in his hand was a different thing entirely. His pistol was the twin of mine.

D-Mag. Signature gun.

Find the esoteric bullets in the corpse and you find your killer too. As for ballistics, all he had to do was swap his D-Mag barrel for mine after the shooting was over. Assuming, of course, that he left my body anywhere it would be found.

Fiora and Maggie hadn't turned toward Harvey

yet. They both were still transfixed, staring in horror at what had been Olin Nickelaw.

"I've got mine," Harvey said, turning his D-Mag on me. "Where's yours?"

Harvey was a cop. He wasn't going to make the same mistake Nickelaw had.

"In the small of my back," I said.

"Turn around."

The muzzle of the D-Mag didn't waver. A shot from it would have hit me in the left eye. I turned around. A few seconds later I felt Harvey's hand grope beneath the vest until he found the butt of my gun. He unsnapped the keeper with his thumb and jerked the weapon from its holster.

"Thanks," he said, backing up. "I'll change the barrels later. Turn around."

"Nice shot, Harvey," I said, turning by increments so that my left side was in relative darkness. "Of course, it's no great feat with a D-Mag."

Fiora jerked and looked away from Nickelaw.

"You don't need to point that at Fiddler," she said quickly. "Nickelaw was the one waving a gun and making threats, not us."

"She doesn't get it, does she?" Harvey said, laughing. The gun muzzle continued to stare unwaveringly at me. "And here I thought she was supposed to be so goddamn smart."

The tone of his voice must have told Fiora that she had misjudged Harvey's motives from the beginning as badly as I had. She reached out to me reflexively. I moved a step away from her, trying to open some distance between us, making Harvey's shooting angles more difficult.

"Harvey's not a cop," I said to Fiora. "Not any more. He's just one more stinking asshole with a badge."

Instantly Harvey's smile became a grimace of anger. He was wired on adrenaline, balanced on the fine edge of self-control.

"Take another step and you're dead," he snarled.

I stopped moving.

"Back up."

I backed up.

"More."

When I was far enough away from Nickelaw's corpse to suit Harvey, he walked over and picked up the Walther. He pointed it at me as he lowered the Detonics. If he noticed Maggie's silent, inch-by-inch retreat toward a partially completed display of Nambe pottery, he didn't mention it.

He must not have noticed the fake O'Keeffes high above Nickelaw's corpse, either. If he had, we would already be dead and Harvey would be on the way to the airport, headed for a country that had no extradition treaty with the United States.

It was up to me to make sure Harvey didn't look up and see our death warrants glued to the wall.

"That's the gun Harvey's planning to kill us with," I said to Fiora, nodding at the Walther. "But he's not going to do it here. He'll take us out on the desert somewhere. Way out. He wants to make sure we're never found. That way the cops will have somebody to blame for killing Nickelaw. A missing painting worth millions, Nickelaw dead of a D-Mag bullet, and me with a brand new D-Mag registered to my name."

Fiora looked at me oddly, but I kept talking.

"You see, if you and I just vanish, the cops will assume that we stole the missing painting, sold it, and got in the wind. They'll never think to look in shallow graves or ask why a woman who makes millions would be satisfied with a painting that couldn't be sold for six cents on the open mar—"

"Shut up," Harvey interrupted, realizing too late that I wasn't running off at the mouth from a fit of nerves.

"Why? Don't you want Fiora to know what you've planned for her? Do you want her to be nice and cooperative up until the instant you put a bullet—"

"Shut up!"

The gun had switched to cover Fiora. I stopped talking. She stared at the gun and then at Harvey.

"Why?" she asked.

"Because I got sick and tired of rich bitches like you looking down their noses at me. Because I got sick and tired of slick pricks like Nickelaw making a monkey out of me in court. Because I got sick and tired of subsidizing rich bastards like Valenti. Why shouldn't they pay me for once?" Harvey laughed. "Nickelaw wanted to grab the painting, burn it, and collect the insurance. But Valenti will pay a lot more than a million bucks to get his hands on the painting, burn it, and be certain that the world will never know how badly he was suckered."

The last piece fell into place, answering the last niggling questions. When Nickelaw had decided to settle for the insurance money, Vikki had gotten greedy. She had run to Harvey, promising him vengeance and money and exotic varieties of carnal gratification.

"All you needed was the painting, right?" I asked. "Nickelaw searched Maggie's place and came up empty. Then Vikki gets her bright idea—or was it yours? Either way, you come up winners. Once you get the painting, you can blackmail Valenti out of millions and finally get a really spectacular piece of ass in the bargain."

Harvey was looking unhappy with me. Fiora offered herself as a distraction.

"Vikki wouldn't use Harvey for toilet paper."

Fiora's cool, precise tones enraged Harvey. Even in the shadowy gallery light, I could see the glitter of his narrowed eyes. With an inarticulate snarl he turned toward Fiora.

"Don't let Fiora outsmart you again," I said quickly. "You see her game, don't you? You shoot her here and Newport PD starts typing blood spots and bingo, there's strange blood to explain and your little scenario of theft and flight goes down the toilet. You can't afford to shoot her here. You can't afford to shoot anyone here. You need to slow down and think."

I wasn't getting through to Harvey. I could see him watching Fiora, his hand getting tighter and tighter, and I was much too far away to change the outcome even if I threw myself at him.

"It's not too late to be a hero," I said urgently. "We can help you explain everything: how you nailed Nickelaw, and the O'Keeffe scam and—"

A woman's unexpected, savage scream clawed apart the silence. A clay pot hurtled out of nowhere, spinning through blades of light and darkness. Harvey got a glimpse of the pot at the edge of his vision and ducked reflexively, taking the brunt of the force with his shoulder. The pot shattered, surprising him more than hurting him.

I was yelling at Fiora to get down and at the same time throwing myself behind a group of waist-high alabaster sculptures. Fiora dove in the opposite direction, pushing a display stand toward Harvey as she went. I hit the floor and rolled, digging for the Beretta in my boot.

Harvey snapped two shots in Maggie's direction. Both of them went wild. Off-balance, distracted, he fired the Walther again and dug the Detonics out of his belt at the same time.

The D-Mag's first slug screamed off a bronze two feet from my head. The Walther's smaller slug exploded a statue next to me, sending shards of stone flying everywhere. One of them drew a red-hot line across my eyebrow.

More shots came, punctuated by the sound of more pottery shattering. I rolled over again as a bullet ricocheted nearby. When I stopped rolling, the Beretta was in my hand.

Adrenaline put the brakes to time. Everything moved in stop motion but me. The Beretta felt insignificant compared to my kinesthetic memory of the D-Mag, but the Beretta was all I had. As its slender barrel came up I saw the distended muzzle of Harvey's weapon come to bear on me. The instant after I took aim, the vision in my left eye was clouded by blood pouring from my forehead.

The Beretta went off just before the D-Mag. Harvey shot once. I kept the Beretta's trigger down until the magazine was empty and the slide locked back and I wished to hell I had more tiny little bullets to spend. Only then did I realize that Harvey wasn't returning my fire.

The world snapped back into normal time. I pushed myself to my feet and went over to where Harvey lay on the floor. The Beretta might not have had much punch, but at close range it was as accurate as Harvey was dead—each of the bullets had gone into his wide-open mouth.

"Fiddler?" asked Maggie.

"It's all right. He's dead and we're not."

Fiora came out of the shadows, threw herself into my arms, and held onto me with her surprising strength. I held her in return, listening to our ragged breaths fill the ringing silence that follows gunfire.

In the distance came the rising wail of sirens. The security guard had finally figured out something was wrong.

ePILOGUE

Maggie, Fiora, and I had enough time to get our stories straight before the police arrived. Even so, we spent a lot of time answering questions. Harvey's buddies from the IRS weren't real happy about pinning a rose on his corpse, but they didn't have any choice. The case against Olin Nickelaw had been officially closed for months, which meant that Harvey had been kicking ass and taking names in a personal and unofficial quest for early wealthy retirement.

In the end the IRS and I agreed to paint Harvey as a bloody hero; it raised less questions that way. As a reward for our good citizenship, the living IRS agents agreed to put a high gloss on Fiora's reputation as an honest investment counselor.

The one and a half O'Keeffes stayed on the wall of Valenti's museum until a man with a chain saw came and cut them free. It took a week to repair the damage. Five days later the museum opened with a small ceremony. The wing Roger Valenti donated had a plaque in the wall that read: Museum of Southwest Art, North Suite.

As for Valenti himself . . .

"Ready?" I asked Fiora.

She turned away from the mirror, stepped into four-inch heels, smoothed her black silk business armor into place, and nodded her head.

At Valenti's office we didn't wait for the secretary to usher us into the august presence. I simply ignored the woman's protests, opened the inner door, and followed Fiora into Valenti's lair. The secretary crowded in, apologizing six times to the breath.

"Get her out of here," I said to Valenti.

No wonder he was a billionaire. It took him about three tenths of a second to figure out all the possible plays and arrive at the one that would cost him the least.

"Thank you, Sarah. These people have an appointment."

The secretary was no slouch at bottom lines either. She was out of the room and closing the door behind her before Valenti finished speaking.

"What do you want?" Valenti asked.

"You're going to drop your suit against Pacific Rim Investments," Fiora said.

Valenti tilted his head as though thinking it over, then said, "There has been too much adverse publicity. Someone has to be blamed for bad investment advice, shady tax write-offs, and recommending Nickelaw and the fake O'Keeffe." He shrugged. "Tag, you're it. And if you think I'm intimidated by your live-in gorilla, you're mistaken. I buy and sell men like him every day."

Valenti smiled gently.

"I'm going to ruin you, Fiora, and I'm going to enjoy every minute of it. You'll rue the day your muscle-bound gigolo glued those fake O'Keeffes to my museum walls."

Fiora turned, looked at me, and said huskily, "You were right to the last full stop. I bow to your superior understanding of human slime."

"Thank you. Now go make sure the secretary doesn't have her finger on the intercom."

"I'd rather you held him while I cut his throat."

"Unfortunately, he's more use to you alive."

Fiora tapped one fingernail against her small leather purse while she thought it over. After a moment she sighed and left the room, closing the door firmly behind her. Before Valenti could say anything he would regret, I tossed a sheaf of papers onto his desk.

"You're good at bottom lines," I said. "Find 'em and sign."

Valenti glanced at the top sheet, read swiftly, frowned, and read some more. His frown grew deeper as he peeled away the lawyerese and read the unflinching demand beneath: he was to drop his suit against Fiora and apologize in print for ever having doubted her integrity and business acumen.

"Why would I sign this?"

"Simple. If you don't, Maggie Tenorio will sign a deposition stating that you were the one who had the bright idea of faking an O'Keeffe, that you co-erced Nickelaw into doing it, and then you got cold feet and stole the painting yourself when old Harvey panted onto the scene. You do remember Harvey, don't you—the civic hero?''

Valenti became very still. He didn't bother telling me I couldn't get away with it. I could, and he knew it. Even if the allegation never flew in court, the press would destroy him.

In silence Valenti signed all four copies. I took three of them with me and left.

Five days later a huge crate arrived from Santa Fe. I pulled apart the boards, Fiora cleared away the packing, and we both stood motionless, admiring the powerful black curves of the stone bear. He was even more magnificent than I had remembered.

In silence I ran my fingertips over cool midnight stone. A Nickelaw Gallery note card was taped to the bear's back where a medicine bag would normally have gone. I freed the card, opened it, and read:

How did you know that the O'Keeffe was Valenti's idea?

I tucked the card into my jeans pocket and went back to stroking the black bear.

''Is it true?'' Fiora asked.

I traded the cold polished stone for a surface that was warmer, softer. Fiora's breath washed over my fingers as I tested the resilience of her lips.

''Fiddler?''

''Appearance is the only reality that matters, remember?''

''But if it were true . . . my God, I can almost

feel sorry for Nickelaw, caught between Harvey on one side and Roger on the other."

"Save your sympathy. What goes around comes around."

"Does that apply to us?" she asked, tasting my fingertips.

Gravity doubled as I reached for Fiora, lifted her, and felt the familiar pressure of her body along mine.

"Fiddler?"

"One day at a time," I said against her neck. "That's the secret of the art of survival, love. One day at a time."

 HarperPaperbacks *By Mail*

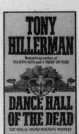

LISTENING WOMAN. An incredible murder investigation carries the Navajo Tribal Police from a dead man's secret to a kidnap scheme, to a conspiracy that stretches back more than one hundred years.

THE DARK WIND. Sgt. Jim Chee is trapped in the deadly web of a cunningly spun plot driven by Navajo sorcery and white man's greed.

A THIEF OF TIME. Lt. Joe Leaphorn and Officer Jim Chee must plunge into the past to unearth the astonishing truth behind a mystifying series of horrific murders.

DANCE HALL OF THE DEAD. Compelling, terrifying and highly suspenseful, DANCE HALL OF THE DEAD never relents from first page till last.

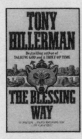

THE BLESSING WAY. When Lt. Joe Leaphorn of the Navajo Tribal Police discovers a corpse with a mouthful of sand at a crime scene seemingly without tracks or clues, he is ready to suspect a supernatural killer.

SKINWALKERS. Brimming with Navajo lore and sizzling with suspense, SKINWALKERS brings Chee and Leaphorn together for the first time.

THE FLY ON THE WALL. A dead reporters secret notebook tell of a scandel involving a senatorial candidate, a million-dollar scam and murder. Soon John Cotton hears the deadly footsteps of powerful people with something to hide.

Visa and MasterCard holders—call

1-800 331-3761

for fastest service!

SEVEN TONY HILLERMAN MYSTERIES

M Y S T E R I E S

YOU WON'T BE ABLE TO PUT DOWN

Tony Hillerman's novels are all best sellers. All his books are unique, riveting and highly suspenseful. Be sure not to miss any of these brilliant and original mysteries filled with Navajo lore sizzling suspense.

Buy 4 or More and $ave

When you buy 4 or more books from Harper Paperbacks, the Postage and Handling is FREE.

MAIL TO: **Harper Collins Publishers, P. O. Box 588, Dunmore, PA 18512-0588, Tel: (800) 331-3761**

YES, send me the Tony Hillerman mysteries I have checked:

Skinwalkers
0-06-100017-5....$5.99

Dance Hall Of The Dead
0-06-100002-7 ...$5.99

The Blessing Way
0-06-100001-9....$5.99

The Dark Wind
0-06-100003-5 ...$5.99

A Thief Of Time
0-06-100004-3 ...$5.99

Listening Woman
0-06-100029-9 ...$5.99

The Fly On The Wall
0-06-100028-0 ...$5.99

SUBTOTAL . . . . $_____

POSTAGE AND HANDLING* . . . . $_____

SALES TAX (NJ, NY, PA residents) . . . . $_____

Remit in US funds, do not send cash

TOTAL: $_____

Name_____

Address_____

City_____

State_____Zip_____

Allow up to 6 weeks delivery. Prices subject to change.

*Add $1 postage/handling for up to 3 books...
FREE postage/handling if you buy 4 or more.

H0061

▇ HarperPaperbacks *By Mail*

READ THE NOVELS
THE CRITICS ARE RAVING ABOUT!

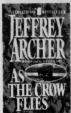

AS THE CROW FLIES
Jeffrey Archer

When Charlie Trumper inherits his grandfather's vegetable barrow, he also inherits his enterprising spirit. But before Charlie can realize his greatest success, he must embark on an epic journey that carries him across three continents and through the triumphs and disasters of the twentieth century.

"Archer is a master entertainer."
— *Time* magazine

FAMILY PICTURES
Sue Miller

Over the course of forty years, the Eberhardt family struggles to survive a flood tide of upheaval and heartbreak, love and betrayal, passion and pain...hoping they can someday heal their hearts and return to the perfect family in the pictures from the past.

"Absolutely flawless." — *Chicago Tribune*

PALINDROME
Stuart Woods

Seeking an escape from her brutal ex-husband, photographer Liz Barwick retreats to an island paradise off Georgia's coast. But when a killer launches a series of gruesome murders, Liz discovers that there is no place to hide—not even in her lover's arms.

"Moves along with hurricane velocity."
— *Los Angeles Times Book Review*

THE CROWN OF COLUMBUS
Louise Erdrich • Michael Dorris

Vivian Twostar—single, very pregnant, Native American anthropologist—has found Columbus' legendary lost diary in the basement of the Dartmouth Library. Together with her teenage son Nash and Roger Williams—consummate academic and father of her baby—Vivian follows the riddle of the diary on a quest for "the greatest treasure of Europe."

"Compelling entertainment."
— *The New York Times*

BILLY BATHGATE
E.L. Doctorow

In the poverty-stricken Bronx of the Depression era, gangster Dutch Schultz takes young Billy Bathgate under his crooked wing. With grace and vivid realism, Billy Bathgate recounts his extraordinary education in crime, love, life, and death in the dazzling and decadent world of a big-time rackets empire about to crumble.

"Spellbinding." — *The Boston Herald*

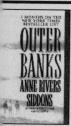

OUTER BANKS
Anne Rivers Siddons

Four sorority sisters bound by friendship spent two idyllic spring breaks at Nag's Head, North Carolina. Now, thirty years later, they are coming back to recapture the magic of those early years and confront the betrayal that shaped four young girls into women and set them all adrift on the Outer Banks.

"A wonderful saga." — *Cosmopolitan*

MAGIC HOUR
Susan Isaacs

A witty mixture of murder, satire, and romance set in the fashionable Hamptons, Long Island's beach resort of choice. Movie producer Sy Spencer has been shot dead beside his pool. Topping the list of suspects is Sy's ex-wife, Bonnie. But it isn't before long that Detective Steve Brady is ignoring all the rules and evidence to save her.

"Vintage Susan Isaacs."
— *The New York Times Book Review*

ANY WOMAN'S BLUES
Erica Jong

Leila Sand's life has left her feeling betrayed and empty. Her efforts to change result in a sensual and spiritual odyssey that takes her from Alcoholics Anonymous meetings to glittering parties to a liaison with a millionaire antiques merchant. Along the way, she learns the rules of love and the secret of happiness.

"A very timely and important book...Jong's greatest heroine." — *Elle*

For Fastest Service—Visa and MasterCard Holders Call

1-800-331-3761 refer to offer HO471

MAIL TO: **Harper Collins Publishers**
P. O. Box 588 Dunmore, PA 18512-0588
OR CALL FOR FASTEST SERVICE: (800) 331-3761

Yes, please send me the books I have checked:

☐ AS THE CROW FLIES (0-06-109934-1) $6.50
☐ FAMILY PICTURES (0-06-109925-2) $5.95
☐ PALINDROME (0-06-109936-8) $5.99
☐ THE CROWN OF COLUMBUS (0-06-109957-0) $5.99
☐ BILLY BATHGATE (0-06-100007-8) $5.95
☐ OUTER BANKS (0-06-109973-2) $5.99
☐ MAGIC HOUR (0-06-109948-1) $5.99
☐ ANY WOMAN'S BLUES (0-06-109916-3) $5.95

SUBTOTAL .... $_____
POSTAGE AND HANDLING .... $ 2.00*
SALES TAX (Add state sales tax) .... $_____
                          TOTAL: $_____
                                   (Remit in US funds.
                                   Do not send cash.)

Name _____

Address _____

City _____

State _____ Zip _____ Allow up to 6 weeks delivery.
                                   Prices subject to change.

*FREE postage & handling if you buy four or more books! Valid in U.S./CAN only.   HO471